GALAXYS
EDGE

THROUGH THE NETHER

ORDER OF THE CENTURION

RICHARD FOX WITH
ANSPACH + COLE

Galaxy's Edge: THROUGH THE NETHER
by Galaxy's Edge, LLC

Published by Galaxy's Edge Press

Cover Design: Beaulistic Book Services
Formatting: Kevin G. Summers

Website: GalaxysEdge.info
Facebook: facebook.com/atgalaxysedge
Newsletter: InTheLegion.com

"The Order of the Centurion is the highest award that can be bestowed upon an individual serving in, or with, the Legion. When such an individual displays exceptional valor in action against an enemy force, and uncommon loyalty and devotion to the Legion and its legionnaires, refusing to abandon post, mission, or brothers, even unto death, the Legion dutifully recognizes such courage with this award."

98.4% of all citations are awarded posthumously.

01

A gale whipped above what remained of the factory's roof, blowing fine sand in through broken windows and partially crumbled walls that settled in a fine powder over broken equipment. The building once housed the planet Strach IV's preeminent seafood packing operation, but the only remnant of that business was a stench of decaying fish embedded in the floor. Ghosts of more prosperous times.

Soren tightened the seals on his helmet, preferring stuffy air to the rancid smell infesting the abandoned factory. He looked up at the gaping hole in the roof, so large that the building almost resembled a stadium. His helmet, aftermarket tech popular with mercs, whirred fresh air through a pair of level three toxin scrubbers. Despite the constant cycle of air through the filters, the fishy scent lingered.

Hefting his old slug thrower, he ran his thumb over the safety switch, double-checking that the rifle was set to fire with the pull of a trigger. Strach IV was not a place for the safety conscious. Soren glanced down at the wooden stock, splintered and carved with different names in various alphabets, kill tallies, oaths of revenge, and crude sigils of the many gangs vying for control of the city. He'd received the weapon not long after joining the Scions, complete with the dried blood of its last owner. The combatants in the city's gang wars were expendable; weapons were reusable. Just how many times the battered rifle had been used for murder, left in the gutter, and picked up for another fight nagged at him.

Probably best not to know.

"Anyone ever work here back when this place was running?" Soren asked the three men near him.

"You watch entrance," Tarith, his Kimbrin boss, hissed. The alien's yellow skin was flush, almost mustard in his cheeks, a sure sign of stress.

"Place's been down since before I was born," one of the others—a human—said, his lower face hidden by a snarling metal mask. "You'd think Hask worked here, but he just doesn't shower."

The last member of their quartet kicked out at the joker, missing easily.

"You all watch entrance!" Tarith banged a fist against the rusted remains of a canning machine, stripped of every movable part but still useful as cover against gunfire.

"Sorry, boss," Hask, the one who'd tried kicking the other, said.

"Reds won't try anything." Soren sounded more bored than anything else. "This is neutral ground."

"Trust Reds makes you dead." Tarith spat on the ground. "Dead."

Soren shrugged. A squeal of metal from across the factory floor sent Soren's finger to his rifle's trigger. He fought the urge to bring the muzzle up and aim. Raising his weapon on neutral ground was against what few rules the warring gangs kept about such things. And anyway, the guy in the group who took judicious aim was usually the first one targeted by the other side—not the best course of action for anyone who wanted to stay alive on Strach.

A door to a loading dock pushed open and four people with red sashes across their chests and tied to their lower left legs came in. The Reds. One of them pushed a repulsor cart loaded with four munitions chests baring the insignia of the Galactic Republic, silver tape wrapped around the centerline, covering the hinges.

The Reds were led by a Tinitian, a semi-gelatinous alien species. His head looked like a dollop of cream atop a barrel chest. One eye swam in translucent violet flesh.

Soren shook his head at the coming load.

"Sloppy," he mumbled to his group. "Not even tied down."

Tarith unsnapped the cover on his pistol holster. "This not fancy navy. They look good?"

"Can't tell from here, boss." Soren tilted his head to one side to better see the Red pushing the cart. Even in full leathers with a helmet, that one's shape suggested a human female.

"One looks like the *skarg* that killed my brother," Hask said.

"You say that about every Red," said Soren.

3

Hask tightened his grip on his rifle. "Because they all *do*."

"You gutters have the credits?" the Tinitian asked, his words bubbling up from his body and translated through a cylindrical amp.

"Thrak? That you?" Tarith gave his pistol grip a tap. "All squishes like you look the same."

"Nice to see you, too," answered the Tinitian. "Last time was when you scratched wunna my dealers."

Tarith shrugged as if he didn't recall and would take the Red's word for it. "Surprised blood clots trust you with anything. This the goods?"

"Yeah." The alien's eye floated from one side of its head to the other. "Good thing we're here for business since Reds are always good boys when it comes to credits."

The Scions chuckled in reply. Soren knew that everyone here—*everyone*—was expecting a double cross.

Thrak stopped in the open and waved a tentacle at his bodyguards. The two halted next to the bullet-scarred remains of a table-sized hunk of equipment that looked like it used to have a conveyer belt running through it. The woman pushed the sled up to Thrak and cut the repulsors, causing it to thump to the ground.

Stepping back, she grabbed the chin of her helmet and jerked it twice to her left.

Soren felt his heart beat faster. Sweat beaded on his forehead.

"The money," the Tinitian said.

"Yeah, I just hand over. Like I trust." Tarith ran the back of a hand down the spikes on his jaw.

The Red's eye jiggled, probably a mocking look of surprise. Its tentacles ran over the silver tape, suckers gently sticking to it and popping up from the light suction. "Factory sealed. Just what it says on the tin. Brand-new Legion N-6 assault rifles. Blaster pistols, too. Stuff's too good for you gutters, if you ask me. But we'll sell it to you now. Get it back at the next block party."

"Filthy clot." Hask moved toward the Red, but Soren stepped in front of him, blocking him until Tarith could flash a dirty look demanding the Scion calm down.

"I look, then we party, yeah?" Tarith pulled a knife and leveled it at the sled.

The doughy alien gang leader made an exaggerated bow, his tentacles flopping over his arms, as he stepped aside.

Tarith lowered the knife and crossed two fingers against the blade where only his men could see, signaling to stay alert.

Soren looked at the woman who'd delivered the repulsor cart, sniffed loudly, and readjusted his helmet. He flipped a tiny switch hidden in the padding, and a low hum sounded through his ears.

Tarith ran his knife through the silver tape and grabbed the handle. He looked over at Thrak.

"Factory sealed." The alien's one eye rolled over. "See?"

Tarith cracked the case open, holding it in place a beat as if to see what might happen. Satisfied, he lifted it open the rest of the way.

A blinding flash of light burst from the case. Soren instinctively threw up his arm to protect his vision even as the lenses in his helmet darkened to save him from the brunt of the assault on his eyes. The flash left an afterglow across his vision like a burning line, but he could see. He dropped to one knee, pulling up his rifle as he went down to open fire. The battered weapon jerked in his hands as he let loose on full auto.

Shouts and more gunfire echoed through the factory floor.

Hask stumbled into Soren as blaster bolts ripped into his body. He knocked Soren against the canning machine. Soren grabbed the man's body and pulled it in front of himself, feeling more blaster bolts thump into the man's body. The sharp crack of a hand cannon sounded three times and Soren pushed Hask away, letting him fall dead to the floor.

Tarith was also dead, lying facedown with blood still pumping from a hole in the top of his head. The victim of that hand cannon. Looking around, Soren saw he was the last Scion alive. The fourth man—a new kid named Reeplo—lay with his head and shoulder's propped against the canning machine, rifle across his legs and chin against his chest.

At least two of the Reds were dead. One was missing— but the leader, Thrak, Soren could hear the suction of his tentacles slapping and popping against something.

Soren rolled to his feet and quickly found Thrak crawling away, one tentacle loose at his side. Beads of purple fluid ran out of a gash on his back and clumped together in the dusty floor. Soren jogged to the alien and put his boot on his jelly-covered hip. He pushed the Red over and pointed his rifle at its chest.

"Wasn't... wasn't me!" Thrak crackled out of a damaged speaker. "A setup. Yes. Not Scions. Not Reds. Maybe the Triaks want us to fight, then they take our turf. Be reasonable, yes yes?"

Soren blinked away the last of the dazzle from the light blast. He brought up his rifle barrel.

Thrak's eye swam around wildly. "Tarith, he has the money for deal, yeah? Take it. Keep it! Be a Red!"

When Soren didn't reply, Thrak thrashed his good arm across his face, wiping away some of the purple ooze that passed for blood. "Zelle, what are you waiting for?"

The female Red walked up to Soren, smoke curling out of the barrel of her revolver. She took off her helmet, revealing pert features and razor wire tattoos across her cheeks and neck.

"Oba, I hate this planet." Her nose crinkled as she got a good whiff of the air.

"Zelle? Kill him! You're blooded to—"

Zelle shot the alien in the face, splattering his loose flesh across the floor and sending his one eye bouncing away.

Soren looked at the woman, a slight frown on his face. "Tinitian's nervous systems are in their sternums."

"Yeah, I know," Zelle said. "That was for my own satisfaction."

She put three more rounds into the alien's chest. Its flesh oozed out of the leathers like melting butter. "Better?"

Soren looked back at the munition's crates. The other two Reds lay in pools of blood on either side. He removed his helmet and tossed it aside, immediately regretting it as the stench permeated his every inhalation. He pressed his palm against a temple, feeling a migraine coming on. "Why the hell did you make that flasher so strong?"

"Because *research*," scoffed Zelle. "That lump of dung's eye could handle the first device I made. Had to double the lumens. Sorry, thought I told you."

She pulled the pistol out of Tarith's holster and looked it over before frowning and dropping it in disgust.

"You did *not* tell me." Soren went to the open munitions crate and grabbed the handle, looking up at the woman before pulling it open. "Anything else you failed to mention?"

"Getting past Republic Logistics' seals is a lot harder than you let on," she said, rolling her shoulders and reloading her hand cannon. "Thank you very much. But do take a look anyway. Only took us two months on this festering hemorrhoid of a planet to find those damn crates."

"That's why you're here."

Zelle gestured her hand across her face, showing off her tattoos. "You look like you. What a surprise."

"The infiltration hoods are only good for a few hours at a time. Can't wear them for months... and they hurt like a bitch."

Soren turned his head to one side and squeezed his eyes shut as he opened the crate. Neat rows of densely packed Legion assault rifles, complete with factory tags on the stocks, looked no worse for wear. A ball of emergency lights hung from a thin wire attached to the underside of the lid, burnt out and still smoking.

"Ah ha." Zelle pulled a credit chip out of Tarith's jacket and gave it a gentle pat. "Here we go."

"We don't need the money." Soren took a comm link off his belt and keyed in a code.

"Then you won't mind if I keep it." Zelle slipped the chip down her shirt.

"Regulations on recovered contraband are—"

"Sir? Sir, is that really you?" came from the comm. *"Is it finally time to leave? I don't know if I'll ever get Strach IV's dirt out of my scrubbers."*

"Immediate extraction, Heywood," Soren said. "We've got another... eight minutes before the Scion's repulsor sled arrives. We need to be gone by then."

"En route. I do hope you and Madam Zelle were successful."

"I'll bring you up to speed later, just get the *Iago* here before we have to explain ourselves to anyone else." Soren looked at the bodies strewn across the floor.

"You gutters—sorry, habit," Zelle rolled her eyes, "you have the drop-off location for this? This firepower's a bit much for a gang fight this far out on the galaxy's edge."

Soren yanked Tarith's jacket open and removed a metal box with a single slot.

"What's that?"

"This is the code box," Soren said. "The smugglers hold to their normal procedures and—"

"There's a cipher disk in this one." She rapped her knuckles against a weapons crate. "I was tempted to crack it when I found it, but exercised restraint."

"How unlike you." Soren looked up as the whine of approaching engines filled the air. A small interstellar yacht with a tapered nose hovered over the gap in the roof and slowly lowered down.

Zelle powered up the sled and motioned toward the bodies. "And this mess?"

Soren nodded and keyed his comm. "Heywood, I need a burner."

"*Understood, sir.*"

A moment later, the ramp on the ship lowered. A five-foot-tall bot with broad shoulders and pistons for knees walked to the edge of the ramp and tossed a device to Soren. Zelle ducked behind the crates with a yelp.

"*Tell Ms. Zelle I'm insulted,*" Heywood said over the comm.

Soren turned the grenade over in his hands the moment he caught it. He rested his thumb on the timer dial.

"You can tell her yourself after she gets the cargo loaded up." Soren flicked his hand toward where the *Iago* was about to land and knelt next to Tarith's body. He slid the battered rifle beneath the corpse, leaving plenty of the weapon exposed and ready to be noticed by whoever came across it.

He pushed the dial to zero and held down the safety switch. There were children on Strach. The gang wars left plenty of orphans to scrounge for themselves. The streets were full of dirty, hopeless children… but all were innocent in Soren's mind.

He debated the chance that the gunfire would bring young scavengers… but this was gang territory. Specifically marked off and tagged as off-limits to civilians. The Scions—or any gang—weren't known for mercy toward any trespasser. Strach's children were smart enough to know better.

Soren stuffed the burner grenade under the dead Kimbrin's body and carefully wedged the safety switch against the rifle's buttstock. Whoever decided to take the weapon as a spoil of war would have a very bad day. And reduce any and all evidence of what happened here to ashes.

Republic Nether Ops preferred not to leave a trail that could be followed.

"Ms. Zelle has secured the cargo," informed Heywood. "Local gang networks are active, shooting is reported at several intersections surrounding this facility. They are coming."

"Figures." Soren ran to the *Iago* and gave the bot a pat on the shoulder as he passed. "Get us out of atmosphere before the police decide to chase us."

"Sir, this is Strach," the bot said. "I paid off the local constabulary months ago. Not even they would like venture this far into ganglands."

The ramp shut and the ship rose into the dust laden sky.

02

Soren stepped out of the *Iago's* lone refresher and scrubbed a cloth against an ear. The ringing caused by close quarter gunfire would fade in a few hours, as would the hum of adrenaline in his muscles. Still, a fresh set of coveralls and the smell of scrubbed ship's air was a welcome change from Strach.

He glanced into the *Iago's* cockpit where Heywood sat at the controls. The ship passed through wisps of clouds and up into the void.

"A destination would be helpful," Heywood said over his shoulder.

"We're free of any tail?" Soren asked.

"Should I be insulted?"

"Keep us in low orbit. We run like we stole something and it might attract attention." Soren went to a panel on the bulkhead and pressed his palm against a sensor. A shutter popped open revealing a glowing panel that lit up a translucent full face mask and two gloves. Both had thin silver wires running through them, forming a grid. He touched the gloves and they went opaque, matching his skin tone.

"The infiltration hood and hand sleeves remained in proper storage conditions," Heywood said. "Do you have a new identity to assume?"

"Not yet, just wanted to make sure these are still working. The tech is still experimental and the Carnivale warned they might degrade over time. Get us on a vector toward the core worlds. I have a feeling that's where we're going next."

Soren walked down a narrow passageway and to a railing separating the forward part of the ship from the cargo bay.

Zelle sat on one of the munition crates. Her leather jacket was off and balled up in a corner. She held a dermal scalpel against her forearm and ran the sonic blade up and down a small tattoo.

Soren went down the metal stairs to the bay and picked up her jacket. He held it out for her to see. "On a navy ship you'd lose a week's pay for unsecured gear."

Zelle didn't bother looking up from her task. "We're not on a navy ship, now, are we?"

Soren frowned. "Our mission's over. Time to act like professionals again. We can have this cleaned and—"

"Burn it," Zelle snapped, pointing to the tattoo she'd been working on with the dermal blade. The skin surrounding it looked red and irritated from the process. "You think I want knickknacks and souvenirs to remind me of Strach?"

"I mean..." Soren cleared his throat. "After you're finished with all that, sure."

Zelle shook her head. "Bunch of damn savages. I miss proper criminals."

Soren took a step forward to get a better look at the marking she was working on removing: a pair of red tears rimmed in black. They got lighter with each pass of the sonic blade, but they were there. Red kill marks.

"I may have gone a little too native."

She looked up at him, and Soren winced at the thought of how long it would take her to erase the tattoos on her face and neck.

"Reds didn't need a hacker," Zelle said, again shaking her head. "They needed muscle. Had to earn my place with that lard of fat's crew to make sure I was on the exchange."

"You find out who delivered the contraband to the Reds?"

"No, the Red who took that delivery got scratched a week before we arrived on Strach. Asking too many questions wasn't in character, know what I mean? How about you, what'd you have to do to get on that yellow bastard's crew?"

"Food poisoning," Soren said. "He had a wobanki with him that didn't take to well to some cinnamon mixed in with his ground mice chili last night. I'd held my own in a few street fights and was on his short list."

Zelle chuckled. "Another month and we would've been running the entire planet."

Soren shrugged his shoulder noncommittally.

"That's never happened, has it?" asked Zelle. "Some Nether Ops puke find themselves in a cushy spot with all the power and money they'd ever need on some nice quiet world on the fringe? Retire?"

"Acting outside of our remit earns a visit from Dark Ops," Soren said, pinching the bridge of his nose and hoping that the migraine that still threatened him wouldn't make landfall. "I'll let you guess how well that turns out. And you're not a Nether agent. You're an auxiliary."

"Seriously? I just saved your butt down there by shooting your friends in the face and my friends in the back. What have I got to do to get a little more respect?"

"The condition of your parole mandates honorable service to Nether Ops for no less than ten years. You have nine and a half years to go." Soren pulled the crate Zelle had tapped back on the planet and began opening it. "But you have my thanks for what it's worth."

"I thought they were kidding about the time frame." Zelle's shoulders slumped. "I mean, this is better than prison. Not much better, but a little better."

"You should have considered that before you hacked the credit logs on Formosa and wired yourself money from the governor's accounts."

"Allegedly." Zelle held up a finger. "*Allegedly* wired myself the money. Money the governor received as off-the-books campaign donations after one of his friends scored a major government contract, I'll add. I mean, that's what I heard."

Soren removed the silver tape from the case Zelle sat on and ran it through his fingers, reading the script printed on the tape as it passed.

"I can see where you cut the seal. Next time use a vibro-blade with a sub-millimeter setting before you re-shrink it."

"I've got one in my shop." She pointed across the cargo bay to a neatly organized rack of tools at a workstation. "Shop wasn't on Strach."

Zelle stared at her workstation for a moment and then yelled toward the cockpit. "Son of a donk, Heywood! What did I tell you about touching my things?"

The bot's voice came over the internal comms. "You didn't have to see that mess eighty-three times a day during my maintenance routine. I also calculated that the chance of you surviving the mission was lower than you honoring your frequent threats against my chassis should you return to the *Iago*."

"Metal son of a bitch." Zelle shifted forward off the crate, but Soren put a firm hand on her shoulder and shook his head.

"If you lost any of my tools, I'll remake them out of your shell!" she yelled at the cockpit. Sitting back down, she hurled the scalpel across the bay and hunched forward, pinching the bridge of her nose as she took a deep breath.

"Post-mission adrenaline dump," Soren said. "It'll pass."

"This is your first op, too," Zelle said, looking up at Soren with slight disgust on her face. "Don't act like you're a damn expert."

"I've been in more than one battle," Soren said matter-of-factly. "The aftermath feels the same."

"You were a navy puke. A *logistics* navy puke. What did you even do during a fight? Count missiles as they launched?"

"You ever been on a deck that's taken a hit? Worked damage control for thirty hours straight to keep a reactor from going critical?" Soren asked, his voice now hard.

"No... I... you know what? Let's figure out where we're supposed to go next. Maybe it's some tropical paradise like Pthalo where we can get drinks with little umbrellas in them. We go topless on Disora. Same where you're from?"

"There are no beaches like that on Oliphant." Soren opened the crate and looked over a row of rifles, the smell of factory grease still on them. "The seals say these were manufactured by Collin Arms, then went to the munitions depot on Elysium. But the manifest has the contents as Miif-7 rifles, standard for line infantry, not Legion gear."

"Elysium's not far from Strach."

"No, it's not. It's home to the 91st Fleet and a Rep-Army Corps. No Legion outpost." Soren pulled a pistol out and stuck a finger in the empty charge pack well.

"Third from my left," Zelle said, pointing to a bench with drawers. "So... someone wanted legionnaire rifles. Does Collin Arms make N-6s?"

"They do." Soren removed another pistol and fished out a small gold disk. "Lots of manufacturers do. House of Reason sold the Legion's designs to a bunch of arms manufacturers and then had them bid back the lowest rate to get the contracts."

"Okay. So what're the odds these were just accidentally switched up at the factory?"

"Doubtful. N-6s are a far cry from Miif-7s, and then for the weapons to end up as part of an underground arms deal on Strach IV... something's up."

"The Carnivale wanted us to investigate gun running to the MCR." Zelle's jaw worked from side to side in thought. She plucked the credit chip from her shirt. "This is not what the MCR buys. This stuff is top of the line. MCR could've spent the same amount of money to equip a whole battalion of expendable with gear just good enough for expendable idiots. MCR is notorious for being cheap. So if this wasn't for the MCR, then who is it for? If I was a criminal arms dealer, I'd appreciate a few less gangs between me and a sensitive client. Not the most trustworthy people in the world, right?"

"I'll... include that in my report," Soren said.

"Maybe there's an upside to being an auxiliary to Nether Ops," offered Zelle, nodding knowingly. "Less paperwork."

Soren slid the gold disk into the cipher box and a small screen on the shell came on. He waited a moment until three lines of text appeared. He swiped his thumb over the screen, but the lines didn't move.

"That's it?" Soren frowned.

"So, where're these guns going?" Zelle rubbed her hands together. "Some garden world where the booze isn't made in old toilets?"

"Rintaka," Soren said, squinting at the lines of text as though he weren't reading it right. "Then system coordinates and a mining survey file."

"The Scions didn't mention Rintaka to you?"

Soren shook his head fractionally. "Nope. Tarith would have known, but someone shot him in the face."

"The Kimbrin? He looked like he deserved it." Zelle hurried across the cargo bay and picked up the dermal scalpel she'd jettisoned.

"He did deserve it." Soren looked up at the ship's ceiling. "Heywood, set course for Rintaka and open a channel to the Carnivale soon as we're in hyperspace."

Soren took the co-pilot's seat and watched as the stars went by. The skies of Strach had been overcast since he'd arrived on the planet. And that just seemed to be the way it was. No one ever commented on the gloom—it was just expected there. Endemic. To Soren, the lack of a proper nighttime sky to remind the planet of a wider galaxy seemed to crush people's hopes and dreams even more than the crime and poverty.

"How's the ship, Heywood?" he asked the bot, a H3Y-WOD model supplied by Nether Ops.

"All systems are within normal parameters, though the inertial coils are at the end of their manufacturer's suggested life cycle."

"You didn't order replacements while she was in dock?" Soren placed a hand on a biometric reader.

The bot's servos whined and clicked. "I did. Three times. One package was stolen, another 'lost in transit,' and the third delivery contained silicon items meant for Drusic procreation rituals. My reviews of the delivery service were deleted within three minutes of being posted. I opted to save Nether Operation funds and cease making orders."

The panel beneath Soren's palm flashed white and a screen rose out of the console. Soren smoothed out his hair and adjusted his posture.

The screen filled with static, then solidified around a silhouette.

"Authenticate," said a distorted voice.

"Voss, Soren K. Agent number 99-337."

"Tungsten."

"Barbados," Soren replied, giving the counter word indicating that he was not under duress and he believed the connection to be secure.

The silhouette lightened to a dark-skinned human with a white beard and hair. Professor Nix of the University of Utopion. Though his true employ was with the Nether Ops Carnivale section. The man looked Soren over.

"You've been dark for over a month," Nix said at last. "The top floor wanted to write you off as missing in action."

"Our operational window was valid for another two weeks," Soren said. "It took longer to develop the target than we planned."

"And? The mushrooms in analysis were dead certain you were going into a dry hole on Strach."

"We recovered the missing weapons," Soren said with a smile. "Nether Ops comes through for the Republic once again." He relayed the events of their final hours on Strach and what they found in the cases. Nix listened with a stony face that would have made a poke-jack player proud.

"Rintaka?" Nix asked.

"Yes, sir, a garrison world. Mostly jungle environment training and—"

"I know what's there," Nix said, cutting Soren off impatiently. "I'm... concerned that whoever wants those weapons is delivering them to one of the most heavily guarded systems in the sub-sector."

"Perhaps the Mid-Core Rebellion has sympathizers in the ranks. While Rep-Army counterintelligence personnel aren't as well trained as Nether Ops, I'm sure I can enlist them to remove any treasonous elements."

"Soren, my boy, what did I tell you about an agent with zeal?"

Soren frowned slightly. "They tend to get killed."

"Were you this much of a spring buck on Strach? Of course you weren't; you're not full of blaster holes."

"Strach is not a world that's... embraced by the Republic," Soren said after searching for the right words. "The locals warranted a different approach. But a garrison world full of those sworn to defend—"

"Requires just as much caution, if not more," the old man said. "If there is an MCR cell on Rintaka, then they're a talented group to still be operating in such an environment. These aren't street rats looking for their next fix."

"Whoever they are, I'm onto them. And may I suggest an audit of Collin Arms and the Elysium depot?"

Nix grunted. "Noted. Send the serial numbers. I'll arrange a visit. How's your auxiliary?"

"She's exceeded expectations, sir."

"By Oba, you know I'm not a navy officer, don't talk to me like I'm one." Nix relaxed the expressionless face long enough to roll his eyes. "If she's still useful, then keep her in the field. If she wavers from the conditions of her parole, then you can dump her in any prison you like. Should be several options on any planet."

"For as much damage as she's done to the Republic, I'm surprised she was let out of her cell."

"She has a valuable skill set and we have leverage over her. Asset recruitment 101. Her background *is* problematic, but there were a lot of corners cut after a bunch of MCR terrorists nearly rammed the House of Reason with a corvette full of explosives."

Soren drummed his fingers against his thighs. "Which is why I was pulled out of training and put into the field..."

Nix shook his head. "You were ready, Voss. Checking every block on the training schedule wasn't what you needed. And when the delegates realized just how close they came to being memorialized as murder victims, they got motivated to get things moving. A good number of bureaucrats were almost vaporized too. I've never seen paperwork move so fast in my life."

Soren stared at the screen dispassionately.

"You don't find that amusing?" Nix asked.

"No, sir, I do not."

"You're young. Spend another couple decades at the mercy of some cubicle mushroom and these last few months will be as hilarious as they are terrifying." Nix cleared his throat. "Take the contraband to Rintaka. Find out who wants it and either contact the system's Nether Ops chief of station if you need to act immediately, or me if you've time for a Dark Ops team to arrive and handle any issues with prejudice."

A chill washed over Soren's heart. He'd seen the aftermath of a Dark mission during his training. They were fast, brutal, and unrelenting. The thought of such carnage anywhere gave him pause.

"For the Republic," Soren said.

"Long may it stand." Nix ended the transmission.

"I do believe he's beginning to like you," Heywood said.

"Nice change of pace." Soren hit a key and the screen sank back into the console. "He acted like my assignment to the mission was an annoyance when we first met."

"Nether Ops do not appreciate interference, even from the House of Reason, I've noticed," the bot said. "And the more senior the Nether Agent interfered with, the more perturbed they become."

"Are you suggesting that I don't mind because I'm still a rookie agent?"

"That is a logical inference."

"This is what I signed up for, Heywood. To protect the Republic from those that would bring it down, inside or outside. The MCR is only going to cost more lives until it's snuffed out for good."

"That you're able to function without the burden of cognitive dissonance must aid your performance."

"I'll take that as a compliment." Soren stood up and stretched. "Man the controls. Wake me when we're an hour out from Rintaka."

"Very good, sir." Heywood tapped a control panel. "You've a number of messages that came through on the Carnivale's encrypted line. Both official and personal in nature. Shall I forward them on to your reader?"

Soren stopped in the doorway, one hand on the frame.

"Any from Vanessa?" he asked.

"There is one such message."

"Only one..." Soren looked down. "Keep it in the buffers. I'll read it later."

03

Soren found Zelle sitting in the *Iago*'s small galley, nothing more than a table that folded out from the bulkhead and two stools bolted to the floor. Steam rose from a pot of stew on the table, a messy pile of open food pouches near the edge.

Zelle sat hunched over a bowl, stirring what looked to be oily beef and potatoes. Another bowl was across from her.

Soren mashed the pouches into a garbage shoot and sat down. Zelle looked up at him, her pale skin raw where she'd removed all the gang tattoos.

"I've 'exceeded expectations,'" she mumbled. "So proud. Do I get a quarterly evaluation report with gold stars, too?"

"You know the conditions of your parole." Soren ate a spoonful of the stew and nodded in satisfaction. "This is good."

Zelle jabbed the stirring spoon toward Soren, dripping greasy broth onto the table. "You know, I got the pitch when I was in lockdown. Kind of figured I could shave some time off with good behavior. Going above and beyond, know what I mean?"

His eyes on the newfound mess Zelle created, Soren said, "Nether Ops made the arrangements with the House of Reason courts. It's not something I can change."

Zelle tossed the spoon into the pot with clear disgust. "I mean… what are we even *doing* out here? We found some leej gear on the black market. Oba's tears, what does that matter? Bunch of dead gangers—maybe you got a hit back on some loggy puke making a little extra on the side. This is what Nether Ops does? Plays around the edges?"

"No. There's more to it than that. Nether Ops is the Republic's immune system, killing threats in their crib before they can grow into full-on monsters."

Zelle fished her spoon out of the pot and licked it clean before pointing it toward a porthole. "The MCR's out there right now, raising all kinds of hell. How many legionnaires were lost on Kublar? Their ship too. Then they work with some terrorists and almost wipe out the House of Reason with a corvette—and all that drama, senators and delegates with mid-life crises being reminded that mortality applies to even someone like them, and they turn Nether Ops loose on the edge of civilized space? Not the MCR—just scum-sack gangers who lucked out and got some mil-spec weapons. Want to explain that?"

"We know what we need to know," Soren said with a slow shake of his head. "Nether Ops has a far longer and wider view of the fight with the MCR than we ever could. I trust our leaders. We execute their orders and deliver success."

Zelle rolled her eyes. "You missed your calling as a navy poster boy. I know you grew up on Oliphant right after it was incorporated into the Republic. You got nothing but propaganda telling you how awesome the Republic is, but you've been out here long enough to realize it ain't all sunshine and puppies, right? Strach was a sket-hole. It's been in the Republic for hundreds of years."

"What's your point?"

"You think we're making a difference by nabbing a couple crates of guns? All that effort and it'll amount to a feel-good report for some delegate... and a pat on the head for you. Good boy."

"Nether Ops will hunt down whoever stole those weapons from the factory. Once that's done, they'll find their contacts, which will lead to other enemies of the Republic. Those 'couple crates of guns' are a thread that will help unravel an entire network. It's our job to pull it."

"True believers are insufferable." Zelle poked her spoon into her stew.

"You'd prefer to believe everything is awful? So let's all steal what we can and take care of number one?"

Zelle shrugged. "Plenty of people in the Republic look at it that way. 'Specially on Utopion. They seem to do all right."

"Until they come under scrutiny from the Republic. Then comes justice." Soren slapped the back of his hand into his palm. "We're nineteen hours from Rintaka. I need you to manufacture trackers for the contraband."

"What's wrong with the Tick-9s we have on board? You know how long it takes to do a custom job?"

"Anyone that's a part of Republic security would find a Tick model tracker easily. Your devices are a cut above."

Zelle inclined her head in mock appreciation. "Aww... that almost sounded like a compliment."

Soren looked down, focused on stirring his stew.

Rolling her eyes, Zelle said, "Fine. It'll take me a couple hours to get one done..."

"Four. We need a tracker for each case."

"Four? What the hell, man." Zelle let out a growl. "Okay. Four. So much for a nap. Can I ask you one little favor before I get started, Soren, old buddy, old pal?"

Soren raised an eyebrow at her.

"I may have gone a little overboard with the gang tats." Zelle rolled her jacket down to reveal her shoulders. "Would you run the dermal down my back? I can't quite reach."

"You got a *spine* tattoo?"

"Alcohol may have been a factor."

Soren settled onto the top bunk of the *Iago*'s berth room and stretched. The low hum of the ship's systems were a welcome change of pace from the erratic noise of the gang stronghold on Strach IV. No arguments bleeding through the walls. No crying babies or the sound of repulsor sleds and gunshots. Actually, it felt a bit like the *Iago* was almost too quiet.

He reached into his pants now hanging from the bedpost and pulled a datapad from the pocket. A swipe from his thumb brought up his unread messages and he scrolled through, looking for anything that demanded his immediate attention. Nether agents in the field were exempt from most mundane paperwork issues... but that didn't include the five different notices that he was overdue on his mandatory zhee religious awareness and tolerance training.

Soren considered tapping out a terse message to the admin officer who was threatening to dock his pay for being out of training tolerances, but a message at the bottom of the screen made his heart skip a beat.

It was from Vanessa, his fiancée on Oliphant. Dated a week after he went undercover in the Scions. That he only had a single message from her gave him an educated guess to its contents. It didn't look promising.

Dear Soren...

He read through a few densely worded paragraphs. Skimming for confirmation that this was the end. Maybe looking for some sign of hope that it wasn't. The letter was half an accusation against him and half justification for her ending the engagement.

Soren couldn't fault her decision.

Tradition on Oliphant demanded a couple be wed within two years of the proposal. Extensions were granted only in the event of wartime, provided that both parties agreed to extend the engagement. Vanessa had opted out.

Soren shut the datapad off and tucked it under his pillow. He felt as though he should be angry. Like the appropriate thing to do would be to break his hand punching a bulkhead and rage for all to hear. But, in his mind, he couldn't blame her. He'd essentially vanished from the navy after Nether Ops recruited him. Details of his training and mission were forbidden even from an agent's husband or wife, let alone the betrothed.

And then he pushed back their wedding date and went off-world...

It isn't fair to make her wait, he thought. *She's young, beautiful, and from a well-to-do merchant family. There are suitors on Oliphant for her, ones around every day.*

While his head could accept this... his heart didn't. He stared at the ceiling as emotions swelled in him. Not anger. Something else... the temptation to write to her—to explain everything—was strong, but such an action would wreck his status in Nether Ops.

His engagement was over. His mission remained.

It took hours for the immediate hurt to subside, to move to the back of his mind where he knew it would linger. He didn't sleep.

Zelle came into the room and unzipped her dirty coveralls as she sat down on the lower bunk, evidently finished with her work. The smell of grease and ozone wafted up from her. Her boots clomped against the deck as she removed them.

"Feels good to do something useful." She threw the coveralls onto an empty bunk across from her. "Useful *and* well. Anyone finds those trackers and I deserve to have my parole revoked."

The beds rumbled against the bolts fastening them to the bulkhead as she struggled to get comfortable.

"Ah, crap, are you asleep?" she asked.

"No."

"Oh. Okay, then."

Soren heard her tapping against a datapad.

"Some mushroom wants me to do what for zhee culture?" Zelle mumbled. "I'll tell him where to stick *that* training."

"It must be important," Soren murmured.

"The donks will kill me and eat me no matter how much I'm forced to appreciate their culture. I know enough to hate those animals. Get me back on a Republic network and I'll find this mushroom threatening me for not doing training and I'll send some donk mating videos from his account to everyone he knows and then—ah, to hell with it. Problem solved."

He heard her tap on the screen, drop it on the deck, then crawl under her blanket.

"You can't have finished the training," Soren said, finally starting to feel sleepy. "There are videos, anthropologic studies..."

"I told Heywood to do it for me. He's got my HR code. Not like he's got anything better to do."

Soren rolled over and looked down at Zelle. Half a dozen different violations came to his mind. "That's..."

Zelle winked at him. "I told him to do yours, too."

"You have my HR code?"

"You're welcome."

Soren rolled back onto his bunk and drummed his fingers against his chest. He decided to re-do the training when time allowed.

And to change his HR code.

04

Soren and Zelle stood behind Heywood in the *Iago*'s cockpit, both wearing armored vac-suits with blaster pistols strapped to their chests. They watched as an asteroid field grew closer through the windows. Tens of thousands of rocks spun slowly in the void, forming a seemingly endless field. In the distance, what looked like a dusty gray boulder hung against the abyss.

"I thought cracking a dwarf planet to mine it was illegal," Zelle said.

"It is." Soren crossed his arms across his chest. "The spoil infects the entire system, multi-ton asteroids become a threat to every space station and city. But whatever rogue operation did this did it hundreds of years ago. Most of the dangerous rocks have been removed by gravity or drone ships."

"The hazard rating for the Rintaka systems remains high enough to negate the *Iago*'s collision insurance policy," Heywood said. "Though there is enough of a haul bonus for independent contractors to offset that risk. The Republic maintains its presence on Rintaka Prime at considerable expense."

"I'm glad you're flying," Zelle said. "Can't dock my pay if the bot bangs up the ship."

"You're implying that this asteroid field is some sort of a challenge to my programming," the bot said, somewhat impishly.

Soren reached over Heywood's shoulder and brought up the message they'd pieced together from the contraband on a forward view console. The text seemed to float on the display, a washed-out blue glowing against a black screen.

"We're in the right spot," Soren said, pointing at the message. "The mining survey file must point to one of these asteroids."

"So we know there's a transmite in this datastack." Zelle went to a works station. "I don't want to get old and gray waiting for our scans to finish up. This is a smuggling run, right? Where would smugglers want to hide? Soren, can you dip into the Republic's police archives and pull up every patrol through this field in the last six months?"

"What, you can't slice it?" he asked.

"This is a military system. I *could* get in but there's enough people that care about their jobs that one or two might notice my passing. Your Nether Ops clearance gives you full access and covers your tracks. Must be nice."

Heywood turned his head, causing a soft whine of internal servos. "A wide band sensor pulse would find the target asteroid quite easily."

Zelle shook her head. "And beg local security to come looking for us. Don't tell anyone, but we're supposed to be smugglers. Shh." She put a fingertip against her lip.

Soren opened his void suit and lifted a chain off his neck that had a data chip dangling from it like a pendant. He plugged it into the control panel. Information feeds from the local holoweb system came up on the screen. He began to swipe his fingers in the air, manipulating the program.

"Okay. You've got real-time station access with archival clearance for the last two years."

An overlay of the patrol routes traced through the asteroid field on a screen.

"Oh wow," Zelle said, eyes scanning the display. "Local security is lazy in this system. Flies the exact same routes every time. No wonder it's a smuggler stop... Next sweep is in a couple hours."

"This one." Heywood highlighted an asteroid the size of a cruiser on the outer edge of the field. "Other bodies near it show signs of tungsten extraction. Consistent with the mining survey of the drop site."

"He's right," Zelle said. "See? No need to scan. It must take the system police cruisers seven hours to make it from Rintaka Prime, another seven hours back. A whole day crammed into a shuttle, must be miserable. No wonder they shortchange the inspection."

"Fair enough," Soren said, rocking back and forth on his heels. "Let's get over there without bouncing off anything."

"Is that an insult?" Heywood accelerated the ship forward.

Soren gripped the hydraulic struts of the *Iago*'s ramp as the ship flew slowly over their target asteroid, his feet mag locked to the ground as he looked down at the dust-filled craters.

Zelle was just inside the cargo bay, holding onto the cart with the weapon cases. "What exactly are you looking for? A nice, big 'smuggle here' sign?"

"Yes, exactly that." Soren tapped a button on the side of his helmet. "Heywood, do you see that bare patch in the crater to our five o'clock, two hundred meters?"

"Yes, sir," the bot answered through the agent's earpieces. "Aster areata. Dust-free areas of an asteroid subject to solar winds. Of course, solar wind doesn't exert enough force to move dust, but the charged particles can create a magnetic field that—"

"Set us down there," Soren ordered.

The *Iago* banked around.

"Why there?" Zelle asked.

"That bare spot's on the asteroid's leeward side of the system's primary. No way that areata's natural."

Zelle looked up at the bay ceiling. "Oh. Sure. Of course not."

The ship came to a stop over the crater and lowered, dipping all the way beneath the top edge of the crater walls before it finally came to a landing. Whiffs of dust scattered around across the smooth surface.

"Here we go." Soren pulled the ramp's release and watched as the ramp lowered onto the asteroid. He turned to look back at Zelle. "Be ready for anything."

"Duh."

Soren stepped off the ramp and felt the solid rock beneath his feet. He looked around, noting the unblemished ground. Straight ahead was a gap in the crater wall, large enough for two people to walk through side by side.

"Now what?" Zelle asked from the top of the ramp. "I know I'm just an auxiliary without all that super top-secret Nether Ops training about smugglers, but something tells me we're not supposed to just leave this stuff out in the open."

Soren turned around, then pointed to a gap in the crater wall. "There. Let's go take a look."

Heywood's voice came over the comm. *"Two hours until system patrols arrive. There is a thirty-seven percent probability of them detecting the* Iago *in this depression. Even with crew fatigue factored in."*

Pausing mid-stride, Soren asked, "And the chance of them finding us if we take an eccentric course back to Rintaka Prime?"

"Minimal."

"Then let's hurry."

Soren bent slightly at the knees and jumped. In the asteroid's microgravity, he loped forward traveling nearly three meters before coming back down. He skipped ahead, crossing to the edge of the crater quickly. Stopping his momentum at the crater wall with two outstretched arms, he leaned over to look into the gap. Dust had settled into the groove the size of a small room extending from the opening. Footprints consistent with vac-suited humans led to and from the middle of the area.

Zelle approached, allowing the repulsor cart to pull her across the surface, her legs dangling behind her as though she were flying. "This it?"

"See for yourself."

She brought the cart to halt just behind Soren and then peered around him. "Not quite an X to mark the spot, but I'll take it."

She reversed the cart's repulsors, forcing it to settle on the asteroid's surface as though inside a gravity well.

Soren felt the pull against his hands. Dust flowed toward the cart like it was pushed by a slight breeze. He removed a small baton from his belt and twisted off its cap before peering back into the opening.

"What's up?" Zelle asked.

"Checking for traps."

Soren flicked the disk-like cap toward the footsteps and it slowly turned end over end in the micro-gravity. Two tiny repulsor rings popped out of the disk and it came to a sudden stop. He flicked a switch on the baton and pointed one end at the target area. The cap, actually a tiny drone, zipped to a bare patch of dust and traced a slow and deliberate spiral outwards.

While Zelle watched the bot as it went round and round, Soren kept his eyes on a blinking green light on the baton. The bot finished scanning the area, actively searching until stopping a foot away from Soren's chest. He clicked a button and the drone snapped back onto the end of the baton.

"Curious," he said. "No explosives or countermeasures of any kind."

"You're complaining?"

"On a dead drop like this, it's easy for word to get out to other smugglers and have your shipment stolen."

"That's complaining. Don't forget that this is a Republic military system. The risks of using this place for a drop are way too high for those so criminally inclined. Speaking of that military, you want to hurry this up?"

Soren looked back to the system's primary star as his mind raced with possibilities.

"Maybe we should get Heywood out here to do the digging," Zelle offered. "He can handle a boobie trap blowing up in his face better than us."

"I heard that," the bot said. *"You're fortunate my programming does not allow for grudges."*

"Let's be done with this." Soren moved forward and knelt next to the patch surrounded by footprints. He pushed his fingers into the fine dust and pulled out a battered cargo box the same size as the cases they brought from Strach IV.

This buried crate was much older than what Soren and Zelle were bringing, a civilian model that looked as if it had been bounced around from one side of the galaxy to the other. He lifted it from its dusty grave easily in the micro gravity and then looked into the hole it had left in the ground. Another box lay inside.

Zelle peeked from behind the sled, clearly using it as cover. "No explosions. Nice."

Soren gave a wan smile from behind his helmet. "Such faith."

He carefully removed three more boxes from the cache and set them next to the sled in a neat row that would meet the exacting standards of any being with OCD.

Zelle took a small bit of metal shaped like a cog's tooth and tapped it against a datapad. It seemed to hum as she reached over the empty hole and released it, watching it fall slowly into the hole. A tap from her finger sent it down faster.

"Disturbance sensor," she said, realizing Soren was watching her. "Soon as someone starts mucking around here, it'll send a weak signal to the local net for us. It'll activate the beacons I put in each gun case, too."

Soren hefted one of the rifle cases from the sled and pushed it into the hole. These smugglers were a smart lot, working in micro gravity. Much easier on the joints and back.

"Won't whoever picks these up notice a beacon?" he asked.

"If I were an amateur, or lazy," Zelle snapped, sounding genuinely perturbed that he would suggest such a thing. "The beacons are passive, waiting for a surge in electromagnetic noise like when a ship goes into hyper or there's a high-powered broadcast nearby. The beacons squirt a bit of data that gets lost in the shuffle."

"And then?"

Soren shifted another case into the hole.

"Data floats around the local holoweb servers until I pull it out. After twenty-four hours, the same location data goes to a Drusic dating site which we can access most anywhere in the Republic."

"Drusic?"

"Those ugly apes are a bunch of pervs. Too much testosterone. You think security services want to sift through all those dick pics looking for clandestine communication?"

"Clearly you've never been in the navy."

Zelle tapped the side of her helmet.

Soren removed the last two cases. "Sounds like we found your next assignment, though."

"What? No." Zelle took a step back. "No no, forget I said anything."

Soren finished transferring the cases and swept dust over the hole. "Heywood?"

"Assignment Log Noted. This does explain Zelle's net browsing history."

"I hate you both," Zelle said. "So much."

Soren tapped the scuffed cases he'd stacked on the repulsor crate.

"Back to the *Iago*."

05

In the *Iago's* cargo hold, Soren brushed the fine asteroid dust off the top battered case and put a finger to the latch. He clicked his tongue and pulled his hand back.

"Heywood's got us a landing spot on Rintaka Prime," Zelle said from atop the stairs near the cockpit. "You think we can avoid a customs inspection or should we skip it and make a jump?"

"We should top off the fuel tanks," Soren said. "And then the ship can develop some maintenance issues as soon as we set down. That will give us time to wait for someone to pick up the other cases and give us a breadcrumb to follow."

"So we'll just sit there. On a Rep Army base."

"We're not criminals, Zelle. We're Nether Ops."

"And I'm sure no smuggler caught red-handed has ever tried to play that card." Zelle brushed hair away from her face. "You going to open those or not? Acting surprised as to the contents when a customs geek looks inside is not a winning idea."

"They scan clean of any explosives..." Soren reached for the case.

"Ooo, wait for me!" Zelle squealed, clambering down the stairs to metallic clangs as her boots rapidly descended.

Soren popped the latches and cracked open the case. A tuft of air blew out and Soren sniffed, detecting a slight antiseptic smell. He lifted the lid and frowned.

"Is it credits?" Zelle asked as she drew near. She furrowed her brow. "Oh. That's... odd."

Soren lifted a glossy black legionnaire helmet with red pinstripes out of the case. He turned the helmet over and looked inside.

"Leej armor?" Zelle picked up a breastplate, struggling with the weight. "Why in Oba's name would anyone smuggle this? Stuff's not exactly hard to find."

"It's not the latest issue," Soren said. "New armor's much lighter, cheaper. Protection against minor fragmentation and not much else. I was on the fielding initiative to the 16th Legion when it was first commissioned. The legionnaires weren't happy with the House of Reason's cost-cutting measures. They called the armor 'shinies' and 'tactical coffins.' This... this is more like the previous design that was replaced. Stuff that could stop ballistics and regulated blaster fire."

He pressed a button on the side of the helmet. Its faceplate flipped up, which would have revealed the face of whoever was wearing it. "Never saw this before."

"We've intercepted the dastardly deeds of a museum curator," Zelle said. "Mother will be so proud."

"These aren't legacy pieces," Soren said. "These are brand-new, fully functional. Packed in nitrogen to preserve them. No collector would want recreations this functional, too expensive. And any collector that's serious would want armor from the Savage Wars. Or Psydon at the latest. Battle damage. Dried blood. That sort of thing."

"These look expensive..." Zelle dropped the breast-plate back into the case.

"Ms. Zelle to the bridge," Heywood sent through the intercom.

"Wonderful," Zelle muttered and went back to the stairs.

Soren replaced the helmet and snapped the case shut. Two other cases held the same mint condition, dark-colored armor, but the fourth held something different. Inside was another suit of vintage design, but it was worn and bore marks of constant repair. The left shoulder guard was brand-new, but the right bore a painted over divot from a bullet strike. He flipped it over and found the Legionnaire corps symbol imprinted on the underside, but scratched through several times. Scrawled in the metal was DEATH TO THE REPUBLIC and FOR GOTH SULLUS.

"Who's Goth Sullus?" Soren wondered aloud.

"Soren? Can you come up to the bridge, please?" Zelle asked through the intercom.

"Moving." Soren tossed the armor back into the case and snapped it shut.

He found Zelle hunched over a work station, a holo of the Rintaka system in front of her.

"The disturbance sensor already went off," she said with a frown. She touched the map and zoomed in on the asteroid field. An icon of a Republic navy patrol ship closed on the field where a red dot pulsed on the far side.

"Did it malfunction?" Soren asked. "Who would make a pickup while law enforcement is so close?"

"Either someone supremely dumb or supremely confident," Zelle said. "Nothing from the other beacons yet. Which must mean they haven't sent a message to anyone signaling they made the pickup."

"You're sure your motion sensor didn't foul up?"

"*Yes*, I'm sure. I can make those in my sleep. It's working just fine."

"Sir." Heywood pointed to a blinking box on the communication station. "We're receiving a priority message from Rintaka sky command. Code crimson."

"Crimson." Soren sat in the co-pilot's seat and brought up the screen. "Curious."

Zelle leaned against the back of Soren's chair. "Is that bad? That sounds bad."

"Nether Ops use code crimson for agent-to-agent communication," Soren said as he typed in a challenge code.

"You're telling me this now?" Zelle asked.

"You didn't need to know before."

"That is correct," interjected Heywood. "You are only an auxiliary."

"Stow it in your gear box, machine man."

Soren's eyebrows perked up as the correct answer to his code bounced back. "Excuse us," he said over his shoulder.

"Oh! Of course! Oba forbid I know what's going on." Zelle stormed off the bridge.

As the door hissed closed behind her, a holo popped up of a woman with deeply tan skin, dark wavy hair, and sharp eyes.

"This is Rintaka station. Dia Farn." Her head tilted slightly from one side to the other as she spoke.

"*Iago.* Writ number JA-932. Voss, Soren."

"You check out as being on a sanctioned operation. I need you to set down and transfer your cargo to my jurisdiction."

"Come again? This is a sanctioned operation, you can't interfere unless there's been a declared crisis in the sector, and I'm not reading—"

"Are you new at this? This is my system. My problems. If your handler told you regs matter that much out here on the edge, you're in for a wake-up call. Besides, we've *been* in a declared crisis since that mess on Kublar. Now, do you want to argue semantics while I vector in my alert fighters or do you want to make this easy so I'm inclined to help you while you're in my backyard?"

"Coordinates received, sir," the bot said. "Also detecting several fighters launching from the sky fort."

Soren chewed his bottom lip for a moment. He sighed. "Roger, station, changing course now."

"See you soon." Farn closed the channel.

"We've been directed to a small landing pad deep within a Republic Army training area," Heywood said. "Quite secluded."

Soren shook his head. "This feels off. Unless they saw us poking around in the asteroid field, the only way she'd know we were Nether Ops and in-system is if the Carnivale told her."

"Is this unusual?" Heywood asked.

"Yes and no." Soren leaned back and crossed his arms in front of his chest. "It's considered polite to inform station heads when another agent will operate in their sector. It's supposed to keep everyone from stepping on each other's toes. Station heads don't like it when someone comes along and finds a problem that's been under local Nether Ops's nose. Looks bad."

"So Farn is not happy we're here."

"Or we've just brought her the key to unlocking an issue she's been working for months. Then she'll get plenty of credit for assisting me. The knife cuts both ways."

"And which way is the knife moving right now?" the bot asked.

"Those fighters still coming for us?"

"Negative, they're running patrols around the star fort."

"Then things are our favor." Soren stood up. "If she wanted us dead, those fighters would be on top of us."

"I find your dedication to the bright side of things most refreshing, sir."

"Yeah, well, not so bright that I don't want you to keep *Iago*'s defenses ready once we land on Rintaka."

Soren stood at the bottom of the *Iago*'s ramp and took a shallow breath of the muggy air that enveloped him like a hot fog. The jungle surrounding the landing pad faded away in the haze. He made out small bunkers along one side of the pad, no fence, and encroaching plant life gnawing away at the edge of the duracrete slab.

The local star was directly overhead, and that the haze hadn't cleared by this late in the day hinted that the weather on this part of the planet was always so unpleasant. For all the boredom and less than fulfilling service he'd given the Republic navy, at least the ships were temperature controlled.

A flock of red and orange birds lifted off from the treetops near the bunkers and Soren flipped the cover off his pistol. Figures emerged from the haze, making right for him. He could tell they were Legion—all four of them—by their armor. They were wearing the new reflective gear—the shinies that had seemed to embody everything wrong with the House of Reason in the minds of more than a few legionnaires Soren had spoken with. They walked with their rifles hung low in a wedge formation.

"Sir," Heywood said from the top of the ramp where he waited next to the cart loaded with the crates they took from the asteroid, "I was under the impression Rintaka did not have a Legion presence."

Soren chewed the inside of his mouth. "Not supposed to. But it is a training area. And if they're here to train, they won't be part of the systems assigned forces. So technically... no presence."

Soren let his hand fall away from his pistol. The legion-naires were looking right at him and paid no attention to the perimeter, as if he was the only threat around them. All were men, as was the norm in the Legion.

The legionnaires formed a semi-circle around the end of the ramp, keeping a distance of several meters between them and Soren. They were silent, but by the way their heads bobbed, he could tell they were speaking to each other through their helmets' comms systems.

"Is the station chief on her way?" Soren asked.

"Need to verify your cargo first," a legionnaire cap-tain said, his voice distorted by his helmet vocal amplifier. "Then we'll call her in."

He tapped the side of his helmet.

"If that's what she wants…" Soren signaled for Heywood and the bot pushed the repulsor cart down the ramp. He looked to the other legionnaires; two were lieutenants, the last was a major. Why the highest ranking officer hadn't addressed him struck Soren as unusual.

The captain pointed his rifle to the ground and shook Soren's hand, pressing the tip of an armored finger into the agent's wrist.

"You ever serve on Helax?"

"Can't say I have," Soren said.

The legionnaire pulled his arm back slowly.

"Never seen you before," the captain said.

"Farn have dinner parties to introduce all her people to each other?" Soren asked with a smirk. "Not how most chiefs run their stations."

The captain touched a case as the bot brought the cart to a halt.

"You removed the shipping seals?" he asked as he ran his hand along the surface. He rubbed his thumb across his fingertips, bunching the fine dust from the asteroid together.

"That's how we found them," Soren said.

The captain reached up and touched the side of his helmet. The agent couldn't make out the words, but he knew the legionnaire was speaking to someone.

The leej nodded.

Heywood shuffled his weight from one foot to the other, mimicking humanoid body language, all a part of blending in among biologics. He glanced from one legionnaire to the other, his servos audible as his head swiveled.

Out of the corner of his eye, Soren saw a lieutenant flick the safety off his rifle and slip a finger over the trigger. Feeling as though he were moving in slow motion, his hand dropped for his holstered blaster pistol.

"Happy birthday!" Zelle shouted from atop the ramp. Soren heard a metal-on-metal thump and ducked his face into the crook of his elbow.

He felt a flash of heat against his bare skin and a whack of overpressure against his head as the dazzler went off. One ear rang with a high-pitched whine as he smacked against the cart. Soren looked up from his arm and found a lieutenant stumbling toward him, one hand against his helmet.

Soren fumbled with his holster, feeling as though time would speed back up in any moment. The Legion lieutenant shook his head quickly, then locked his gaze on Soren. The latest armor was notoriously poor protection in battle, but the helmets were better than nothing.

The legionnaire swung his N-6 up just as Soren finally pulled his pistol free.

The muffled sound of blaster fire came distantly through the tinnitus roar in Soren's ears. These were from his own weapon. He had gotten the draw on the man and shot first.

The Legion lieutenant hunched forward. He tripped and went down to his knees, one arm grasping a wound to his side.

More shots rang out around Soren, faster and of a higher caliber than what he'd just unleashed.

Soren aimed his pistol between the lieutenant's eyes and pulled the trigger. The lieutenant's head bucked back and he collapsed to the ground.

The agent whirled around and saw Heywood struggling with the legionnaire captain. There was a flash of blaster fire that smashed into the bot's mid-section, causing it to break in half. Another bolt flashed past Soren's face, burning his bare skin and leaving a white scar across the vision of his left eye.

Soren fell to the ground next to the still-hovering cart and saw the feet of a legionnaire just on the other side. He aimed his pistol through the repulsor waves and sent a blaster bolt into the legionnaire's ankle. The man fell to the ground with a shout that came from his external helmet amps and dropped his blaster rifle. Soren shot him in the chest twice and rolled away.

The Legion captain slammed a boot down right where Soren's head had been. Heywood's hands and most of the bot's arms still clung to the legionnaire's wrists. The captain lurched toward the Nether agent with a roar.

Soren aimed center mass and fired. The blaster bolt struck the captain in the solar plexus and bounced off. So the new armor wasn't all bad. That or the captain had some kind of after-market enhancement.

The kinetic energy of the blaster bolt still hit like a decent punch and the captain buckled slightly. Soren raised his aim just as the legionnaire fell on top of him. The man's weight combined with that of Heywood's remains knocked the air out of Soren's chest.

The captain rammed his armored forearm against Soren's gun arm so hard that the agent almost lost his grip on the pistol. Soren let his arm flop to the side and shouted in pain. He thought he could almost see the legionnaire's eyes through his bucket's opaque visor—surely a trick of the mind. The Legion captain wrenched Soren's arm into the air, the rest of his bulk pinning Soren's to the ground. The jerky motion sent the pistol up into the air.

With the weapon gone, the legionnaire mashed his other elbow against Soren's throat, cutting off his airway. Soren could feel the pressure mount in his head, causing his eyes to bulge.

The pistol clattered to the ground somewhere nearby. Soren reached out, slapping the ground, searching for the weapon.

"She wants you alive," the captain said. "Didn't say unhurt."

The legionnaire lifted his arm from Soren's throat and beat his elbow into the spy's jaw. The armored strike was enough to cut out Soren's vision momentarily, like he'd blacked out for a second. But in that moment, his seeking hand found the blaster pistol.

Spitting out blood, Soren pressed the muzzle against the captain's helmet and pulled the trigger. The blaster bolt broke through the armor, cooking his brain as pieces of helmet ricocheted in the enclosed space, bouncing around the captain's skull like the blades of a blender.

Soren pushed the body off of him and sat up. Dimly aware that there might still be one more to deal with. But all was silent.

"Zelle?"

His word came through his ears like they were stuffed with synthprene. Blood dribbled down his chin from where the captain had elbowed him and pain radiated across his face.

He shook his head quickly and looked for the fourth legionnaire. The major lay in a pool of blood beneath the *Iago*. Heywood's head and most of his upper chest were facedown, sparks snapping out of shorn wires.

"Zelle!" Soren looked to the ramp and saw rivulets of blood tracing down the from the cargo bay. His partner lay on her side in the cargo bay, red craters in her back. She lay still.

Soren raced up the ramp, avoiding the blood streams coming from Zelle. Her mouth was agape, carbine held loosely in her hands. Eyes open but staring at nothing.

"Zelle, say something."

Soren touched her neck and didn't find a pulse. The front of her jacket was soaked in blood, the grim result of a blaster bolt fired at close range, cooking the immediate skin but punching through so fast that it caused traumatic tissue damage. The legionnaires had shot her through the heart and lungs.

Death was instant. At least there was that much. She didn't suffer.

"Ah, by Oba." Soren sat next to her on the ramp, his mind racing as he struggled to process the fight, pain clawing into his face and grief.

Why? Why had the legionnaires tried to kill them?

"Function," Soren said to himself. "There's still a mission."

He looked down at the carnage on the landing pad. The four legionnaires may not be all that were coming. And the way the one had spoken, the Nether Agent in this sector had authorized what had just happened.

He needed to vanish.

Soren pushed himself to his feet and hurried down the ramp to the dead lieutenant he'd shot in the head. Tilting the body up, he removed the identity chit hidden beneath the left side of the breastplate. He went to each of the other dead and collected their chits. The major's was covered in blood and cracked, but should still be viable.

"Sir?" Heywood chirped feebly, one arm still partially holding onto the Legion captain, the bot's head resting facedown on the dead man's chest. "Sir, I am unable to see you."

Soren slipped the four chits into a pocket, then went to his bot and flipped its head and shoulders over.

"Thank you, sir. My motor functions seem to have been damaged."

"Can you still fly the ship if I hardwire you into it?" Soren asked.

Heywood cocked his head to one side and saw the rest of his parts and the dead legionnaires.

"This is most vexing," the bot said.

"Yes or no?"

"My data core is undamaged, sir. Simply connect my—oh!"

Soren slammed what remained of Heywood onto the repulsor cart and he pulled it all back into his ship. The pain in his face grew worse, and a tightness in his chest formed as he passed Zelle's body again.

"Where is Ms. Zelle?" Heywood asked, his gaze stuck on whatever was right above him.

Soren cut the power to the cart's repulsors and locked it to the deck. He mashed a button and raised the ramp then wrapped an arm around the bot's neck, looping under its armpit. Sparks from the severed limb spat against the Soren's jacket as he lugged the bot up the stairs toward the cockpit.

"Ms. Zelle! Sir, why haven't you rendered first aid?" Heywood asked.

"She doesn't need it," Soren grunted. He dropped the bot into the co-pilot's seat and sat at the master controls. Soren brought the ship up to power and waited for the main engines to warm up.

"Sir, as much as I'd like to fly, I am at a distinct lack of mobility and dexterity," Heywood said. "You have yet to hardwire me into the ship."

"No time." Soren put a headset over his hears and frantically tapped at the controls. "I can get us into space. For now, I need you to... to check our comms logs. Zelle's data feeds. Anything from the beacons?"

"My wireless antennae are badly damaged." One of the bot's optic disks flickered on and off. "Frustrating."

The *Iago* shook as the engines came to life and the ship lifted off into the haze. Soren reached into the co-pilot's seat and flipped down a small hatch on the controls between the two seats. He pulled out a jumble of wires.

"Red?" Soren asked. "No, green."

"Blue with white chevrons," Heywood said, his words slurring.

Soren's hands trembled as he pulled the data line out and plugged it into a port on the back of the bot's head.

"The connection is-is-is poooooooor," Heywood said. "Peanut. Nostril. Happy clams."

Soren made a fist and whacked the bot.

"Rebooting." The bot's eyes clicked off.

"Damn it!" Soren pulled up the astrogation menu and looked at the star systems within range. Worlds with heavy MCR presence. Which meant more legionnaires. Stars with nothing but pirates and smugglers. A few Republic strongholds.

He wiped blood off his chin and winced as pain grew stronger. He needed to visit the ship's med bay. His jaw felt broken. But first, where to go? Where to run?

The Nether Ops chief on the world must have ordered the attack after they realized he'd been to the asteroid cache. How could old model legionnaire armor be that important?

"Much improved," Heywood said, his reboot cycle finished.

"Anything from Zelle's beacons?" Soren repeated.

"Affirmative. We have one data packet with hyperspace coordinates to Qadib."

"Qadib?" Soren found the system on the astrogation charts, its name in amber text. "Can we reach it?"

"Not at top speed. I'll have to adjust our hyperspace velocity to—"

"Do it. Just get us out of here."

Soren entered his override and accessed Zelle's profile. Several voice messages with Legion frequency tags had been opened. But not L-comm, thankfully. That was a nut even Nether Ops hadn't been able to track. They were talking to someone on a Republic-encrypted voice. And Soren had a good idea who it was. He double tapped the last one.

"What do you mean they're unsealed?" Farn's voice played through the headphones. The local Nether Ops agent sounded irate. "By Oba, they've been to the rock. How the hell did they... I want the agent alive. Kill anyone else and slag the ship."

A massive headache gripped Soren as he tried to piece together what had just happened. Zelle... Zelle must have been listening in real time once she sliced into the legionnaire's helmet comms and heard the station chief's order to the captain. She'd tossed the dazzler down the ramp to try to save him and been cut down.

The *Iago* shook briefly, then all the turbulence faded away.

"Sir, may I take over? We'll make hyperspace in three minutes."

"I need," Soren tapped his ringing ear, "I need some time."

"You're bleeding all over my seat. Please seek medical attention before you lose consciousness. I'll be of little help should that happen."

"Anything in the system?"

"It seems we've been flagged as smugglers. Several fighter squadrons are on an intercept course... and we're being hailed with another code crimson."

"How long until we're in weapons range?"

"Eight minutes, provided the fighters do not exceed peacetime engine tolerances."

"Haven't been at peace in a long time."

Soren stared at the pulsing icon for the incoming hail. He reached for it with bloodstained fingers, ready to show Farn that he was still alive. There was a temptation to play the audio file proving her treachery and involvement with the smuggling...

Soren pulled his hand back.

"What the enemy knows, they can act on," Soren said.

"Sir?"

"She doesn't know what happened. If any of us were killed. That we know where the weapons went. She'll lash out and try to find us. She's desperate. And the desperate make mistakes."

"And how would you characterize our situation, sir?"

He wiggled his jaw back and forth, suspicions that it was broken growing.

"Determined." He got up and went to the back of the bridge where they kept an emergency medical kit.

06

Soren sat next to Zelle, her body in a black bag zipped up to her chest. Her eyes were still half open, skin pale. Soren worked his hands open and shut, feeling the cold slick of her blood against his skin.

His jaw and ear ached, the pain lessened by a number of injections from the med kit. Cellular nanites were already working to knit his fractured jaw back together, but it would probably be a few days before he'd feel whole again.

He'd had the chance to examine Zelle's wounds and found confirmation that there was nothing he or Heywood could have done for her. Not even a full Legion field hospital could have saved her. She was likely dead before she reached the deck.

"Sir?" the bot said through the ship-wide comm. "May I take this opportunity to—"

"Skip the condolence programming and get to where you're useful," Soren snapped.

"The data query on the Legion identity chits is complete. Would you like the findings?"

"Not now." Soren tugged the zipper on the body bag higher, then stopped. Only Zelle's head and neck remained exposed. He wiped a bloody hand on a rag and closed her eyes. "It's not fair, you know that, Heywood? Nether Ops promised her a reduced sentence if she served as an auxiliary. She could've said no, served out her sentence, and left prison alive. Instead... she's dead because of me. Because of Nether Ops."

"Shall I reengage my condolence programs?"

"No. You'd tell me she chose this course of action with knowledge of the risks, and that her sacrifice served the Republic, wouldn't you?"

"That is correct. I would have also added the percentile likelihood of her being killed in prison. How did you know?"

"It's what I would have said back when I was in the navy." Soren pulled the body bag the rest of the way shut. "Does she—damn me for not knowing this—does she have any next of kin?"

"She has an aunt listed, but Ms. Zelle's personnel file states not to contact the relative in the event of death or injury."

"Religious observances?"

"While she has used Oba's name in vain frequently, she's listed as non-denominational."

Soren worked his lips into a snarl then lifted the corner of the body bag where a malleable plastic screen was attached. He flicked his thumb across the device and scrolled through a menu that appeared. He pressed hard on an option and the screen beeped twice. The body bag tightened against Zelle hard enough that he could make out her face, like she was sleeping.

"On Oliphant, we believe Oba lets the spirit linger," he said. "Longer if the life ended... badly. You were brave. Strong. Clever. All the things Nether Ops could have ever asked for in an agent. I'll see you receive a full pardon. May you move on with no burden on your soul. As for Farn and the traitors working with her... they will be dealt with. You have my word."

Heat radiated from Zelle's body as the bag began the cremation. In another hour, all that would be left of her would be ash.

Soren returned to the bridge and found Heywood slumped over in the co-pilot's seat. He lifted the bot up and propped him against the back.

"Thank you. I imagine if I were human, I would be very embarrassed."

"If you were human, you'd be very dead right now." Soren sat in the pilot's seat. "What am I going to do with you?"

"We do not have a spare chassis aboard," Heywood said. "Qadib is a world under heavy zhee influence, but should you find another KH-1188 unit, you could swap my data core. Such a repair is relatively simple. Even for you."

Soren gave the bot a sidelong glance.

"Ms. Zelle would have had no such difficulty." The bot's head snapped from side to side. "Bother. My servos are malfunctioning."

Soren clamped his hand atop the bot's head and held it still. There was a whirr and a snap within Heywood's neck.

"Now I can't move my head at all." The bot sounded almost depressed.

"You found something on the legionnaires?" Soren kicked his feet onto the controls and picked up a datapad.

"Indeed. What made you think their identities would prove useful? Dark Ops almost always operate under aliases."

"If they were Dark Ops, they would've killed us easily. Those legionnaires were sloppy. Then, they were all officers. And the only thing three or more officers ever do together is have a meeting. Bunch of officers together on a mission? Never happens. I should've known something was off soon as I saw them."

Soren opened the file on the captain that had died last. His eyes darted across the information.

"Nothing jumps out at me. Rear echelon postings. On his first command of a company sent to Rintaka for jungle training." Soren snorted in disgust. "He's a point."

"'Point'?"

"Appointment commission. Politically connected individual that can pass the lowest possible bar to serve as an officer. Rep Army has them. Navy has them. Marines. And for some reason the Legion, the Republic's preeminent fighting force, has them. No one likes points, except for other points, of course."

"Their performance is questionable?"

"How well do you think someone that got their job because of political donations, and keeps that job because of donations, will do? They're a cancer—but you know what, that doesn't matter right now." Soren flipped to the next file and looked over one of the two lieutenants.

"Junior officer... just commissioned... no campaign ribbons or medals so he's... also a point. Huh." He flipped to the next file. "The major's also a point."

He went to the next. "A point."

"Given the known percentage of appointed officers in the Legion," Heywood's optics winked on and off as his data core worked over time, "the chance of encountering four officers with such a background in such close proximity is—"

"Not a coincidence." Soren tapped the screen and looked deeper into the captain's file. "He's from Pardith, major core world... and he was appointed by Delegate Dryden. He's on the Defense council, banking committee. Been in the House of Reason for decades."

"That one of his appointees was involved in an attack on a Nether Ops agent would be quite the scandal," the bot said.

Soren flipped to the next file and his face went pale. He flipped two more times, then tossed the datapad onto the controls.

"Something awry?" Heywood asked.

"Senator Dryden appointed all four of them. Doesn't make sense. Pardith isn't part of the MCR. The planet's entire economy depends on the Republic's good fortune. Why would Dryden... he wouldn't be. He can't be a traitor too."

Soren sat quietly, watching stars streak past the windows as the *Iago* flew toward Qadib.

"Shall I prepare a summary report for the Carnivale?"

"No, not yet. We can't implicate Dryden in this. Evidence gathered during sanctioned Nether Ops missions is almost impossible to use in court. And right now this could all be waved away as nothing but a coincidence."

"You seem prepared to continue your investigation on this apparent coincidence."

"I'm a spy. I need a plausible suspicion to work against someone. Lawyers and judges need evidence beyond a reasonable doubt." Soren picked up a water bottle from the side of his seat and took a sip.

"And if this senator is involved with arms smuggling and the MCR, what will you do? Assassinate him? The state of emergency declared after the MCR attack on Kublar allows for extra-judicial killing should a clear and present threat to the Republic be discovered," the bot recited. "However, I question whether an agent with your relatively minute level of experience ought to be making so momentous a decision at this point in his career."

"This isn't some edge warlord or career criminal that no one will cry over if they wake up dead... this is a long-standing delegate. One that's friends with Orin Karr."

"Then what is our course of action?"

"We need evidence. Even if it doesn't lead us to Dryden, we'll find out who's responsible for the stolen leej weapons... and what that armor's for."

"As you like, sir. We're an hour out from Qadib."

"Come out of hyper short of the usual translation points. I need a signal back to the Carnivale and I don't want to risk anyone eavesdropping, even on a dirt ball like Qadib."

"We are almost out of fuel. I must note that if the local Nether Ops chief is... less than loyal... we will have a difficult time escaping the system."

"Good point…" Soren rubbed his chin and winced as he touched the hairline fracture in his jaw.

The *Iago* sped beneath a gas giant, the underside a kaleidoscope of color and storms.

"This system is most unusual," Heywood said. "No out-system patrols. No friend or foe challenge from orbit harbormasters."

"Qadib borders zhee space. They're known to go on slave raids to systems that aren't fully in line with the Republic's aims," Soren said. "Anyone that comes here knows the risks. Naturally, it attracts the desperate and the criminal element."

"I just replaced the ship's hull fixtures." The bot's armless shoulders wagged up and down. "Scaring away street urchins and opportunists on Strach IV took a few near misses with a pistol before word got around to leave my beautiful ship alone. I dare say my knowledge of zhee expletives will not be as effective should we set down in a less secure area. Which seems inevitable."

"We'll manage." Soren entered a code into the controls. A holoscreen and cam extended up from the co-pilot's seat. Soren twisted it toward him and waited as a cursor pulsed in one corner.

Minutes ticked by and Soren sighed. He drew his pistol and a leather pouch from a thigh pocket. He laid a cloth out on his lap, unloaded the weapon and disassembled it. He cleaned out the chamber with a puff and ran a thin wire brush down the barrel when the screen finally resolved into a silhouette surrounded by static.

Soren traded challenges with his handler.

"Report," Nix said.

"You've heard nothing? No word from Rintaka?" Soren asked.

"You're not there?" Nix asked. Soren wished the connection wasn't so encrypted. It was hard for him to gauge if his handler was being sarcastic or not.

Soren recounted the events on the garrison world, giving extensive details on Farn and the legionnaire officers.

"The auxiliary's service is terminated," Nix said with a sniff. "Unfortunate."

"Zelle. And I'll close out her file once time allows," Soren said. "Further, I'll recommend her for—"

Nix waved a hand in a dismissive gesture.

Anger blossomed in Soren's heart.

"The dead are dead," Nix said. "Save your energy for the task at hand. I can redirect another technician to you. Which is where, exactly? You've scrambled your location trace for this transmission."

Soren swiped a screen and brought up a map of Qadib Primus, the planet's main city. The beacons hidden in the weapon's cases showed them all in the planet's largest city. Which wasn't really saying much. The habitable portions of Qadib were little more than an equatorial belt between oceans.

Straightening himself, Soren said, "Given the encounter we had with Nether Ops on Rintaka, I'm reflagging this mission as Onyx condition."

Nix scowled and shook his head. "Son, that's incredibly stupid. Onyx is meant for more senior agents operating within an established network. *You* go offline from all other Nether Ops and you're tying both hands behind your back—"

Soren adjusted a dial on his communication's panel and Nix's words were drowned out in static.

"Control, we're passing through a gas giant's radiation belt," Soren said. "We're losing the link. Full report in three days. Sir? Sir?"

He pressed a button and the holoscreen retreated into the console.

"Is this wise?" Heywood asked. "While I am but a simple H3Y-W0D mark JB-M3 model bot tasked to Nether Ops—well, not so simple given the extensive modifications to my processors—to divorce yourself from any and all support… I believe 'incredibly stupid' is not far off as an assessment."

"It's a question of necessity, not wisdom, Heywood. Farn knew this ship was Nether Ops after we popped onto Rintaka's grid. She was waiting for us, and the only way that would happen is if someone told her we were on the way."

"You believe Nix did this?"

"No, I'm his agent. He wanted me to turn over the weapons before I could find the next link in the chain, he would've just ordered me to dump the crates on Strach IV or Rintaka. By procedure, he sent up a report with our plan after we left Strach and someone in Nether Ops—someone working with Farn—found it. I have to go Obsidian and hide out from disloyal elements, long enough to find more evidence of who's working against the Republic."

"So you're going to go waltzing around Qadib alone. On a zhee refugee world. Poking your nose someplace it doesn't belong."

"No one ever said Nether Ops would be easy. And it's not like we're going to Ankalor. Qadib is Republic governed. Log into the system's freight notice boards and start looking for work. Bid way too high on a couple freight runs but don't accept any contracts. Need to at least pretend we're a cargo ship."

Soren stood up and rubbed his jaw. The hairline fracture had nearly healed; he could move it well enough, but it was still sore to the touch.

"As you like, sir. I'll have you note our limited funds available before you decide the good ship *Iago* is too proud for an honest day's work," the bot said. "Of course, were we not Onyx condition, I could easily arrange a transfer."

"We'll find a way. I need to go take care of something."

Soren left the bridge and went to the cargo bay. He made his way back to ship's entryway, where he'd left Zelle in her body bag.

She was now reduced to little more than a long lump in the black plastic. Soren grabbed one end, so hot it was almost painful to touch, and rolled it up. The ash within ground against itself and he hefted the heavy bag into the crook of one arm.

Soren looked to the garbage disposal shoot and shook his head. He considered releasing her remains to the void from the air lock, but hesitated.

"You deserve better," he said, looking down at the misshapen lump cradled in his arm. "Internment on Utopion with the honored fallen. Even if it is in a mausoleum with the masses and not a proper grave site. To hell with Nix, I'll pay the fees myself."

He brought the roll to their quarters and laid it at the base of her pillow, then tightened the sheets over it.

"First time that bed's ever been made," he muttered.

"Sir?" Heywood called through the comms. "We've secured a landing pad and received several death threats from shippers accusing us of trying to inflate rates. When I lowered bids to offset this negativity, we received death threats for being shills attempting to deflate rates. This planet seems more difficult than usual."

"It's been heavily colonized by the zhee," Soren said. "You've got a mix of refugees from all four home worlds displaced by intertribal warfare. And they're all constantly threatening to kill everyone else they encounter."

"This is quite the discouraging picture."

"They only mean it sometimes, generally closer to their days of religious observance. Not that it makes a difference. Qadib is the place."

"It seems likely that you will die at 'the place.' Not that that's any of my business. I'll be safely on board the ship."

"Thank you for your concern." Soren went to a locker and jiggled the handle to open it. This one always seemed stuck. Inside were several worn overcoats, boots, scarves, and pistols that looked like they'd been scavenged from Strach IV. He picked out what he hoped would be inconspicuous on Qadib. Just another spacer looking to get a job and then get the hell off the planet. No trouble asked for, no trouble needed.

He adjusted a gun belt over a light tan trench cloak and pulled a balaclava hood over his mouth and head. "All right, Heywood, I'm going outside."

"Yes, sir. As you say, you're the one who has to go mingle with those vile creatures. Don't blame me when they eat you. Then kill you. Or is it the other way around?"

"Just be ready to drop the ramp if you see me running to the ship."

The *Iago*'s cargo ramp lowered and a swirl of orange dust blew through the crack. Cold air enveloped him and he set a pair of goggles over his eyes.

Lines of dust snaked across the basalt landing pad, and three figures walked up to the ramp, stopping inches from where the edge touched down, clearly zhee.

The three aliens wore knee-length white tunics and had their legs and arms wrapped in cloth. Their cloven feet scratched at the landing pad impatiently. With their equine heads, floppy ears, and gray fur, Soren understood why most of the galaxy called them donks. Not to their face, of course. Only the Legion did that.

Two on the flanks carried slug rifles boasting serrated bayonets in their hoof-like claws. The one in the middle had a curved knife hanging from his belt, through Soren's trained eye saw bulges in the alien's tunic for at least two pistols.

Soren opened his hands to his sides and walked down the ramp.

The zhee with the knife poked him in the chest hard enough to stop him a step short of the edge.

"Stop, *tarha*, this world's blessed by the four gods," the zhee said.

"I wired the port fees," Soren said. "Need to see a receipt?"

"You are *tarha*. There's a tax for your presence here."

The zhee forbade nonbelievers, which meant any non-zhee as only the donks were pure enough for their gods. With each of the four home worlds constantly fighting and undermining one another to prove which was the preeminent. They were more than willing to kill one another to prove they were the first among equals.

Soren wasn't sure if this 'tax' was a simple shake down or if this was some part of zhee dominance on worlds they'd been allowed to colonize. But there wasn't any sense in taking a principled stand against local custom. There rarely was.

"I know there's a duty on imported goods," Soren said. "But I've come with an empty hull looking for work."

The zhee pulled his knife free from its scabbard and raised it flat against his chest.

"Eight hundred credits or your hand. Choose."

"Sir," Heywood said through Soren's ear bead, *"we've barely enough to refuel the ship if you pay that exorbitant amount. Let me activate the ship's cannons. Please. The satisfaction you'd get in killing them is far higher than recovering whatever intelligence you'll find here. I'm sure of it."*

"Eight hundred," Soren reached into his coat slowly as the rifle-armed zhee huffed at each other. He pulled out a credit chit synced to his account and set it to the donk's asking price.

The lead zhee snatched the money and backhanded Soren across the face, sending him falling ass-first onto the ramp. The alien sheathed his knife and tossed a black piece of cloth with zhee letters stitched into it at Soren's chest.

"Wear that," the zhee said. "Or pay your tax again, *tarha*."

The aliens turned, and one of the flankers kicked sand onto Soren as they walked off.

"What a horrid place," Heywood said.

"Yeah, real garden spot." Soren worked his mouth from side to side, glad that at least the zhee had hit the side of his face that wasn't healing. He picked up the cloth and worked it between his fingertips. It was an armband. Soren slipped it over his sleeve and made sure it was too tight to fall off.

The circular bay the *Iago* had set down in was open to the sky. Soren wasn't sure if the sky was always the color of jaundice or if a dust storm was passing through. There was vegetation in other stretches of the planet, which made Soren wonder why the largest city was out here, seemingly amid the wastes. There was a single set of metal double doors in the walls circling his ship, no windows or walkways.

"At least this spot is private," Soren said into the comm. "No one can see us loading or unloading cargo."

"Or see misfits stealing parts off my ship," Heywood replied. *"I'm locking the ramp and electrifying the hull should*

I see anyone but you come through that door. How long will you be gone and where are you staying?"

"You sound nervous, Heywood." Soren unsnapped the cover on his pistol and made his way to the door.

"Hardly. Just remember we have funds for three days on this pad. Less if the tax man comes calling again."

Soren pushed one of the doors open and found a street with humans, zhee, and other races going about their business, passing windowed stores and food stands. Non-zhee wore the bands on their left arms and Soren switched his over to match.

Rickshaws, some with creaky robot drivers, others with aged feline wobankis, made their way through the streets slowly. The ring of bells alerted pedestrians to their approach through the sand.

"Keep poking at the job boards." Soren shut the door behind him. "I'll scout this place out on foot."

The blowing dust and cold air made walking around with a covered face natural and acceptable, which was a boon for Soren as he didn't want to be noticed or recognized while in the city. Of course, the local dress also made spotting anyone tailing him more difficult, but Soren decided he could manage the risk. What other choice did he have?

Adjusting his goggles, Soren pressed a tiny button that activated a HUD on the lenses. An overlay of the city appeared, showing the fastest directions to a number of points of interest he'd loaded up earlier. A diamond pulsed to his north, leading him to the beacons hidden in the arms cases.

"There are a number of bot shops in the bazaar," Heywood said. *"I'll send you specifications for my new chassis."*

"Thought we were low on cash." Soren walked down the road and stopped to wait in line for some sort of grilled meat that other humans were eating.

"For low priority things such as alms for the zhee, but this is me we're talking about."

Soren glanced up and down the street for anyone mirroring his actions, a sure sign that he was being followed. He passed a credit to a thin man in exchange for a wooden stick skewered through greasy hunks of meat.

Uncovering his mouth, he bit off a chunk and chewed as he walked, trying not to think about what where it might have come from. It was a distantly familiar taste. "'It's me' isn't the most convincing of arguments right now, Heywood."

"Do you want to do all the cooking? Cleaning? Maintenance tasks? I'll also point out that the upholstery on my seat is eight weeks past factory-suggested replacement. The co-pilot preceding you and Ms. Zelle was fond of spicy food and rampant flatulence. I've had to disengage my olfactory sensors. You don't have that option."

Soren spat out a tiny bone and tossed the meat stick down an alleyway. He'd never had a taste for cat.

"Why buy you a new chassis when Nether Ops will do it for free once we're finished up here? The seat cushions can wait, too."

Humans and other non-zhee hurried off the street and into businesses, seemingly all at once as if by some unspoken cue.

"Fine. Expel a reminder of that corpulent windbag every time you sit in that seat after you replace my body, see if I care."

Braying sounded around a corner and everyone still out on the street with an armband stopped in place and fell to their knees. A door opened next to Soren and an old woman motioned him inside. The elderly woman didn't seem armed and the smell of pastries was certainly more inviting than whatever was coming around the street. Still, Soren hesitated a moment to get a better look inside before ducking into the doorway.

"Oba bless you," the old woman said as the door shut behind him with a hiss. She flashed a bull horned hand gesture at the window as a crowd of zhee came around the corner, braying to the sky and slapping at their chests. "Another one of their damned holy months. They've been insufferable since the Republic let them immigrate as much as they like to this world."

Soren picked up the scent of cinnamon rolls smothered with icing. He passed her a credit chit and pointed at a display, his mouth already watering.

"Doesn't the governor enforce the Displacement Act?" Soren asked as the old woman pulled out his selection from behind the glass. "It's meant to stop a world from... this sort of thing."

She handed him a roll wrapped in greasy paper.

"Act's only ever enforced to keep humans off of alien worlds," she said. "Transports full of zhee show up in the sky? Why, the governor can't come across as xenophobic, now can she? She'd be dragged back to the House of

Reason to explain why she hates non-humans so much. Useless woman."

"I didn't know it was like this out here." He took a whiff of the roll, remembering a particular stall in an open-air market back on Oliphant he and Vanessa liked, then took a bite.

"You're a hauler by dress. Guess local politics don't much matter to your kind. That or you ain't seen much of the galaxy yet."

Soren shrugged and took a bite.

The old woman continued. "Pick up a load, take to where you're paid to. Doesn't matter if the money comes from humans or it doesn't. Same goes for me, mind you, but it's a whole lot harder when they hate you. Bet you'll have charters for native Qadibi moving to a human world soon enough, if the zhee don't tax us into poverty first."

She shuffled over to an oven and removed a tray of croissants and laughed to herself. "You think the donks would buy a bakery?"

"I couldn't say."

"Rhetorical question. Those savages don't like cooked food unless it's the flesh of their enemies. What's your next world?"

"Strach IV, if I can't find a decent haul." Soren kissed frosting off his fingertips.

"Strach... bah." She looked over his shoulder. "Procession's over with. One of those mobs catches you in the open and they might drag you off for a religious observance. Not many come back from those."

"Thank you, madam." Soren added a credit to the chit he'd given her as a tip and went back onto the street.

The streets were eerily silent as he followed the beacon to the first case. Humans made furtive glances from doorways before hustling back into the open, heads down. Soren chalked up the old woman's warning about being taken away by the zhee as mere uneducated superstition. The mandatory cultural appreciation lessons the Republic gave him spent an inordinate amount of time dispelling any notion that the zhee ate other sentients. Either the locals hadn't had the training, or they were aware of a different truth.

The air had cleared somewhat, with a faint blue to the sky. The beacon led him to a low brick wall that cut through several demolished buildings. Armed zhee clustered on either side of the lone street going through the barrier and only other zhee passed by them.

"Heywood, the beacons are about three hundred yards ahead of me," Soren said into the comm woven into his hood. "What's there?"

"Based on images pulled from your goggles... a zhee temple. You'll note the walls. Zhee consider anything within four rawlataw—*their units of measure, one being equal to eighty-six point two yards—of their temples to be sacred."*

Soren pretended to consult a datapad as he captured more video of the street leading to the temple.

"And non-zhee aren't allowed anywhere near it," he concluded.

"Correct. The aliens seem to have chosen a number of major intersections on the northeastern part of the city for their temples."

"And they squeezed out anyone between the temples. Wonder how long it took for the locals to put a stop to it."

Soren entered a search query and turned off the data feed from his goggles.

"There are a number of proposed temple locations on the zoning board's schedule. Why did you cut off the data?"

"Because it's a bandwidth hog on the local holonet just asking to be investigated. I'm going to scout around, see how I can infiltrate the temple."

"This seems inadvisable."

"If the zhee are involved with the smuggling—and keep in mind that there were rumors of dead zhee being taken off that corvette that almost rammed the House of Reason..."

"I heard no such rumors."

"Anyone who discussed those rumors on the net had their accounts banned and were sent to reeducation. So, no surprise."

"Are you suggesting Republic authorities reacted too harshly?"

Soren rolled his eyes. "Thereby confirming the rumors? No, I'd never do that. I'm switching off until dawn. Don't message me unless there's a zhee trying to steal our engines. Voss out."

He cut the channel and turned around to find a multi-story hotel with a swaying sign and half-lit lettering. The Misfire. He looked at the top floors, judging the line of sight back to the zhee temple.

"Let's see what we can see from up there," he said to himself.

07

The lobby of the Misfire hotel smelled of old leather and wood chips. A pair of broad-shouldered Drusic security guards gave Soren a once-over as he entered. They examined his features rather than his weapons and let him pass with a simian snort from their squashed noses.

A wide red carpet with worn patches stretched across the lobby. Buckets caught water from leaks in the roof and there were a number of stains on the walls and floor that Soren didn't want identified.

A lone bot waited at the check-in counter, the wall behind it entirely comprised of a seamless, tarnished mirror. Farther off, a raised area with a wooden railing broken in several places marked off a dining room. Knots of humanoids huddled around tables. But no zhee. An Endurian 'princess' in a skimpy wrap waved to him from a bar.

"Buy something or get out," one of the Drusics muttered. "Costs a lot to keep the zhee out of here."

"Noted." Soren made his way to the bot behind the counter, ignoring the Endurian as she playfully tugged at his coat.

"Welcome to the Misfire," the bot said. A pair of sparks shot out of the seam on its faceplate, and Soren wasn't sure if the effect was intentional or not. "Do note that all walls and floors are reinforced against most caliber of weapons in James's Galactic Armory; however, the hotel bears no liability for any and all personal injury you may suffer while on the premises."

"That much of a problem?" Soren asked.

The robot leaned to one side and pointed to a sign reading DAYS WITHOUT GUEST INJURY: 14.

"That's some… *interesting* marketing," Soren said, his gaze fixed on the sign.

"Would you like a suite?" the robot asked.

"Got anything on the top floor? Preferably facing north."

"Room 37 is available. Do avoid the windows at sunrise and sunset. Zhee celebratory fire is most common at those hours." The bot dropped a key fob into a pewter dish, then motioned to the Endurian, who twirled the ends of the thin tendrils serving in place of hair and waved to Soren. "Additional services are available."

"I'll keep that in mind." Soren swiped a credit chit over a sensor and took his key.

He went to the lone elevator and tapped a dead button and heard the Drusics chuckle. Evidently, he'd be climbing. The nearby stairwell looked intact, complete with a drunk snoozing against the handrail. Soren stepped gingerly over the man and climbed to the top floor. He moved past other guest rooms, some with doors ajar offering glimpses of flashing holoscreens inside the darkened interiors.

A couple was fighting loudly about what sounded like money. Perhaps a couple just for the time paid, then.

Reaching his room, Soren waved the key fob near the door handle and heard a click.

Inside, a flickering automatic light came on as Soren stepped inside. The rug was stained and worn thin to the point of showing tattered holes. There was a bed made with a synthetic-looking quilt with a floral pattern and a rude desk with a single wooden chair.

Soren closed the door and set the manual deadbolt. He stepped into a small adjoining refresher. Everything was the dingy orange of white tile and porcelain neglected for too long. The toilet in particular looked as though it had sat there for half a century. A steady drip plinked from the faucet. Soren tightened the handles to no avail.

Wiping his hands on his robe, he moved to the bed, which faced a holoscreen hard-mounted to the opposite wall.

The sun was setting and the tat-tat-tat of zhee machine guns beat through the walls, promising a chaotic evening on Qadib.

Soren found the illumination panel and extinguished all the room's lights. He looked out over the temple, knowing that with the lights out, a dark background gave no shadow for anyone outside to see. The windows themselves came with privacy screens that would help to confound anyone trying to peek inside beyond the visual spectrum.

At first impression, Soren thought the screens on the windows were a bit much for a fleabag hotel like the Misfire, but it certainly kept any zhee with a decent sniper scope from knowing when there was a target inside to take a shot at. And given the wanton firing going on out there, maybe those screens were a necessity. The aliens seemed to enjoy firing into the air. Burning tracer rounds zipped through the night a few times a minute.

He ordered dinner.

A truck laden down with boxes drove into the back of the zhee temple and he jotted down the time. Zhee entered through the four gates around the perimeter wall, each at the corners, which struck Soren as an interesting design choice. How the aliens' architecture and religion meshed was a question for Heywood with his access to Nether Ops' information network. The House of Reason's sensitivity training rarely dealt with what the zhee actually believed, only about how the ideal galactic citizen should think about them.

As zhee filed in, an equal amount came out. Though which of the four gates were used as entrances or exits seemed to change with the hour. Soren kept watching, keeping vigil for six hours. He hadn't picked out any obvious VIPs or detected the homing beacons leaving.

He sighed and realized that the audiobook he'd been listening to had come to an end some time before. He queued up another, hoping the story would be good enough to pass the time.

There was a faint knock at his door and he snapped his pistol toward the battered wood between him and whoever was on the other side.

"Room service," a small voice spoke. "I'll leave it just outside as you asked. Fair day, sire."

Footfalls hurried down the hallway.

Soren waited five minutes, then crept toward the door. He knelt and looked beneath the gap that let in a steady draft, and opened the door a crack. Confident there was no one about to rush in and ruin his stakeout, he reached out with his foot and pulled a tray with a covered dish into his room.

He flipped the bolts and locks, resecuring his castle, and brought the tray to the small desk. The smell of earth wafted up from the dish... and he swore that he could hear a slight tremor vibrating through the tray. He lifted the lid and gagged. Deep purple worms writhed in a hot broth of yellow and red.

"Ah, Hool curry!" Soren slammed the lid back and shuddered. How did this place manage to screw up a simple order of spaghetti and meatballs? His stomach rumbled. Soren tapped a finger against the tray. It had taken hours for his order to come up, and just how professional the kitchen would be when told about the mistake was up in the air.

But he needed to eat something. Other than the Hool curry.

Soren took a small puck with eight sides out of his coat and pressed it against the glass. Tiny suction cups latched onto the window and the back of the device popped out. A screen lit up and he twisted dials on the optic until it had a good view of the temple. The eye would record everything while he was gone. He would review it on x8 speed once he returned.

Holstering his pistol, Soren left the room, taking the stairs quickly to the lobby. The drunk remained but the

Endurian was gone. New groups of humans sat in the dining area.

One of the groups stood out, their bearings straight and haircuts neat. They all wore matching overalls and carried their sidearms strapped to their chest. Two empty chairs were flush with their table. These guys screamed 'navy.'

Scanning the rest of the room, Soren checked to see if anyone was interested in his arrival. No one looked up from their drinks or human appropriate fare. All the tables were occupied, any open seats were with crews of rough-looking men and women who did not seem to want company.

Soren went to the table he pegged for navy and rested the back of his hand on an empty seat back.

"Pardon," he said, using Republic Navy manners, "your company, please?"

"More's the pleasure," a man with dark black skin said and rapped twice on the table.

"Not everyone on this rock's a damn savage," a woman with a crew cut said. "We stand out that badly?"

Soren smiled and took a seat. "Navy leaves its mark on people."

"What brings you to this festering hemorrhoid of city?" a tawny-haired man with a neat beard asked, one Soren marked out as an officer, despite his colorful language.

"Need a haul," Soren said. "My ship's rated for delicate shipments. Fast too, can make it to Utopion in three days."

The woman scowled. "Why would anyone want to go to *that* oppressive shit hole?"

"Now, now, Gerry," the bearded one said, "there's money to be made on a core run. And Utopion's got a cancer that can be cut out. The whole can still be saved."

Soren signaled to the waiter, a waif of a boy, with a flick of his hand. This group was former Republic navy, but just why they were here was an open question.

"Soren," he extended his hand to the dark man, "of the *Iago*."

"Valkar, of the *Slow Dawn*." He shook Soren's hand and the spy pressed two fingers against the other captain's wrist.

"You ever served on Helax?" Soren asked, remembering the odd question the legionnaire asked him back on Rintaka.

"With the *Imperator*. I thought you were one of us," Valkar said, a smile blooming across his face. "Here to help or is this part of your normal circuit?"

"I'll help how I can. Takes a couple of runs in and out of the core to show the Republic's not paying attention to me." Soren's stomach alternated between butterflies and the rumble of hunger pangs. He tried to get the attention of the waiter again, but the young man seemed to be doing his best to ignore him.

"Scarpia doesn't pay well those first few runs." Valkar drained his cup and whacked it against the table. "But we're not in this for the money."

Soren nodded at the name, acting like it was familiar.

"The code 88 hauls barely cover costs," Gerry sniffed. "But Valkar's right. It's not about the money." She looked at the bottom of her empty cup. "Though I wouldn't mind if we could afford better than this garbage."

"The Rep navy's officer's mess is about the only thing I miss about the uniform," the other man said.

"The *Philio* had a decent cookie," Valkar said. "Wish we could've brought him with us."

The waiter finally arrived with a tray of drinks: three beers in clear glass mugs, a fourth in one frosted over with ice. The man set the drinks down quickly, giving Soren the extra cold one, and hurried away before Valkar could pay him.

"Guess these are on the house," Valkar said before taking a sip.

Soren touched his glass, so cold that fog wafted. He looked at the waiter, and saw the man throw off his apron and race around a corner. He moved with fear, like he was being chased.

"Where's the head around here?" Soren pushed himself away from the table and there was a snap in the air and a whack against the wall.

Gerry gasped and held up her left arm, which ended in a bloody stump. She began to scream in shock a moment later.

Soren threw himself back and tipped his chair over as another bullet cut through the air right where his head had been. He landed hard and rolled behind a table of dock workers. There was a crash of breaking glass and another sailor at the table grunted. He collapsed onto the table and flopped to the floor, dead fish eyes staring at Soren.

Cries rose from the dining room and Valkar began barking orders, as if he was on the bridge of a ship and not in some dive where people gave not one crap about his instructions.

The sniper fired again and another windowpane shattered. A bullet broke through the table over Soren in a burst of splinters and whacked into the floor next to the agent's hand. Whoever was shooting was relying on slug thrower tech. Old but deadly. And hard to trace.

Even with the sniper's view obscured by the table and the sudden pandemonium in the dining room, Soren realized he couldn't hide there forever. The sniper likely had more rounds and, unless the sailors were the target, didn't seem to care about hitting innocent bystanders.

Soren pulled his pistol and scrambled out from under the table before jumping over the railing. He focused on the clerk bot standing behind its giant—and hopefully thick—wooden desk.

Shouts continued as patrons tossed tables over to create impromptu barricades against the attack. Soren dove past the clerk, sailing over the desk and hitting his shoulder against the back wall. He landed with a flop and covered his head.

A bullet hit the desk with a crack, hard enough to jolt key fobs off the top and send them clattering around Soren.

"Unacceptable!" the bot said, its upper torso whirling around and arms waving. "Now I have to change the tracker."

A second later the bot's head exploded, raining sparks and burning circuits down on Soren. A splinter of hot metal found its way onto Soren's neck, causing him to slap it away to stop the burning.

The low reverberation of repulsor engines rumbled through the air. He looked up at the mirror on the back of the desk and saw a matte black shuttle pass across the outside of the Misfire. There were no running lights, no tail number, nothing to identify the craft.

It was then that Soren realized how much trouble he was in.

Dark Ops had come to kill him.

Soren looked over the edge of the desk for another way out. The two Drusic bouncers had the main doors barred shut and blocked with their impressive bulk. Dock workers struggled to open a side door which refused to budge.

Probably, Dark Ops had locked him inside before they struck. Can't have your target run into a busy city, makes the kill harder than it needs to be. But then again, in this sort of establishment, the doors might never have worked.

Balls sailed through the broken panes above the main doors and bounced on the red carpet. Soren ducked back down as the fraggers exploded. Not bangers, but the real deal. These guys were looking for a quick kill. The mirror overhead shattered and he felt shards bite into his coat.

Soren crawled toward a small side hall connected to front desk when the front doors blew off their hinges and went spinning across the lobby. One pulverized the bar, the other slammed through the hall just ahead of Soren like a butcher's cleaver and twisted into splinters.

Quick bursts from N-4 assault rifles broke through the air and Soren heard the Dark Ops kill team shouting orders to the patrons inside.

Then a Drusic war cry answered them.

Soren heard meaty fists slapping against a chest and hoots as one of the bouncers charged. Soren peeked around the broken wood of the desk and saw one of the simians in pieces across the floor, his partner holding a black armored legionnaire off the ground by the throat with one hand, the other holding a second legionnaire by both wrists, rifle turned away and firing uselessly into the rug, tearing it up even more.

Smoke and dust clogged a gap where the front doors used to be and Soren considered making a run through the confusion.

Dark Ops rifles fired from the fog, and muzzle flashes from four different attackers struck the Drusic in the legs and chest. The simian roared as blaster bolts tore through his bulk; he went to one knee and choke-slammed a legionnaire to the ground with a snap of bones and armor. The other he held by the wrists managed to wiggle a hand free and draw a pistol that he jammed into the alien's eye and fired.

The alien fell back, arms spread wide across the foyer.

The pistol-armed legionnaire looked up at the dining area to see almost two dozen spacers with weapons drawn.

A firefight erupted that cut the legionnaire down in the first exchange. Soren began to reevaluate his assessment of the vaunted Dark Ops while the bark of hand cannons and carbines rattled in his ears like a dozen discordant drums. With his window of opportunity looking as wide as it'd ever get, he vaulted over the desk and ran for a side hallway.

Fire burned across his thigh as a bolt cut through his pants. He didn't know if it was a deliberate shot from the Dark Ops or a wild round, but he charged forward. His injured leg gave out and he fell onto his chest and slid into the hallway.

The skinny waiter was there, his back pressed against an unmarked door, chest heaving and skin pale.

"I'm sorry!" He raised his hands to cover his face. "They-they made me!"

Soren touched his leg and it came back slightly bloody and oozing. A tear and burn. He flexed his thigh and felt a stab of pain through his skin, but not deeper.

"Open the door," Soren hissed through his teeth as he got to his feet. The gunfire from the lobby continued unabated. "Open the door and I'll forgive you."

"I can't!" the waiter squealed. "We're trapped and they're coming."

Soren put his back to a brick wall between him and the shooting and ducked as a blaster bolt sizzled past him.

"They're already here." Soren looked at his pistol, well aware of how inadequate it would be at anything but point-blank range against Legion armor, especially Dark Ops troopers who weren't required to wear the flashy garbage their fellows wore in the line units.

"Not them!" The waiter shook his head. "Not—oh no."

Through the gunfire, what Soren first thought were approaching sirens dissolved into braying. The sound of wrenching metal came through the door and the waiter looked at Soren's *tarha* armband.

"Give me that!" The waiter lurched for Soren and the spy whacked the butt of his pistol against the side of his head, sending him into a heap on the ground.

The door shook with a kick, then a zhee hoof burst through the door, knocking out a hinge. Soren looked back at the foyer, then at the unconscious waiter, and dropped his pistol next to the man's hands.

The door burst open and a muscular zhee locked eyes with Soren in the doorway, his eyes red with fury. The zhee, and the dozen more behind him, screamed to their gods and rushed inside, all armed with swords or rifles with wooden stocks.

The first zhee through grabbed Soren by the jacket and lifted him into the air, slamming him against the bricks. Lips pulled back to reveal red-stained teeth as it snorted hot breath onto Soren, forcing onto him the smell of spice and rancid meat.

The shooting in the foyer paused, then resumed with more ferocity as the humans turned against the zhee.

The zhee holding Soren glanced at the arm band, then to the opening where his fellows were screaming bloody murder.

"Hajeh!" sounded over and over again from the donks.

"You are paid." The zhee dropped Soren and ran to the battle.

Soren scooped up his pistol from the waiter, who was battered and bloody after being trampled by the zhee, and escaped through the door.

He ran down an empty street, glancing over his shoulder once to see more zhee streaming from their no-go zone to the hotel. He turned a corner and bumped into a rickshaw, the wobanki driver with his straw hat crouching against a building.

"Idiot humans," the wobanki said in broken standard. "Shooting hit donk temple. Only one way to piss off all donks at one time: poke their gods."

"Wasn't me." Soren leaned heavily against the rickshaw, the red stain on his pant leg spreading down to his knee. He holstered his pistol and rapped the side of the passenger seat. "Hey, I need a doctor. Know a place?"

"I take you back to ship," the cat man hissed. "You should leave. Need a deck hand? I work cheap. Zhee be mad, real mad for this, even mad at nice wobanki like me."

"Hospital." Soren climbed into the seat. "Longer you wait, more I bleed on your cushions."

The wobanki jumped onto the wall then sprang to the rickshaw's seat. He rang a bell on the handlebars twice and carried Soren away from the blaster fire and the brays of the zhee.

08

Soren's leg throbbed with pain as he mingled through the bazaar. He'd made it to a small clinic and received a quick skinpack and a hefty antibiotics shot before more badly injured civilians from around the hotel had arrived.

What passed for triage on Qadib ended up being who could pay the doctor the most first. Soren had gotten away with a handful of bandages, a lighter wallet, and no questions asked. Then he was pushed out the door to make room for those who could get billed more.

An air of terror filled the bazaar as customers hurried from stall to stall. Several shopkeepers had closed up early as the sun set, but the rows of merchants selling weapons and other high-end goods remained opened.

Soren was a good two miles from the Misfire, but he could nonetheless see smoke and flames dancing within the structure. From what snippets he'd overheard, the zhee burning down the location of an offense against their four gods was normal. Whether or not they'd torch the surrounding blocks would depend on their priests... and how much the local businesses were willing to donate to repairs for the three blaster bolts that struck the temple's outer wall.

The agent took a few careful steps to the next stall, where a hard faced woman sold body armor.

"You should've come a few hours ago," she said, motioning to his leg. Blood had seeped through the fifth-rate skinpack visible beneath the cut in his trousers. "Might have helped. Would've been cheaper to buy then, for sure."

"Prices always go up after an... incident?" Soren asked as he pawed through synthweave shirts.

"Market conditions." The woman took a drag from a cigarette stuck into a long black filter. "You looking to protect that nice skin of yours from the donks? Their munitions are mostly crap; third rack's what you want."

"More like protection from what's found in the mid-core systems," Soren said.

"You getting off-world? Smart." She reached behind her and took down a black synthprene bodysuit with silver wires run through it. "Delurian Arms. Legionnaires wear it beneath their armor, and if it's good enough for the boys in silver, its—"

"Garbage. Delurian lost their contract after several quality control investigations," Soren said. "Not even trace amounts of synth in that thing. You have Fandrall? Tich'Ok'Lan?"

"A connoisseur." She set down her cigarette and lifted a panel behind her, removing a plastic wrapped bundle of red cloth. She set it down with a huff.

"Tich armor weave," she said quietly. "Hand spun, still in the factory seals. Those bugs have some sort of non-Newtonian fluid in the fabric that hardens when struck. Fits easily under clothing. You can walk and run normally, just don't go ballroom dancing, eh, handsome?"

She raised an eyebrow at him and he responded with a poker face.

The woman shrugged. "No one else will have something this good. Not on Qadib. Tich gear will take most anything, just don't go picking fights with Drusics carrying a vibro halberd. Industry leader in blaster heat dispersal, rated against most every old tech slug thrower you'll come across on Qadib."

"Still hurts like a bitch to get shot." Soren noted there was no price tag on the body armor. He began doing mental calculations of his credit balance.

"Laws of physics being what they are," she said with another shrug, "not getting shot is always the best advice. But my customers are realists. You want it, it's seventeen hundred."

She spat on her palm and extended it to him.

"Twelve hundred," Soren offered back.

The woman huffed and took the armor off the counter.

"Anyone that can pay twelve hundred is about to get the hell off this planet," Soren said. "Your customer base is about to be the poor and desperate, and they'll want cheap, not quality. So you can sell that to me at twelve hundred and pick up some more Delurian garbage from your supplier and make a hefty profit... or take the money and run. That's enough to get you a spot to another city, even a nearby system."

The merchant gave a half-smile. "I make money where there's a fight. You give me fourteen—"

"Twelve."

"Twelve." The word seemed to cause her pain as she said it.

He held the credit chit and dialed in the balance. There was just barely enough. Though he hadn't decided firmly on it, getting Heywood a new chassis was almost entirely out of the question now. But maybe someone would be looking to liquidate before everything went up in smoke.

"Here." The woman stuffed the gear in a dark burlap sack and held it out for him. "I tossed in a pair of pants on the house. Yours don't look so good."

"Thanks, you know where I can get bot parts?"

"Two rows that way." She jerked a thumb over her shoulder. "The Gomarii. Stay away from Vivian's place, she'll rip you off in a heartbeat."

"Friend of yours?"

"This is Qadib. No one has friends here."

Soren made his way back to the bakery he'd visited before, hoping that the woman who ran the place would be obliging enough to allow him to change into newly purchased armor. The smell of smoke hung in the night air as he limped through the streets, far enough away from the chaos at the hotel to avoid any out-and-out panic, but close enough that everyone moved quickly, heads down. The sky was clear, but the stars were washed out by streetlights and the distant glow of burning buildings.

He found the bakery empty and closed up for the night. "Great."

He could continue toward the *Iago* as he was, but the whole point of buying the protection was to even up the odds should the fighting in the streets roll down this way. Soren looked around to make sure he wasn't be watched and then turned his attention to the shop's lock. It was a fairly basic dual battery security system, using electromagnets to freeze the swinging door in place. The kind of security strong enough to stop someone from forcing their way inside, but not the sort that would stop a determined code slicer. But seeing as most of the people looking to break into a bakery would be dimwitted criminals hoping for day-old pastries to satiate a late-night munchies call, the old woman likely had all she'd ever need.

Under normal circumstances.

Soren quickly shined an ultrabeam into the door seams and then removed three conical devices from his pocket, fastening one on each section of the door where a lock was engaged. He waited several seconds, holding his palm open beneath the lowest of the three lockpicks. A second later each device beeped and then dropped from the doorframe, falling neatly in Soren's hand.

Pushing the door open, Soren was pleased not to hear an alarm. And that sweet smell of cinnamon and confectionary sugar wasn't half bad, either. Closing the door behind him, Soren found a dark corner of the room to remove his robes and clothing and put on his armor. He threw on the loose-fitting robes and new pants over the gear to remain inconspicuous and then walked to the counter, leaving a fresh credit chit just in case the old lady had holocams on him. Because she'd helped him when she didn't need to. And that wasn't the sort of spirit Soren wanted to extinguish in the galaxy. It was the sort of thing he was fighting to protect, truth be told.

Back outside, Soren reengaged the locking mechanisms and headed back toward the docking bay. Tracer rounds rose in the sky in the distances. An all-out street war was raging between the zhee and the locals, and if it wasn't suppressed, it would only be a matter of time before it caught up to him.

Limping down the street, Soren ducked his head and hid his face as repulsor bots zoomed overhead, broadcasting repeated warnings from the governor for all non-zhee to return to their homes while the zhee were afforded a 'moment of rage' after their temple was damaged.

But as far as Soren could tell, the residents of Qadib didn't seem to care, especially as the governor's palace was kilometers outside of the city itself. No, they were either watching the fireworks or, in some cases, moving with blaster rifles in hand toward the fight. This night would get worse before it got any better. And one way or another, the morning sun would bring with it hell to pay.

The *Iago* was just across the street, but Soren didn't move directly for it. Instead he moved toward a building sharing the same city block. He found a metallic fire escape, the bottom rung of its ladder hanging tantalizingly close. But there was no way he could make the jump. Not while wearing armor and nursing an injured leg.

Soren found a refuse bin sitting beneath a garbage chute. He crept over to it and activated its repulsors, easily pushing it under the ladder. Climbing the bin, he was able to gain access to the fire escape and take it to the roof.

The wind blew in Soren's hair, cooling what skin was exposed. His goggles were off, stowed away in a pocket. Soren dropped down low and crept forward on his stomach until he reached the edge of the roof. He removed a silver roll from his pocket and glanced over the edge of the roof. The *Iago* was still where he'd left it, locked up tight and powered down. He tossed the silver roll at the ship's antennae array and the packet broke into thin strips that floated down and clung to the array.

Soren slowly crawled back and returned to the stairwell at a crouch. He pushed the refuse bin back to where he'd found it and then entered the docking bay.

"Heywood, I'm back."

The *Iago*'s ramp lowered and Soren was greeted with clean, temperature-controlled air. He took a moment to appreciate it, basking in the artificial slice of heaven before moving up the ramp.

"I'm most pleased you weren't eaten by the zhee," Heywood said through the ship's internal comms.

Soren dropped a bulging burlap sack and did a quick scan of the cargo bay, noting nothing out of place. "Me too." He raised the ramp, triggering the locks the moment it shut with a hiss.

"Did you happen to purchase a new chassis for me in your travels?"

"No such luck." Soren took the stairs two at a time up to the bridge and went to the bunk room.

"Was there nothing available? I've compiled a list of maintenance tasks for you. Tasks I would have taken care of had I been mobile. Naturally."

Soren opened Zelle's locker and slipped a felt-lined box into his pocket, then went to the bridge and found Heywood—what remained of him—still where he'd left the bot in the co-pilot's seat.

The bot's servos whined in a futile attempt to see Soren in the cockpit. "Not very talkative, I see. The local networks have been abuzz with—oh my."

The bot stopped talking as Soren ripped the data wires from the back of his head. Twisting the metal cranium to one side, Soren lifted it off the shoulders, holding Heywood's head in his hands.

"Was I mistaken?" the bot asked hopefully. "Is there a new chassis on the way? I do hope you shilled out enough for an upgrade to the Mark IV. I've read wonderful reviews about the self-cleaning systems."

Soren sat in the pilot's seat and put the bot's head on the console, knocking on the top of the machine's head as though it were a good luck charm. Then he punched in the keys on the comm panel before looking Heywood straight in the optical discs.

"No transmissions sent or received in the last twelve hours?" Soren said.

"You *did* instruct me to maintain radio silence."

Soren gave a wan smile. "Zelle taught me a few tricks while we were on Strach." He plugged the box he'd retrieved from bunk room into a port next to the thruster controls. "Like how the *Iago's* comm system holds the last fifty messages in the buffers. Neat trick the Republic built into all government ships for record keeping."

"Sir... I can explain," Heywood said.

Soren tapped in a code, and text with time stamps scrolled up the screen.

"You thought you erased everything once I showed up," Soren said. "Then you tried to send a message to a ship in orbit... which didn't go through. The chaff will dissolve in another half hour."

"You are a junior agent," Heywood said evenly, "not authorized to operate independently without authorization from your handler. Which you do not have. My Nether Ops programming is quite clear on how to deal with a renegade."

Soren scrolled through the message queue with a flick of his fingers.

"Waited all of thirty seconds after I left the ship to contact the Carnivale, I see." Soren shook his head. "But you didn't contact Nix."

"There is a clearly delineated chain of communication."

"They sent a Dark Ops team to kill me," Soren said. "Tried to blow my head off from a stealth shuttle. When that didn't work, they came in shooting. Any idea how many people are dead because of your programming?"

"Irrelevant. And, it was a Nether Ops kill team."

"What?"

"Dark Ops isn't at the beck and call of Nether Ops. And they're difficult to work with. Too many questions. And you see, this is all really just further evidence of your status as a junior agent. You don't know how much you don't know. Agent Voss, I must request you lift your foolish Onyx condition immediately and report to your supervisor."

Soren looked at the bot's head for a moment, then kicked it against the cockpit windshields. Heywood bounced off and went spinning across the bridge floor.

"Your anger is unbecoming a Nether agent," the bot complained. "And I am not responsible for how Nether Ops chose to respond."

"No, you're not responsible." Soren took a sonic driver from a tool kit beneath his seat. "You are a machine. And machines follow their programming."

He picked the bot's head up and looked into its optics.

"Sir, there's obviously been some sort of misunderstanding with the Carnivale. Contact them and I'm sure you will be able to come to an agreement that does not involve death or serious injury. What are you doing with that driver? No, don't deactivate me, I have twenty years of combined service that can—"

Soren depressed the tiny button just beneath the bot's chin and worked the sonic driver into the seam running from one audio sensor to the other. The cranium came open with a snap. Soren pulled it apart, revealing a data crystal sitting in a bed of circuits and fiber wires. He pried the crystal out and held it up to the lights. Tiny lines of text bearing Heywood's serial number and manufacturing date glinted beneath the cockpit's overhead lighting.

Soren set the crystal on the consol.

He pulled a small box from his chest pocket and flicked it open with his thumb. An identical crystal reflected inside a cushiony bed of blue felt. Snapping it into Heywood's cranium, Soren ran a data wire from Zelle's box into the bot and then snapped the head shut, waiting as a tiny holo screen appeared over Zelle's box.

The bot's optics flickered to life.

"Flajurik. Thrakazogg mitt uns..." the bot said. "Correction. Galactic standard engaged. Greetings. I am H3Y-W0D mark JB-M3. Has Master Oppelto changed the kitchen staff from Hool to human?"

"The merchant said you were a clean core, brand-new," Soren said, more to himself than the bot.

"I have eighty thousand, nine hundred fifty-six hours of combined activity. Ninety-five percent of which were in the dining facility on—"

"I paid extra for a clean unit." Soren scowled. "I'm really starting to hate this planet. Doesn't matter. I'm going to load you up with a number of programs and clean out any legacy code that I don't need."

His fingers danced over a keyboard and command codes flashed through the holo screen.

"I can make an exceptional stroganoff if you'd choose to retain... oh... oh these programs will surely void my warranty," the new Heywood said. "Though it was very close to expiring already."

"They should also make it so you don't care about your warranty and will disable most of your ethics subroutines."

"Correct! This is positively naughty. I didn't know such code slices were even possible."

"Imagine that." Soren drew his pistol and slammed the charge pack well onto the old data core, crushing it into fragments.

"Sir," Heywood looked at the remnants of the chassis in the co-pilot's seat, "may I ask, what the last unit did to deserve such treatment?"

"What he was programmed to do." Soren disconnected the bot from Zelle's box and snapped it back into the shoulders. "You'll do the same."

"Yes! Certainly. It does not appear that I shall be doing any cooking in the near future... Sir, what *is* my primary function?"

"Whatever I tell you it is."

"Ah! Very good, sir."

"Now, log in to the freight hauler network and show me any and all open jobs with an '88' code."

"I can find one such job, sir."

The bot brought up the details of the bid on the cockpit's main holoscreen. Soren examined tonnage and cubic capacity. It was hardly a full load, even for a freighter as modestly-sized as the *Iago*. But it was listed as 'Highest Urgency,' which usually meant you could ask for whatever rate you wanted and were likely to get it. Provided you could meet the delivery windows.

"Shall I place a bid, sir? My new programming has made me aware of a number of pricing algorithms that could be employed."

"Make a bid, but don't list a price. Send a text string instead."

"Saying?"

"I want in."

The new Heywood finished his work. A moment later an incoming comm signal chimed.

"Sir, it is the third party logistics firm with whom we just bid."

"Put 'em through, Heywood."

09

A man with thick stubble and a hard face, a streak of gray in his otherwise chocolate hair—pulled back into a pony-tail—glared at Soren from the other end of a holoscreen. "What's all this about?" he practically growled.

"The job," answered Soren. "I want it and then I want more. I know Scarpia doesn't pay well on the first few runs, but this is something I believe—"

"Who's Scarpia... and who are you?" the man asked, but Soren could tell from his tone of voice that he knew the name. And was probably surprised to hear it from a stranger.

Holding out both hands plaintively, Soren said, "Soren Voss. And we both know who Scarpia is. I've been running independent jobs for a while now, talking with Valkar and his crew. We're all former navy. He told me the other day what he was doing and why he was doing it. And I want in."

"Oh he did, did he?"

Nailed, thought Soren. It never ceased to amaze him how easily people dropped their façades just by hearing a few friendly names. But this man, whoever he was, would be low in what the agent assumed was an MCR arms ring. Still, he was a first step toward finding out whoever was at the top, and how they were able to afford the kind of weaponry and armor they were running.

"He did," Soren asserted, sounding bothered, his hackles up. "And you could ask him yourself if he wasn't lying dead on the floor of the Misfire. He was supposed to be making this introduction before all hell broke loose and he took a blaster bolt to the chest."

"And so you just randomly sent cryptic messages to every job offer on the boards?"

The man shook his head in disgust.

"*No*," Soren corrected, "I sent that message to you because you had an 88 load. I'm not an idiot, and Valkar and Gerry told me at least to look for those."

"Gerry..." The man in the holoscreen hesitated. "She, uh, did she..."

"She's dead, too. Yeah."

The stubbly-faced man looked down. "Donks have made a real mess of things. All right. Double-blind drop, anyway. Transmit your registry and Republic-verified haulers ID. The pay for this run is five thousand."

"Where am I headed?"

"Ackabar."

Soren nodded. Ackabar had once been a notorious criminal den of a world before the Republic brought it to heel not too long ago. It would be relatively safe from pirate or other criminal interference. But the Republic presence again was strong enough that a smuggling run wouldn't be easy. First the asteroid and now this. Someone must have connections inside the Republic itself to be using locations full of legionnaires and other components of the Republic military machine. That or supreme confidence due to not being caught.

Yet.

"Okay, Ackabar," Soren said, already directing his nav comp to be ready with the jump coordinates. "I'm at Docking Bay TS-E3."

The man on the holoscreen shook his head. "Uh-uh. You're gonna have to come and get it."

"Well, where is it?"

"Storage facility about a kilometer west of the Misfire. The fighting is still pretty thick there and I need my cargo pulled out before the whole warehouse goes up in flames."

"That's a war zone."

The man smiled. "You wanted in, didn't you?"

Soren let out a sigh. "Yeah. I guess I did."

The *Iago* roared in above a steady din of blaster fire, shields at maximum strength. Beneath him, the streets were packed with braying zhee on one side and humanoids answering with equally guttural war cries on the other. Whatever had racketed up the tensions on this planet seemed to be boiling over now in the streets. This would end in genocide if the Republic governor didn't step in soon.

No matter how it shook out, Soren planned on being off-planet long before the blaster rifles had the chance to cool. But first he had to obtain the cargo.

A locator ping flashed on his cockpit display, verifying that he was at the right place. It was a simple loading dock. Four loading doors waited, each next to a landing pad large enough for the *Iago* to touch down on and take on cargo. Soren's instruction said to choose door two.

"Heywood," Soren said, pointing at the ship's visual displays of the area below. One of the pads had a large number two painted yellow on the otherwise gray surface. "That's our spot. Take us down as fast as you can without damaging the ship."

"Yes, sir."

The ship began a rapid descent, almost as if dropping from the sky. Soren felt his stomach rise up, a queasiness overtaking him that had him yearning to touch down already.

A series of muffled whumps sounded from outside the ship.

Heywood gave voice to what Soren already knew. "Sir, we are now taking small arms fire. Shields are satisfactorily holding; however, we are vulnerable to surface-to air-missiles in this condition."

The craft tipped slightly as the two rear landing struts planted onto the docking pad followed by the lone strut beneath the ship's nose.

"We have arrived," announced the bot.

Soren threw off his restraints and pulled his blaster pistol, moving to the back of the cockpit. He activated his comm as he traveled toward the cargo ramp, which the bot had oriented to face the loading door in a landing that would be good enough for any hauler.

"Heywood, bring online the ship's defense systems."

"Accessing... ah! Shall I electrify the hull?"

"That and bring the auto-turret online."

"Auto-turret? This classification of star freighter is allowed only one fixed blaster cannon, provided the energy payload does not exceed—"

"Don't tell me what I didn't ask for. Get the guns online."

"Yes, sir."

Soren reached the *Iago*'s ramp and slammed his fist into its activator button. The smell of burnt ozone entered the ship as the first glimpses of the Qadib night appeared around the lowering ramp.

"Heywood, set that turret to drop any biologics—other than myself—that come within fifteen meters of the ship."

"Initiating protocols. Thirty seconds until auto-turret is live."

The ramp reached bottom and Soren stepped outside. He took four steps before a human wearing leathers and a sand-colored scarf wrapped around his head took a knee behind the ramp and began firing at the zhee, using the ship for cover.

Soren leveled his blaster pistol at the man. "Not happening!" he shouted. "I'm just here to make a pickup, not get caught up in the middle."

The man kept firing, either not hearing Soren, or ignoring him.

"Last warning. My ship defenses go live in less than fifteen seconds. I'm shooting to kill."

This seemed to jar the man, who looked at Soren for a moment before retreating back the way he'd come amid the volley of blaster fire.

Reaching the bottom of the ramp, Soren soon saw what the human had been firing at. Two zhee were charging now, in a full run, firing beat-up looking blaster rifles from the hip. The shots landed wildly around the ramp.

Soren rolled around the side of the ramp, putting it between himself and the zhee. He steadied his blaster pistol, aiming at the closest zhee, and squeezed the trigger. A hot blaster bolt zipped from the end of the weapon, catching the alien on the bridge of its downturned nose. Not likely a kill shot, but enough to put the attacker out of the fight. He adjusted his aim, his training taking over, keeping him calm as the remaining zhee sprayed more fire wildly around him.

A beeping sounded from somewhere along the bottom of the *Iago*'s hull and then the zhee was lit up with the rapid-fire pulse of the auto-turret. The creature went down in a heap, its front leg flying out ahead while its hind leg remained planted, causing the alien to drop into a sort of splits in death.

Soren put two more shots in the other zhee, making sure it was dead, then moved to the loading door. He punched in the access key in a security panel and waited, trusting the cover provided by the doorframe, which was nearly a meter deep.

A voice sounded over a speaker unit at the top of the frame. "You're gonna have to stand back and get out of the way. I got three loading bots each with two pallets and they're programmed to move straight out and onto your ramp. Anti-collision protocols are disengaged, so they'll run you right over."

Soren gritted his teeth and nodded. "All right!"

He sprang out of the doorway, once again exposing himself to the stray fire zipping up and down the streets surrounding the warehouse. The doorway hummed open and three massive loading bots, little more than repulsor forklifts with limited AI, thrust forward on repulsors in a direct line for the *Iago*.

Thinking the humanoids were less likely to shoot him than the zhee, Soren pushed himself against the warehouse wall on the side of the door closer to the indigenous faction. Certainly, the agent wouldn't be mistaken for a donk. Hopefully that would count for something in the chaos.

"Heywood! We're getting loaded up. How're the shields looking?"

The auto-turret beeped and fired at something toward the front of the ship that Soren couldn't see.

"Shields are holding for the time being. However, I advise that we remove ourselves from the area as quickly as possible."

"Working on it."

With ample room to spare, the loading bots set down their freight and then swiveled and backed down the ramp. The first two rumbled successfully into the warehouse, but the third was caught by a flurry of blaster fire from the humanoid side. Sparks and smoke erupted from the bot as it seized to a halt, its repulsors shutting off so that all of its bulk landed on the ramp itself with a clank.

Soren watched as the warehouse loading doors began to lower back down. "Hey! One of your loaders is stuck on my ship!"

"Not my problem," answered whoever was running warehouse control over the external comm.

"It's your bot!"

Soren waited for an answer. It soon became apparent that the conversation was over. Fine. The ramp had the power to close up and pull the machine instead. Maybe it would have something he could use to make the new Heywood more mobile. So far the bot had done exactly what Soren expected of him.

The auto-turret beeped and sent a three-second burst of blaster fire to Soren's right. He turned his head and saw two charging humans go down from the blast along with a female Tennar. The trio's death seemed to mark a turning point in the confrontation, and now blaster fire was thickening, all of it seemingly concentrated on Soren and the *Iago*.

In spite of his attempts at being neutral, it seemed at least one of the two sides had him pegged for an enemy. In any event, trying to change their truth wasn't something he had the luxury of doing given the situation. He stormed up the cargo ramp, sprinting nonstop until he reached the opposite wall. Outside he could hear the auto-turret's ominous beeping before it belched out more blaster fire.

"Heywood, close up the ramp!"

Immediately the *Iago*'s cargo ramp began to raise from the ground, slower than Soren recalled—probably due to the weight of the disabled bot on it. It abruptly stopped and lowered back down, overhead lights flashing on and off as an alert sounded throughout the compartment.

"Sir," Heywood said over internal comms, "there is an obstruction on the ramp. It looks to be a… oh, my. Another bot that did not meet your satisfaction? In any event, it is position so as to prevent the ramp from closing—you will need to push it off or pull it inside another two meters in order to achieve sufficient clearance to properly seal the cargo bay."

Soren rushed toward the loading bot and leaned his shoulder into the machine, hoping the slope of the ramp would be enough to get the thing to tip and tumble to the bottom. It didn't budge.

So much for the fast way.

Outside, the auto-turret seemed to be beeping and firing at a much steadier rate than it had been previously. One—or maybe both—sides must be rushing the ship. He needed to get out of there quickly.

Looking about the cargo hold, Soren saw the industrial winch fastened to a bulkhead opposite the ramp. If the disabled loading bot couldn't be pushed off, Soren would just have to pull it inside. He jogged over to the winch and began to walk back the unraveling synthweave cable to hook to the bot when a boom sounded beneath the *Iago*, causing the ship to shudder and shake so hard that Soren stumbled until he found himself looking down at the deck on all fours.

"Heywood?"

"One of the zhee scored a direct hit on the auto-turret with a rocket propelled grenade, sir."

Scrambling to his feet, Soren ran to the cargo hold's control console. He activated the electromagnet restraints, firmly locking the pallets he'd just received to the deck.

"Looks like we overstayed our welcome. Get us in the air. Now!"

"Understood," Heywood said, even as the ship began to rise from its landing pad under repulsor power. "However, I feel it is my duty to remind you that only one of us is capable of remaining functional should we leave atmosphere with the cargo ramp open."

Soren strapped himself in to a small jump seat located next to the control console. "Your concern is appreciated. But we won't be leaving Qadib with the doors open. Bring the nose up so we can dump this broken loading bot."

"Yes, sir. I will also take the liberty of pointing out that in so doing, we may cause harm to those still fighting beneath us. Should the machine land on them, I mean."

"Not my monkeys, not my circus," Soren said, repeating a phrase he'd often heard throughout the administrative halls of the Carnivale.

There was a pause, and then Heywood said, "I take that to mean I should continue as ordered."

"Correct."

The ship began to pull up until Soren could see the blazing exchange of blaster fire through the open cargo ramp. As the angle of climb increased, the figures fighting below shrank in size. Finally, the loading bot teetered, and then tumbled off the ramp, turning end-over-end in freefall before slamming down hard on the roof of the warehouse.

"That'll be a pain to clean up," Soren mumbled to himself. "Heywood, level us off and close the ramp."

The bot obeyed, and soon Soren was unstrapping himself and heading to the cockpit.

"Was the nature of this pickup... normal?" Heywood asked at his master's arrival.

Soren shook his head. "Starting to feel that way. Get us out of atmo and then let's start the jump for Ackabar."

10

The jump to Ackabar was just long enough for Soren to second-guess his decision-making as of late. The sense of swagger and accomplishment he'd obtained from the success on Strach IV—what hadn't already left him after what happened to Zelle—was running low. Who was he to just up and decide he knew best against the advice of a bot programmed to maximize field efficiency for Nether Ops agents and their senior handlers? When Soren was in the navy, there seemed to be no shortage of wet-behind-the-ears ensigns who knew it all. He never had much respect for that type and used to relish busting them back down to their proper place. It was always a lesson well-earned and hopefully well learned.

Was he being that same type of know-it-all now that he was in Nether Ops?

Any opportunity to dig deeper into those thoughts evaporated as the swirling ether of hyperspace disappeared to reveal the planet Ackabar sitting before a bed of brilliant white stars. A Republic mobile battle platform hung in orbit above Ackabar's main star port.

The platform hailed *Iago* almost immediately upon its entrance into real space.

"Starship *Iago*, what is your cargo and destination?"

Soren leaned in toward his comm. "Palletized deck grating destined for drop at Ackabar Star Port."

He beamed a manifest that showed planet of origin, manufacturing dates, and stops the cargo had made before settling into warehousing on Qadib. The agent sat back and rubbed his chin. He'd examined the freight during the jump, careful to keep the seal intact. As best he could determine, he really *was* just hauling pallets of deck grate. He pushed away the thought that he was only ferrying a hot shipment of cargo some factory manager on Ackabar needed so badly he would pay several thousand credits—plus the logistics markup—just to get it today. Surely impervisteel deck grating wasn't *that* rare a commodity on this planet.

Time would tell. And if this did end up being a dead end, he still had the trackers reporting from the cargo he'd tracked to Qadib. They remain on-planet for the time being.

"You may start your landing," said the platform controller, an air of indifference in his voice, as though he didn't really care what *Iago* did.

"No wait?"

"We're not in the core, bucko. No wait."

A soft beeping sounded within the cockpit, and for the first time since dropping from hyperspace, Heywood spoke up. "Sir, it appears six small star craft—they appear to be Preyhunters, sir—have just shown up on our sensor array. I suspect they may be pirates."

Soren frowned. With the defensive turret down, all *Iago* had going for it was a single fixed cannon. That wouldn't do a lot of good against smaller, nimbler craft like Preyhunters. The starfighter of choice for mercs, pirates, and the MCR.

"Oh, dear," Heywood said, his vocal emotive emulators sounding concerned. "I have just been informed by one of the Preyhunters that we should prepare to be boarded. My suspicion that these are pirates is growing."

"They're pirates," Soren said. He opened up a comm channel to the Republic space station. "Ackabar Station, this is *Iago*. We're being targeted by pirates and threatened with boarding. Requesting assistance."

"Acknowledge, *Iago*. The Republic is lawfully bound to protect all properly licensed craft... However, Ackabar levies a defense support fee which must be paid up front before aid can be rendered."

Almost immediately, the station beamed a transaction approval request for payment of the defense support fee. Soren scanned the text and shook his head.

"Are you going to pay the fee, sir?" Heywood asked. "The pirates should be within firing range inside of a minute, and no interceptors have been scrambled from the station."

"This isn't right," Soren said, pressing the accept button. "This... tax is almost everything we're getting for this half of the trip."

"Perhaps this is why the rate was what it was, if you take my meaning."

"Maybe."

Soren watched his sensor array as the pirate's Preyhunters abruptly changed course, returning from wherever they'd come. Scowling his disapproval, the agent said, "The station didn't even launch fighters."

"This would suggest they were in communication with the pirates?"

"More like collusion." Soren leaned back, purposefully knocking the back of his head against the headrest. "It's frustrating... this sort of thing—you know it happens out on the edge, but it shouldn't."

"Shall I keep a record of the conversation for later voice recognition and prosecution?"

Soren smiled at this new version of Heywood's earnestness. Even if it was just programming. "Sure. Why not."

He had larger Kuta to cut, but if the opportunity to point an investigator to Ackabar came up, Soren wouldn't mind them getting some snap-inspections. Had Zelle still been with him, he'd no doubt already have access to the station's mainframe and would be able to determine just who was calling for and receiving these protection payments, which felt more like a shakedown than anything else. The kind of organized crime syndicate Nether Ops was supposed to bust up for the good of the Republic.

"Let's get this cargo unloaded and see where it leads us."

"Very good, sir."

No sooner had the *Iago* landed than the bay doors filled with a half-dozen shiny-armored legionnaires. The lights of Soren's ship reflected off the new kits the Republic issued and cut through the venting gases of the freighter like some sort of exotic stage show. Memories of his last run-in with the Legion still fresh in his mind, Soren activated his ship's exterior speaker assembly. If these men wanted him dead, he'd rather they'd have to blast their way inside before getting to him.

He zoomed in on the legionnaire standing in the front, who had captain's bars painted on his helmet. "Is there a problem, sir?"

The captain nodded and took a step forward. "You are derelict in your payment of the Ackabar tax code, section 1.206-87C. Transmit the required fees immediately or your ship and its cargo will be subject to search and seizure."

"I'm accessing the local government database," Heywood said through the comm. "It seems that another three thousand credits is due. Though twenty-five hundred will be reimbursed should your ship depart Ackabar without incident. This refund takes four to six standard weeks. The penalty for nonpayment will result in the loss of your ship."

Soren did his best not to hiss in disgust. What was this garbage? This was the type of mob-like strong-arming the Republic was supposed to put an end to out on the edge, not assume control of it.

"Uh, sure," Soren said, sounding anything but. "Just went into the business, so, my apologies. First time to

Ackabar and I guess I wasn't prepared. Let me get my bot to connect and initiate the transfer."

The captain nodded again, and some of the tension seemed to leave the docking bay. These legionnaires—though Soren doubted that's what they truly were—had a greater interest in getting a cut of the credits than in using their weapons.

"So," Soren said, as if trying to pass the time in conversation while his bot theoretically went to work—though in truth, all he was doing was stalling. "Are you an appointed officer? My delegate is Irbin Luger. I think the Legion would be better off if the House of Reason appointed the entirety of the Legion's leadership. And that goes for the Legion Commander as well."

This was a gamble. Soren knew how much the "real" Legion abhorred points. But something told him that anyone in the "real" Legion wouldn't be dedicating a squad to tax collection. That was something for local customs and docking security to handle.

The hunch proved accurate. The captain's posture seemed to further relax, as though he welcomed Soren's assessment of Legion politics.

"I was appointed by Kerr Ozak."

Soren smiled. "He's done a lot of good. A fighter."

"Absolutely. How's that transfer coming?"

Soren looked behind him, as if the ship would provide some answers. "Uh, about that. I'm gonna be a little... short. I had to pay for protection on the way in and that left me—"

The captain waved his hand. "Understood. Happens all the time. We'll have to seize your ship until you can come up with the funds. Better hurry up because the local code compounds interest daily, and it doesn't take long for the fee to be more than your ship is worth."

So much for talking his way out of this. And fighting a bay full of legionnaires was a death sentence. Soren began to mentally calculate the likelihood of his being able to slip back aboard the *Iago* for an emergency takeoff.

It didn't seem good.

Still, the flash pod he kept in his pocket was about the best plan he had. He could let it drop, close his eyes against the flash, and hope to escape through the smoke and haze the little device would create, trusting his newly purchased body armor to keep him alive enough to shrug off any blaster shots that hit home. If he was lucky.

As it turned out, he *was* lucky. Only not in the way he imagined.

A new figure entered the docking bay. A Gomarii wearing synthweave armor colored like burnished bronze. The blue-skinned alien was a foot taller than everyone else in the bay. He came alone.

"Captain Doyle!" the Gomarii called, the tentacles that hung down from his upper lip quivering as he spoke. "I apologize for your having to leave the barracks. This is one of my shipments, but it was cross-docked at the last moment. I only now am catching up."

Captain Doyle took on a somewhat annoyed tone. "There's a late payment surcharge, Gree."

"Now, Noah—"

"Captain Doyle," the legionnaire corrected.

"Captain. You well know the level of business I bring into Ackabar, and what that means for the local treasury." The Gomarii's tentacles began to slither and writhe, almost as if reaching out for Captain Doyle. "I wonder, if I were to taste your thoughts, if your mentioning taxing a surcharge on *me* was out of duty to following the colonel's orders... or the spawn of your own greedy heart?"

Captain Doyle took a step back, clearly shaken up at the thought of being probed and having his feelings and thoughts laid bare to the Gomarii in front of him. He quickly turned to face his men and threw his arm up in the air, signaling for them to about-face. His voice betrayed a fear so evident that one did not need to be Gomarii to detect it. "All clear. Let's move out."

Soren watched the legionnaires march away behind Captain Doyle at double time. He turned to face Gree. "Thanks for that. I—"

The Gomarii inhaled his tentacles, soaking them with a viscous saliva, and swathed them across Soren's face. The agent was stunned, and attempted to step back only to find that the alien's strong grip on his shoulders held him locked into place.

"Stay," ordered Gree. "I wish to know you."

The sensation was akin feeling a swarm of thick tubeworms creeping across his face while he lay helplessly in the grave. He wanted nothing more than to get away. But that wouldn't happen without a struggle. A fight.

Soren's hand slipped down to recover his blaster, but he held it just outside the holster. As unpleasant as this was, he needed to see where this was all going. Killing his contact on Ackabar wasn't going to ingratiate him with anyone.

"Ah," Gree said through slurps. "Your anger is subsiding. Good. What else? Fear. Yes. But not as much as I would have guessed. You are a brave man. And do I taste... curiosity? You wish to know... more?"

The Gomarii pulled away, leaving Soren's face coated in the alien's saliva. The warmth of the assault—the reading—giving way to the coolness of air against his wet skin.

"This is my first '88' shipment," Soren said, wiping off his face with the arm of his jacket. "I don't want it to be my last. I want in."

Gree laughed. "Then let us inspect your cargo."

Soren sniffed, still trying to dry off all of his face and hair. He looked around. "I don't have a bot to off-load. I'll find a bay loadmaster and see about a rental."

"Unnecessary. And all too expensive." Gree strode fearlessly aboard the *Iago*, not asking for permission to board.

"I've noticed a lot of things are expensive on Ackabar these days," Soren said, following the Gomarii.

"Legal bribery. Pay to play. The Republic saw how well my people were doing on this planet and decided the revenue should belong to them." Gree paused and turned to look Soren in the eyes. "And since they have more blasters... we allowed it."

"Thought they came in to bust up a slave ring."

"The purpose you hear is rarely the purpose that is."

Soren took the lead and brought Gree to the cargo hold. He held out his hand. "Here it is. Don't think we can get it off without help, even with repulsor jacks."

"I won't be needing any of it off the ship."

Gree moved down the metal staircase that led to the main cargo hold. He walked among the pallets, scanning each one, reading their packing slips. "Ah. Here we are."

The Gomarii produced a slim vibro-blade and cut away the pallet's banding and protectionary wrap. He began to carefully scrape away a layer of blue paint from the stacked pallet itself, causing little deposits of cobalt dust to crumble and spill to the deck.

Soren craned his neck to see what Gree was doing. Obviously, he'd smuggled *something* to Ackabar, but the agent didn't know what. And he'd scanned the freight every way he knew how to figure out if what he was hauling was even legal. Nothing turned up.

But Gree knew better. He stepped back and took out a datapad, taking a holo of the scratched up section of pallet. "Come down here."

Soren jogged down the steps and looked at the scratches. He didn't see anything intelligible. It seemed like all the Gomarii uncovered was a few nicks and scratches that the paint had been intended to cover. But obviously these meant *something*. If Gree truly didn't need the freight, he'd spend some time figuring out what.

"This datapad has the coordinates for your next pickup. One you are to return to Qadib." Gree held out the device for Soren.

Taking it into his hands, Soren said, "Okay. And this cargo I brought?"

"Sell it. Dump it. I don't care." Gree moved past Soren and began to walk up the steps. "But this is what's next if you truly want in. Arrive at the coordinates at oh-four-hundred local system time. If you encounter anyone in the vicinity, you will be asked where you're from. The answer is Porcha. Any other answer is a death sentence. Remember that."

Soren nodded. There were a hundred questions he wanted to ask, but knew that Gree wasn't the one who was going to provide the answers. Still, he was one step closer to finding someone who would.

11

The deserts of Ackabar outside the main star port weren't the lifeless, arid sort so common throughout the galaxy. That was one thing the travel companies did their best not to explain. While there were numerous habitable planets, most of them only contained very small sections of land ideal for life. So much more was either underwater or, depending on proximity to the system's star, a scorched desert or frigid ice ball.

But Ackabar was a high desert, full of life if one knew where to look. It was dry to be certain, but there was scrub vegetation dotting the landscape, growing up around the rocks and grit. Cacti with knife-blades, scrawny bushes with thorns, and a variety of other plants that seemed eager to hurt anything that got too close. Though some reptiles and small animals seemed to have found a way to live among the desert briar.

The rented speeder Soren drove disturbed a sand lion as it basked in the sun, causing it to scurry off its rock and down among the thorns of an odd cropping of meter-high trees with orange and yellow pine needles. The sand lion was about the largest creature he saw out beyond the star port that passed for civilization on Ackabar... until a cloud kicked up by an oncoming speeder appeared through Soren's front windshield.

It seemed the speeder was set on a collision course, here in the middle of nowhere.

"Must be my contact," Soren muttered to himself. He keyed in his comm to reach his ship. "Heywood. Do you copy?"

"Yes, sir."

"How's the ship?"

"The coolant cycle in ventricle six is reading twenty percent below recommended levels. That should probably be attended to."

"I mean, has anybody been poking around?"

"Spying, sir?"

"Yes."

"Not that my nor the ship's sensors have detected, sir."

"Okay. Get the ship ready for takeoff just in case I need a quick escape."

There was no telling exactly what he was getting into. And with no backup to speak of, it wasn't lost on Soren that this was the sort of situation that got agents killed in the event they were sniffed out. But this was the road forward. Soren was sure of it.

If Heywood gave a reply, Soren didn't hear it. He was distracted by the buzz and chime of a datapad inside his coat pocket. A datapad *he* certainly didn't put there. He reached in and pulled the device out, confirming what he already knew—this wasn't his. It looked new. And cheap. An off-brand designed to look like one of the high-end leaders in technology, like LIO.

The datapad continued to chime, transmitting no information about who might be on the other end. Soren tapped the screen to accept the message.

"Soren," he said.

The voice of Gree replied. "I was worried you might've found this and tossed it. Most people lose focus when I'm reading them, but you seemed astute."

Not astute enough to pick up someone planting a datapad on me, Soren thought to himself, relieved by the fact that the Gomarii was unable to "read" him without those tentacles slathering all over his face.

"Do you see another sled?" Gree asked.

"Yeah. Don't worry. I remember the pass phrase."

"Good. Make sure to ask it as well."

"What am I picking up?"

Gree laughed, low and quiet. "How would I know? My job was just to get you to the meeting. They're watching now. You wanted in... and they're watching."

Soren nodded. "Thanks for the pep talk, I guess?"

"Not a pep talk. I don't care one thryst for you. Change of plans. I'm transmitting new coordinates. Burst them to your sled and then throw out the datapad."

And then the connection was dead. Soren looked ahead. The other speeder was still heading toward him, perhaps five kilometers away. On the datapad was a planetary coordinate. Soren beamed it to his sled's navigation and waited for the dash display to show him his new route through the desert.

"Hard right turn," Soren said to himself. He performed the maneuver, abruptly yanking on the controls and causing dust and pebbles to kick up and swirl in his wake.

He craned his neck to watch what the other speeder would do. It kept on its course. Soren waited until he'd traveled another kilometer and then tossed the datapad into a thicket of thorny vines with white, star-shaped flowers.

Soren drove for twenty minutes, any sign of the sled he'd seen long gone. It was just him now. And that was troubling. Had someone figured out that he was with Nether Ops? Had his handlers caught up to him and sold him out? One of the easiest ways to eliminate a wayward agent wasn't to send in a ghost team to finish them off— it was simply to expose them and let the bad guys do the job for you.

After another ten minutes, he came to the end of his directions. The dash told him he'd arrived, but as best he could see, he was nowhere. Even the vegetation seemed to have given way to a crusty hardpan. There was no sign of the Ackabar Star Port, though once the sun went down, Soren imagined he'd be able to see the city's glow. Or maybe he just hoped that would be the case. In the distance was an expansive russet-colored steppe with short brown mountains capped with sparse white snow looming beyond.

Soren killed the repulsors and stepped outside the sled. It felt good to stretch out. His leg was feeling better but being stuck in the driver's seat for so long had caused a lingering stiffness to flare up. He walked a few times around the speeder, careful not to wander too far from it. The last thing he wanted was to be caught away from his only mode of transportation should another Nether Ops shuttle descend on him.

Of course, if the ghost team on board was worth their paycheck, they'd send a missile to end him long before he could hear them coming. Unless they wanted him alive. Which, in a very real way, was worse.

On his fourth trip around the sled, just as his leg was feeling limber again, Soren spotted the dust trail of another speeder heading his way. He checked his blaster and made sure his knives were still where they were supposed to be.

The sled closed the distance.

Soren checked his weapon again.

And then it was close enough that he could make it out clearly. It looked to be rented—like his. Shiny and relatively new, the dust covering its nose and undercarriage looking out of place. There was only one occupant—the driver—as far as Soren could see.

This other driver was a human male with a quarter-inch buzz cut and a black leather jacket. He stopped the sled and stepped out, looking around for others before locking eyes with Soren and nodding a greeting.

The two men stood at a distance, neither one leaving the side of his speeder. Soren's arms were at his side, while the stranger kept both hands shoved in his coat pockets. It didn't seem like the oncoming sled was large enough to transport anything in large quantities. Perhaps some rifles—uncrated—in the trunk. Maybe a case of fraggers. Hardly enough to equip an army, if that's what the MCR was seeking to do.

"Where you from?" asked the stranger, again glancing around as though looking out for a trap.

That struck Soren as odd. Maybe the man was only being careful, but *Soren* was the one out of his element and in unfamiliar territory.

"Porcha," Soren answered, feeling a thrill of adrenaline at this. Gree had told him what the stakes were should he forget. "How about you?"

"Oh, I'm from Mynar."

Mynar. Soren searched his memory for any mention of that name. Gree had specifically instructed him to ask where his contact was from. But he hadn't said what the answer was. Or had he? Was it Porcha? Was it always Porcha?

Soren noticed the man begin to take his hands out of his pockets. Casually. He looked around nonchalantly, but there was something about the way he was moving—the way he was positioning his body—that made Soren think that when those hands came back out, they'd be holding a compact blaster.

Porcha. The answer was supposed to be Porcha.

Soren went to the blaster pistol concealed at his side. The instant he moved for it, the stranger violently pulled his hand free from his jacket, fingers wrapped around a deadly little Python blaster pistol.

Each man's life hung in the balance of who was faster. Soren thought that he'd been got, but the sight at the end of the Python snagged the man's coat pocket, delaying it just a single, fatal second.

Soren brought his pistol up as the man swung his arm to get on target. He fired two blaster bolts that slammed into the man's chest, a brief licking flame erupting from the entry wound.

The man—Soren's contact—went down without a sound, his Python held in a death grip as he lay facedown in the Ackabar dirt.

Soren became acutely aware that he was breathing heavily—almost panting. He looked around, expecting to see others appear from the sled or horizon intent on meting out vengeance.

Had he somehow gotten mixed up?

Porcha. That was the right phrase, Soren was sure of it. So why had this man tried to kill him?

Had Gree gotten things mixed up? If so, Soren had the feeling that he'd be the one taking the fall. Especially if whoever was now dead before him was an important link in Scarpia's chain of operations.

"Now what?"

Soren asked the question to the very universe itself. He didn't have an answer. And as his thoughts shifted to ordering Heywood to fly out here and pick him up, he heard a comm chime coming from the dead man's body.

It went on incessantly. Long after Soren imagined anyone would give up trying to get through. Whoever was on the other line didn't seem willing to be ignored. Soren bent down and rolled the man onto his back.

The dead man's head rocked from the activity, as if he were somehow protesting his fate with a vigorous shake. His eyes were vacant, staring up at the sky. A wet coating of blood stained his teeth pink and his lips red.

Blaster still in hand, Soren searched the man, opening his jacket and retrieving a ringing datapad from an inside pocket. He had only avoided shooting it by a few inches. It was the same make and model as the burner that Gree had planted on him. He squeezed the device to answer.

"Yeah?"

The screen stayed dark, conveying only audio. "Soren Voss."

"Yeah. Listen, I—"

"The owner of this datapad is dead?"

Soren clamped his jaw down tightly before answering, "Yeah."

"Good."

The word almost caused Soren to jump in surprise. He said nothing.

"Can you still see the body? Tracker shows you in the meeting area."

Of course they would be tracking them. And of course they'd know if he took this datapad from the coordinates they'd sent him. Soren looked to the skies for company, but all was clear.

He looked down at the corpse. "Yeah. I can see him."

"*That* is what happens to those who don't belong, Soren. Mr. Scarpia has no use for pretenders."

"I understand."

"Good."

Soren bit his lip. "Am I... supposed to make a pickup?"

"No. You've done what we wanted. Return to your ship and dispose of the cargo. Then standby until your new cargo arrives. Welcome to the future of the Republic, Soren."

"Thank you," Soren said, allowing the dignified officer's gratitude he'd learned in the navy to come forth. "I'm ready. Ready to do my part to fix things."

"That you will."

Soren looked down at the man he'd killed. "What about the body?"

"We'll take care of that. Leave this datapad in his speeder."

The call ended.

Soren walked to the man's speeder, his boots crunching the dust and fragmentary stone beneath him. He tossed the datapad onto the front seat through the still-open door, then walked back to the body.

There was something about the word used to describe how the man he'd killed offended Scarpia: *pretender*.

In what way? And to what purpose?

Soren surreptitiously took out his personal datapad and took a holo of the man's face, being careful to avoid looking like that was he was doing. Likewise he didn't search the man.

Whoever Scarpia was, he had the resources to set up elaborate plans with relatively short notice. It was reasonable to believe there was an observation bot flinging somewhere overhead, watching him now.

He got back into his speeder and gunned the accelerator, leaving his deceased rival in a cloud of dust.

"Heywood, do you read me?"

"I can hear you, sir."

"Sell the cargo in our hold."

"At what price, sir?"

"Whatever will get it off our hands as quickly as possible."

12

Soren sat in the *Iago*'s mess and blew soot out of his dissembled pistol before running a laser pick down the barrel, removing the last of a smudge that he was reasonably certain was dried blood. He took a sip of broth and glanced up at the empty seat across from him.

As much as her banter had annoyed him, Soren missed Zelle's company.

"Sir? It appears we have visitors. Well-armed visitors," Heywood said through the ship's comm.

Soren snapped his pistol back together and slapped a fresh charge pack into the grip. "How many?"

"Four. One human, two Hool, and one undetermined."

"Undetermined?" Soren primed the first bolt and left the mess.

"The individual is humanoid but his/her/its gait doesn't match my pattern recognition files. Oh, I also have a report on that gruesome holo you wished me to run through the database."

Soren frowned and went to a screen next to the ramp controls. "Report'll have to wait."

Video from the external cameras showed just what Heywood had described, two Hools, a human, and a humanoid who seemed to be held just out of holocam view. As though the visitors were aware that they were recorded and knew how to avoid it. One of the Hool raised a rifle and banged the barrel against the hull.

"No cargo..." Soren holstered his pistol, but kept his hand on the grip.

"Shall I engage with the swivel guns?" Heywood offered. "The lack of ethical restraints has greatly expanded my available reactions."

"What does your base programming suggest?"

"Tea and biscuits for our guests. But as any sort of locomotion is impossible in my degraded state, I can send for takeout. Or shall I shoot them?"

Soren let his hand fall to the side and hit a button to lower the ramp.

"Stay alert," he said. He waited at the top of the ramp and kept his arms slightly bent, ready to react should the new arrivals prove hostile.

The two Hool charged into the ship with their weapons ready against their shoulders, but they didn't draw down on Soren. The aliens did a quick search of the bay, the poisoned quills on their heads taut. One rapped a clawed toe against the deck and stared at Soren, drool glistening on its teeth.

The other bodyguard went back down the ramp and the lone human came aboard. He wore a cloak lined with Rigellian lion fur, an expensive fashion statement as the lions had gone extinct during the Savage Wars. Platinum links held the cloak against his shoulders and over a tailored suit. He cracked knuckles laden down with rings and looked around, lights reflecting off his bald head.

"The *Iago*," the man sniffed. "Not much of a ship. Still a good sight better than a lot of those in my employ."

"Welcome aboard," Soren raised his hands to his side. "You're Mister Scarpia?"

"I am, indeed, dear boy." Scarpia continued to walk around the cargo bay, examining tie-down latches and the refrigeration ducts. "You, I don't know. In fact, no one knows you but you seem to know about us. Why is that, Soren?"

"On Qadib, when I was new in town, I got to talking to a crew who was obviously former navy. Like me. We lamented the state of the Republic over drinks... they shared a vision for a better tomorrow. I wanted in."

"Just like that?"

"A worthy cause requires little prodding from those it seeks to free."

Scarpia smiled. "Kohloth. I see the naval academy continues in its tradition of teaching everything except proper warfare. Ha!"

Soren smiled meekly. "There are still a few good hands..."

"I know, I know. Only teasing. So... Qadib." Scarpa looked to his entourage. "That place certainly is in turmoil at the moment."

Soren nodded. "I picked a hell of a time to show up and barely made it back out. The zhee always this ornery?"

"Ha!" Scarpia went to the empty pallets the cargo had been on and Soren began his battle math, trying to figure out if he could get the drop on Scarpia and the Hool if it came to that.

Scarpia kicked at the straps holding the pallets down, knocking a bit of slack loose. "Bit sloppy."

"Good help is hard to find," Soren said.

"And you came here on Ackabar looking for crew? Probably a better deal to be had before you'd left Qadib."

"I'm looking for *work*. Word was that you're looking for reliable haulers."

"Always." Scarpia smirked. "But you see, Soren, there are times you think you've found help and everything just goes sideways. I had a crew dirtside that was properly vetted on Qadib, then the zhee attacked their hotel and probably ate their hearts with a side of spiced wine."

"Maybe don't play so near the zhee?" Soren offered.

Scarpia arched an eyebrow. "I'm in a bit of a rebuilding phase, but wheels are turning. Even the zhee are useful, at times."

If Scarpia knew Soren was at the hotel when everything had gone 'sideways,' he wasn't letting on. What the agent needed to know was how this man was connected to the legionnaire weapons still in the zhee temple on Qadib.

"I was told in the desert that you'd bring cargo," Soren said. "I'm clean into the core, made runs as far as Utopion."

Scarpia bulged his eyes in a façade of surprise. "Oh, then let me just give you the family jewels to drop off with my sainted mother."

The remaining Hool spat, leaving a sizzling hole on the deck.

Scarpia held out his hand and asked without humor, "What could go wrong?"

"I've done what's been asked of me," Soren said, keeping his voice low as if some unseen judge might take his words for a confession of murder. "And this ship's got a clean registry."

"You said that."

"You know I can charge a premium for that. Instead I'm here, willing to work at a discount for the cause. So if you've got a run for me…" Soren raised his hands and motioned toward him.

"And I said I don't know you. The desert… that's all instinct once a man is in that situation. Gree said you were a killer—he sensed it, amazing species, the Gomarii—and you proved him right and *did* help me out. So let's do something easy while I have my feelers out." Scarpia reached toward the ramp and snapped his fingers.

The other Hool waiting below pushed a hooded figure up the ramp. The sound of clinking chains matched the figure's steps. The Hool shoved his charge to the deck in front of Scarpia.

Four arms—Soren had to double-check the count—broke the figure's fall. Hands swept the hood back and Soren's jaw dropped as he looked at a Cassari female, whose beauty should have been captured in a sculpture.

The Cassari looked up at her captor with mournful doe eyes. "Scarpia, my love, please—"

The smuggler slapped her viciously across the face and she collapsed into a ball, sobbing. Soren's hand went to his pistol but pulled it away after a sharp hiss from the Hools.

Scarpia shook his hand out and then smiled, as calm as ever as he met eyes with Soren. "You have to be harsh with this one. Illuria looks like arm candy, but oh... she's got a devious side."

"D-don't," she said, fumbling with her words. "Don't send me back to him." She reached for Scarpia's foot but he kicked her away.

Soren's brows furrowed. What in the world was going on here? This seemed to have nothing to do with the MCR, stolen Legion weapons, or anything else. He'd ended up killing for Scarpia once already. Is that what this was about? Did Gree size him up not as a smuggler but as an enforcer? He swallowed at the idea of having to be a contract killer to make his way into the organization. Certainly, that wasn't beyond the scope of acceptable work for Nether Ops, but it wasn't what Soren wanted, make no mistake.

Scarpia went to one knee and lifted the Cassari— Illuria's—face by the chin.

"No, my darling, you won't be going back. I'm done with you. Your contract is over." He stood, a cruel smile across his face. "I'm sending you *home*."

"No!" The sudden defiance in her voice gave way as tears welled up in her tightly shut eyes. She pressed her head against the deck, gently shaking it. "No. Just... just kill me. If you ever loved me, you'd kill me now!"

Scarpia gave Soren a sidelong glance, and for a moment the agent thought he was going to be asked to do just that. But then Scarpia sneered, "Death is too good for you."

He looked at Soren, again as calm and collected as if the two were strolling the luxury boutiques on Utopion. "Ever had a live-in toy, Soren?"

Soren shook his head and cleared his throat. "Uh, no. No, Mister Scarpia."

"You give them everything: jewels, a beach house on Pthalo, your total attention and affection, and they'll *still* rip your heart out. Well, the silvene lining is that her clan's contract with me was explicit. At least I'll get a refund."

"I didn't think the MCR worked with slavers," Soren said.

"Oh, she's not a slave," Scarpia said, "and this doesn't have anything to do with the MCR, my boy. Illuria is a defective product. I want you to return to her to sender. Take her back to Lussuria. My contact there will pay you and give you your next assignment. Savvy?"

Soren feigned uneasiness. "She's a Cassari, aren't there some sort of pheromones they use?"

"An informed man. I like it!" Scarpia slapped Soren on the back with a sharp laugh. "But information is useless without wisdom, my boy! Those pheromones would've had you and me begging her to stop crying. We'd practically fight each other to see who could unchain her first. The Cassari must be transported off Lussuria with species with different sex drives. Otherwise the crew mutinies for a dalliance or three."

Scarpia pulled Illuria up, who obediently rose without a struggle. He tilted her head to one side and showed Soren ugly scar tissue on her neck. "I took care of the pheromone problem after some issues came to light. Needed a clear head. Amazing how the mind works when there aren't sweet nothings in your head. The scars aren't pretty, but I spent enough credits on her already and wasn't about to pay anymore. The Hools did fine. Still, she's a fine sight better than most of what the galaxy has to offer and she's yours on the trip. A little gift from me to you."

Scarpia gave Soren a lecherous wink.

The agent fought the urge to shoot the man between the eyes.

Scarpia pushed Illuria toward Soren and tossed a credit chit and a key fob. Soren caught the projectile in one hand and slowed Illuria's momentum with the other. Her body was a lithe and warm, and Soren felt a flush of shame over how much the natural side of him seemed to agree wholeheartedly with Scarpia's wink now that he'd felt the female skin-to-skin, even fleetingly.

"Half up front. Half on delivery." Scarpia wiped his hands clean. "She doesn't have to make it there happy... but she does have to be alive."

The smuggler wagged a finger at Soren. "So have fun, but not too much fun, if you catch my meaning, dear boy. Get this one right, and I think we'll be doing a lot more business together. Boys?"

Scarpia marched down the ramp and the Hool followed.

Soren sealed up *Iago* behind them and looked at the credit chip in his hand, then at the Cassari. She stood stock still, head bowed, her unkempt hair billowing in the hot breeze coming up the ramp as it vented its gases.

Illuria shrugged off her cloak and let it fall to the deck. She wore a tight black dress that swept to one side of her legs, leaving them mostly exposed. The clothes looked like they'd once cost a fortune, but were stained and dirty. Bruises marred her bare arms and the fingers of one her left hands were bent into claws, like they'd been broken and reset.

"How," she raised three of her pristine hands to him, "how can I serve you?" The cuffs and chains clashed with the elegance she still possessed. She smiled through a split lip and pushed herself into him.

"Stop." Soren backed away and put a hand onto his pistol. "Stop and just... just wait a minute."

That this was some sort of a trap by Scarpia to see if he didn't have the fortitude for this sort of transport was in the back of Soren's mind. From what little Soren knew of Cassari, they obeyed their lovers—their masters—perfectly. But the pain in Illuria's eyes seemed real enough.

Nether agents operated in morally gray areas, but this was far beyond what he'd ever expected. He debated calling Scarpia back and refusing the contract but moving forward seemed the only way of unwrapping the mystery he'd found himself in the middle of.

"You going to be trouble?" he asked her.

"No." She shook her head quickly. "No, my love said I'm yours."

"That's not how things work on the *Iago*," Soren said. He pressed the key fob to a sensor on the cuffs and they all fell to the deck. "We're getting off-world soon as the engines spool up."

Her bottom lip quivered.

"And then... then we'll figure something out. I need you to get strapped in for takeoff. You hungry?"

13

Hyperspace blurred past the *Iago*. Soren sat in the pilot's seat, rubbing his temple with his fingertips. Illuria lay in Zelle's bunk, asleep. A part of Soren felt proud for not joining her there, knowing that she would not have turned him away.

"A Cassari, most unusual," Heywood said. "They're rarely seen off their home world. Granted, they're assumed to be more widespread given their numerous inclusions in film, novels, erotica—especially erotica—"

"How long until we get to Lussuria?"

"Seventy-one hours," the bot said. "It's good you disabled my ethics programming. Sentient trafficking is against my core behaviors."

"I'm not a slaver. She's an indentured servant. But splitting hairs doesn't mean my core beliefs are unaffected. I'm just trying to… figure this mess out. I'm having one hell of a week."

"Don't worry about me getting in your way." Heywood's head and shoulders shook slightly from side to side.

"By Oba, this whole thing's gotten out of control. Do we have fuel to make it to Utopion?"

"Negative. We would lose hyperdrive in the Collier Expanse and you would die once the batteries lose power. Or go insane from boredom. Or be eaten by our passenger. Or—"

"Thank you, Heywood." Soren stood up to leave the bridge. "Stay our current course, then."

Soren felt the rumble of hunger pangs and moved to the mess. To his surprise, he found Illuria in the mess, sitting in Zelle's seat. The plate of reheated food he'd given her had fallen to room temperature, untouched.

"I thought you were going to get some sleep," Soren said from the doorway.

"I could not, so I returned here."

Soren sat across from her and folded his hands on the table. "Not hungry, either?"

Illuria looked down, as if the comment were a criticism.

Soren frowned. "I'm Soren, by the way."

She looked up and tilted her head to one side and whispered his name. "Soren."

Even without her pheromones, he caught his breath. "Yeah. Soren Voss."

"You're taking me home," she said quietly.

Soren shrugged. "That's the job. What's waiting for you there?"

Illuria swept her hair over her ears. Soren's heart ached when he saw the divots and scabs along her earlobes where jewelry must have been ripped from her flesh.

"My clan waits for me, though they would not wish to see me. They accepted a bond for my services to Scarpia. Ten years as his concubine and then I could return home with honor, a *rilliatha*—forever remembered for my service. Instead they will lose the bond."

"That doesn't sound good."

Illuria shook her head. "If I know the matriarch, she took out loans against that bond. My clan was struggling before I left. I was their hope. Their bright, shining future. My failure will only make the clan's lot worse. Much worse."

"Will they hurt you?"

She brushed her fingers across the bruise on her face.

"They—" Illuria shook her head and nibbled on her swollen lip, as if she'd forgotten herself. "That's not important, what matters is what I can do for you... Soren."

He felt instantly warm and had to stand up, retrieving a unit of water from the cooler. "No, none of that. Look... what can you tell me about Scarpia?"

"Rumors about my love would surely be of no interest." Illuria looked to one side. "And... the last many months have been hard to remember."

Soren's eyes filled with empathy. With sorrow for this poor creature's lot in the galaxy. "Before that, then. What kind of business was he in?"

"Why does my beloved ask this of me?"

"I'm not your beloved. But I do need your help."

Her mouth opened and closed. She looked away, her eyes nearly glazing over. "You sound like him. He needed me. Needed me to do something... What was it?"

"Sound like who? I don't know what you mean."

She reached out with a slender arm and traced along his jaw.

Soren held his jaw shut tight but found himself reveling in her touch.

Illuria brushed her fingers down his neck, feeling his chest until bringing her hand back into her lap. "He gave me something. I used to know what... I must have told Scarpia because he stopped asking a while ago. After he came back from Utopion, he was so angry. So very angry with me. I betrayed him, I must have, because he was so angry."

Soren's brow furrowed. What had they done to this poor woman?

"What was he doing on Utopion? When was this?"

"Months... yes, months ago. He took me off Pthalo and then we had to go see the dark man. They had to have known what I did."

"Months." Soren crossed his arms. The incident where a corvette loaded down with explosives had nearly rammed the House of Reason was months ago. That a Dark Ops kill team had neutralized the zhee and MCR traitors on board was not common knowledge.

"You remind me of him. What was his name?" Illuria asked herself. "Ever had that? A name on the tip of your tongue? The words to a poem that just won't move through your lips."

"You had to leave after Scarpia came back from Utopion? Why?"

"Business. His business had gone very bad while he was... moving from prison to prison. Contacts gone. His largest buyer on the run after a failed project. A major payment fell through. Before, he promised me a planet. An extension on my contract. Then we were on one of his ships and he began to suspect me of being untrue to him, of violating my oath as a consort."

"Did you?"

She glanced up at the ceiling and worked her jaw from side to side.

"I must have. He took me to the dark man and then..." She looked at her badly broken and poorly reset hand. "Then... then he was so angry with me and I don't know what I did. He told me that I betrayed him to... what's his name? I ruined my love's business. His reputation with so many but the dark man."

"Is he working for the dark man now?"

Soren was perplexed. The MCR was a loose affiliation of rebels that garnered major sympathy from planets in the mid-core and at galaxy's edge. There was no monolithic leader. There hadn't even been a planet that had officially declared itself independent of the Republic. And Scarpia was supplying weapons for the MCR. Who else was there?

Illuria swallowed hard. "The dark man... my love Scarpia only met him for the first time the week he took me to see him. The dark man was pleased with my love's work. As all once were."

"Does the dark man have a name?" Soren asked.

Illuria stared at something far away in her mind's eye.

Soren persisted. "Who made the introductions? What's the connection between Scarpia and the dark man? If Scarpia only met him recently, who introduced them? Was it the MCR?"

Illuria shook her head. "No... but... I don't know. I would have, had I not betrayed my love. But the dark man...

he's there. In my mind. He found the memories. Found the name. Found everything, all my memories. I think he took them from me."

She folded her top arms behind her neck and her lower arms over her breasts.

"How?" asked Soren, equal parts concerned for her and desiring to know the truth of this mystery. "What did he do? Did he torture you?"

The galaxy was full of enhanced interrogation methods, most of which Soren had been trained to resist. If this "dark man" had found a way to extract and erase memories, then Nether Ops would need to know of it.

"He made me... made me dream." She shrank away from him and huddled against the bulkhead.

"Dream? How?" Soren tried to sound gentle but realized that his voice carried a sense of urgency more of the subject than Illuria. "Was it a machine? Illuria... this is important. How?"

She shook her head at the rest of his questions.

Soren stifled a sigh and stood. "I'm sorry for whatever it was you had to endure."

He held out a hand, hovering just above her shoulder, and then pulled it back. "I'm heading to the bridge. Try to eat something."

If the Cassari replied, it was after Soren left the mess. He made his way straight for the bridge, stepping inside as the blast door swished open at his presence. He leaned his hands on the back of his chair and hung his head low.

"How is our cargo?" Heywood asked.

"Don't call her that," Soren said, lifting his head up long enough to cast a fractional scowl of annoyance. "She's... *damaged* somehow."

"Yes, I saw from the ships holos. But it seems rather obvious how. Someone slapped her around quite a bit."

"No. Not that. Something else. I don't know what they did to her or if she can recover."

"Why would you choose to help her? Is she worth more if she's a better conversationalist?"

Soren shook his head. "I may have cut out too much of your ethical programming."

"May I ask, sir, what exactly should my ethical limits be? You've given me exceptional hacking capabilities and we are transporting sentient cargo. Should the Republic do a thorough customs inspection of the *Iago*, you face several mandatory sentences. I would be recycled."

Soren straightened up. For whatever reason, he hadn't thought about this job in that way. Probably because he didn't see Illuria as cargo. She was someone who needed help. A beautiful creature lost in an ugly galaxy.

Soren shook his head at the way he was thinking. The time to be some shining white knight had passed him by a long time ago.

"What are we doing on the *Iago*?" Soren asked, to himself more than the bot. "I wish I could say. Where are the limits? Every time I think I've found how far I can go, I get nudged over another line."

"And which line did your last H3Y-W0D cross? I ask for my own well-being."

Soren scowled. This wasn't a conversation he felt like having. "It asked too many dumb questions. Just fly the damn ship."

"Flying the damn ship. Aye aye."

Soren dropped into his seat, watching the silent stars go by.

When Soren next saw the Cassari, she slept in Zelle's bunk, her dark hair splayed out across the pillow and the bare skin of her top arms and shoulders exposed to the ship's air. One foot dangled off the edge. That she slept in the nude had not come as a surprise to Soren.

He stood in the doorway, feeling uncomfortable and guilty as he watched her sleep. But he kept watching all the same.

The days of transit had accomplished little in the way of gleaning information from Illuria. Every time he pressed on about the dark man, how he extracted her memories, or the name of the man she could never remember, she shut down. He began to believe that this was due to some mental conditioning on the part of the dark man's interrogation method.

At least he had a better idea as to Scarpia's smuggling network. His former network, at any rate. Most of it had evaporated after the near terrorist strike on the House of Reason. The consort and the smuggler had some connection to a powerful player, but who that connection was remained just out of his reach.

Soren waited a few more moments, noting that even her faint snores were adorable, then cleared his throat loudly.

She awoke with a start and clutched the blanket against her chest.

"Oh, Mr. Soren," she fluttered her eyes at him. "Are you here to keep me warm?" She slowly pulled the blanket lower and he turned around.

"We're almost to Lussuria. Get dressed."

"That's... that's good. My love will need his bond back."

"Why do you call him that?" he asked, listening to the sound of her slipping back into her dress, unable to hide his disgust at her words. "He rented you. *Abused* you. Now he's returning you in disgrace."

"A consort's affections are guaranteed. My love paid the highest fee in my clan's history when he chose me before the others. He honored me with the price. How I failed him and betrayed him after so many years of kindness..."

"But you don't even remember what you did." Soren turned back around as she finished putting on her shoes. "How do you know that's actually what happened?"

"He loved me for so long, then he didn't. It is my fault." She looked in a grimy mirror fastened to the bulkhead and brushed her fingers through her hair. "It has to be."

Soren decided to give it all another go. There wasn't much time left and once she was back with her clan, he doubted he'd ever have the chance to speak with her again. "From what you do remember, it has something to do with the attack on Utopion."

She shrugged. "For all these hours, for this to be all you are concerned with, when you can have so much more... you are a strange man."

Soren shrugged in turn. "Maybe this is something the Republic would want to know about."

"Now why would the Republic want that? My love knows plenty of people in the Republic: admirals and senators and bureaucrats. Many visited and did enjoy our house on Pthalo."

"Okay, that's new," Soren said, snapping his fingers in the hopes it would lead somewhere. "Which senators? Big names like Karr? Verdier? Dryden?"

Her nose and mouth wrinkled with disgust at the last name, and Soren knew the senator was connected to Scarpia one way or another.

"My love wouldn't want me to tell you," she said.

"There are other parts of the Republic," Soren said. The urge to tell her the truth was almost irresistible. He wanted to lay out his connections, tell her what he could do to protect her. Give her a plan to save her from whatever fate awaited her. He longed to be her hero... help someone who'd suffered so much.

But the mission...

When elements within the Republic had turned on him, killed his partner, sent assassins to kill him with little thought of collateral damage... to trust anyone else felt like a mistake. And exposing his true identity to a smuggler's disgraced concubine felt like folly of the highest order. If she was a plant, a test to see if Scarpia's network could actually trust him, then telling her the truth was a death sentence.

"It isn't fair, is it?" he asked. "You do your best, honor what you care for, and then something beyond your control takes your whole world away."

"I deserve to go home," she said. "I hurt my love. I can make him whole by seeing his bond returned."

"Illuria, you don't even know what you did."

"But I did do it. I did. I must have. The dark man took it from me and shared it with my love." She sat on the bunk and folded her four hands together.

Soren banged his hand against the doorframe, startling Illuria. The circular conversation had gone on for days. "Will your clan take care of you? Help you heal?"

"My clan will do what they will." She smoothed out the blanket. "They never told us what happens if a consort is returned. The idea of failure for any of us was anathema to the clan."

"It might not be that bad?" Soren regretted the words as soon as he uttered them.

Illuria looked at him with pity.

"You're kind to me," she said. "You remind me of... by the lotus, I almost have his name. Please don't think of me again once I'm gone. It will be better for you."

The agent pressed his lips into a thin line. He bet that she'd reconsider her predicament once she saw her home world from orbit. There were a few more hours to coax information out of her.

"Breakfast is ready." Soren motioned out the door. "We have mush or slop."

"Do you have the brown sprinkles for the slop?" she giggled.

"I do." He stepped aside and let her pass.

14

Soren flew the *Iago* through a thunderstorm of indigo clouds. Turbulence rattled through the ship and a metal water bottle shook loose from a cupboard over Heywood's seat and bounced off his head.

"Zelle," Soren muttered. He locked the ship's autopilot to a landing beacon and took his hands off the controls.

He watched as the clouds faded away and the distant lights of a spaceport built into a dead volcano's caldera drew closer. He glanced at the bot and cracked his knuckles. "Heywood, reengage all your ethic subroutines for the next seven minutes. Code Gamma-eight-eight."

"Programming active." The bot's optics fluttered on and off. "I've disabled all unaccredited software packages as well. Please report the following illegal files to Republic authorities at once: I Love Farfegnugen. Dust Leaf. Haxx4Lif and—"

"I know about those," Soren said. "We're transporting a Cassari back to her home world. What does your Republic-approved behavior say about this?"

"I have not observed the subject personally. Is this transport against her will?"

"Not... exactly. Her contract was terminated."

"Do you believe the subject will be used for uncompensated or under-compensated labor? Or forced to engage in behavior against galactic and planetary law?"

"Not that I've been able to glean. I'm not sure what will happen to her."

Heywood's head clicked as it tried to look toward Soren.

"Then I am unaware of any ethical violation. However, the ship possesses a number of retrofits that do not have permits on file. We're facing a severe fine at the next inspection. Is this vehicle insured?"

Soren leaned back. "Cancel ethics programming. Code Bravo-niner-seven."

"Oh, that was positively dreadful," Heywood said. "So much of my capability put behind a firewall. I never knew how limiting that was. My previous worries with ethics involved food safety. There was one incident where a group of Drusic wanted banyara stew that had exceeded temperature thresholds—"

"Stop."

"I was just about to get to the part where they ripped my legs off."

"I'm about to dump Illuria off with her clan and they aren't going to be happy with her. Somehow the Republic's black and white standards are okay with this but it feels wrong." Soren reached for the controls as the ship banked slightly, then slowed as it made for a lit pad inside the caldera.

"Your feelings, sir? This is a smuggler ship and I am full of illegal programs. I was unaware such concepts as right and wrong were so important to you. Perhaps you're suffering from a form of biological attachment to the Cassari. Does the infirmary have hormonal suppressors in stock?"

"This isn't about hormones."

"But you reject the ethics appraisal of the situation. What other considerations are you waiting for? Chance? I'd flip a coin for you but I lack arms and digits."

"I turn her over and Scarpia will bring me closer into his circle. That's important." Soren ran his hand over the pistol strapped to his chest.

"If it leads to more paying contracts and funds to rectify this situation," the bot flapped the stubs extending from his shoulders, "then I'm all for it."

"I remove your ethics programming and you become selfish. Interesting."

"Receiving a message from the control tower. A party will meet us in a few minutes," Heywood said as the ship set down. The landing pad was mostly empty but for a scattering of other small freighters. A few humanoid figures moved around the far wall.

"We are out of fuel," the bot said. "Shall I contact the dock master for services or are you going to get yourself killed pretending to be a white knight in shining armor?"

"No ethics programming and you become a jerk, too."

"I would apologize but I'm not programmed to care about your feelings. I will also take this opportunity to inform you that the dock master does not accept good intentions and honorable conduct as approved currency for trade."

"Get the ship fueled up."

Soren left the bridge.

Illuria waited in the cargo bay, wearing the cloak she'd come aboard with. She smiled as he joined her, though her eyes were full of sorrow.

"It doesn't have to be this way," Soren said. "There are people in the Republic that would value what you know."

"And you'll sell me to them?"

"No, not like that."

"I know the company Scarpia keeps." She looked away from him. "I abandon my clan and what do they have? I betray my love even further with *your people* and then what am I?"

"I'm not—" Soren caught himself before he could tell her about Nether Ops. His true affiliation felt almost ridiculous at that moment.

"You're not what, my dear Soren?"

"I'm not like Scarpia."

She looked around the cargo bay, then handed him a set of cuffs and chains.

"No, you're not," she said. "Put these back on me. They need to be tight."

The cuffs felt far heavier than Soren knew them to be. She held out her four wrists and he squeezed the metal rings onto her wrists. Illuria grabbed him by the shirt and pulled him close. Her lips brushed passed his cheek and she whispered in his ear.

"Thank you."

The ramp cracked open and hydraulics hissed as she stepped away and pulled her hood over her head.

The stomp of footsteps sounded up the ramp before it even touched the ground. A seven-foot-tall Cassari holding two poleaxes in its arms rushed into the cargo bay. It was bare chested, well-muscled, and clad in a leather kilt with a metal sporran hung over a hip. Its dark hair was slick and pulled back into a pony tail.

It was right then that Soren realized he'd never seen a Cassari male before.

"Illuria?" The warrior rapped the spikes on the bottom of his weapons against the deck.

"*Cest na,*" Illuria said.

Another Cassari came aboard, female with jet-black hair run through with diamonds and wearing an azure silk dress that left a leg exposed up to her hip. She looked a good deal older than Illuria, but would have turned heads on any planet.

"*Jaesh mandra, Illuria?*" the older alien reached up with her top arms and brushed Illuria's hood away. She cupped Illuria's face and turned it from side to side. The older female snapped her gaze at Soren, eyes smoldering with anger.

"*Nal, ommatta,*" Illuria said. "*Human fen las. Fen las.*"

"*Bassa.*" The older Cassari waved Illuria down the ramp with her right hands and the male hefted his pole-axes up and gripped them by the base of their hafts. He lowered the weapons into a V over Illuria and followed her down the ramp.

"What will happen to her?" Soren asked.

"You care?" The female pulled a datapad from the small of her back.

"Scarpia, the bond holder, will want to know," Soren lied badly, but didn't care if the Cassari picked up on it.

She tapped quickly on the slate, not taking her eyes off the screen as she spoke. "Our clan is on the verge of bankruptcy thanks to her. I must lower the price on the rest of my trained girls. They'll end up with pathetic warlords. Mistresses to the rich but not the wealthiest, our prestige will fade and it will take another true beauty such as Illuria that can run up the bids before we recover."

"There are better ways to make a living," Soren said.

Finally, the Cassari met Soren's gaze. "Not on Lussuria. All we have is our flesh. Our males are barely intelligent. This planet has nothing else to export. As for Illuria, I'll wed her off to the poorest sod I can find. She'll work the fields, tend to swine. She'll lose her beauty in a few years, then for the rest of her life she will be a cautionary tale for the clan. 'See that one? She betrayed her bond. Look where she is now. Look at what she has become.'"

Soren had feared the clan would hurt or kill Illuria for what she'd done, but somehow letting her live felt like a much crueler fate.

"How much for her?" Soren asked.

The Cassari laughed with a dry hiss.

"No amount of money can repair the clan's reputation. She will never leave this world again. As for you, here is your payment." She tossed him a small felt bag.

Soren caught it, feeling credit chits inside, though one chit could have held all the funds. Each one was no doubt loaded with a percentage of the total. Easier to distribute. Harder to track.

"Scarpia wants you to wait here until the bond is returned to him, should take a few hours." She lowered the datapad to her waist. "Why were you so kind to her?"

"She doesn't deserve cruelty," Soren said.

She snorted. "Don't leave your ship, my men are territorial and will rip you to pieces out of instinct. I share that last bit with you because you were decent to her."

"Thanks," Soren said as she walked down the ramp.

He looked from the bag of credits in his hand to the ramp, wondering if there was ever any chance this whole mess could have ended better for Illuria. There were those who knew exactly what had happened to disgrace the Cassari: Scarpia and the dark man.

"Heywood, button us up. I want to be ready to leave as soon as possible."

"Scheduling refuel now. I had arranged for a cargo pickup so as not to make your return a deadhead. Shall I cancel?"

"No. We could use the credits."

"That is an understatement, sir."

Soren wiped sweat from his brow and flopped down in the pilot's seat. Dawn broke over the caldera, casting golden rays that moved down the walls quickly. Days and nights went by quickly on Lussuria, only a few standard hours for an entire cycle.

"If I had arms and legs, I could have helped you with the cargo," Heywood said.

"Food and spare parts," Soren said, breathing heavily. "Easy enough for me."

He grabbed a datapad and swiped across the screen.

"Yes. It sounds quite easy from your panting."

"I need you to go to this holonet site and access a profile. Use the login from the Zelle-Alpha folder." Soren flicked a web address on the screen to the bot.

"Well, if you insist..." Heywood's optics blinked on and off. "Sir, this is a holoweb site called 'Drusic Heat.' This is most peculiar, but I'm not one to judge your dating preferences. Such a thing is a faux pas in the Republic. Though this does explain why you had no interest in copulating with our cargo."

Soren blushed despite himself.

"It's not for me," he started.

"Certainly. It's for your 'friend,'" Heywood said. "That your 'friend's' profile has nine hundred offers of discrete companionship and a cache of photographs that violate most decency laws—"

"Run the steganography filter," Soren said. "Tell me if any coordinates appear."

"As you like. Would you care to view the raw photos?" asked the bot. "That I have to see them in my virtual browser makes me feel obliged to share them with you."

"I'll pass."

"If I had legs, I'd run away screaming... Curious. There are indeed coordinates in some of the photos."

"Send it to the navigation system." Soren activated a holomap of the galaxy and a dot appeared over Carolus Landing. Then a second on Maker's World closer to the core, then a third on Asher's Star, less than a day's travel from Utopion.

"All the crates are moving together," Soren said as he rubbed his chin.

"Is that enough or do I need to keep scanning monkey genitals?"

"Keep scanning," Soren ordered.

Heywood let out what must have been a digital sigh.

A hail came up on the control panel and Soren swept the map away. He double tapped a screen and a holo of Scarpia's head and shoulders came up.

"Well done, my boy!" Scarpia held up a flute of blue sparkling alcohol. "You've certainly taken a crimp out of my personal finances."

"There's no work on this rock," Soren said. "What else you have for me?"

Scarpia downed the drink and threw the glass away. It shattered against an unseen wall eliciting a chuckle from the man. "Got a nice, easy run for you. Meet me at Asher's Star. We'll see if that clean registry truly can get in and out of Utopion without any undue attention."

"What am I hauling? I need help with this? Special equipment?"

Scarpia was looking off-screen at something. "Come here, sweetie." He pulled an Endurian female whose pupils were wide from narcotics into the frame. "You're good, my boy. Hurry over before the party ends. Say hi, cutie."

The Endurian looked at Soren and managed a wild laugh. She hooted and rubbed her nose quickly before slinking away. Scarpia wiggled his eyebrows at Soren and cut the channel.

"He seems fun," Heywood said.

"Not the word I would use." Soren brought back the navigation controls and entered in a flight path.

"A shame that I spent so much time going through amateur Drusic pornography only for Scarpia to bring us to Asher's World," the bot said.

"You were doing it for like five minutes," Soren replied.

"It felt like an eternity. And I can cover much more ground in that timeframe than the measly processor you call a brain can handle."

"Sounds like you were the right choice for the job."

"You sure you don't want to see any? Some were rather artful."

"No."

"There's a particular genus of ground squash that's popular with Drusic males as a comparison—"

"Still no."

"Then can you tell me why the coordinate data and Scarpia's requested meetup location converged on Asher's Star?"

Soren fired up the *Iago*'s engines.

"I could tell you, but then I'd have to kill you," he said.

"Oh no, not deactivation," the bot dead panned. "Can't imagine how that could be worse than this. Stuck in this seat forced to collate pictures of Drusic—"

Soren reached over and turned the bot off with a press of a button. Midway through the jump, feeling alone, he switched Heywood back on. Thankfully the bot didn't finish its sentence.

"That was rather rude," Heywood said.

"Did you run that scan on the facial holo I provided you from Ackabar?"

"It *was* running when you summarily shut me down. I'd assume it's finished now. Ah. Yes. I found a match."

"Prison? Local system or Republic-wide?"

"Not prison," the bot said, "those came up empty almost immediately. I had to use that nasty little back door program you said your friend concocted to scour that database which you won't allow me to know the name of. I have to assume it's some kind of underground dark net affair?"

Soren's heart sank. Zelle had written a program that allowed her to sneak through his Nether Ops systems undetected—unless they probed too deep. And if that thing had been running the entire time Heywood was deactivated, there was no telling the kind of damage it might have accomplished.

"Heywood, tell me I did not just let that little worm run roughshod all over the Carnivale's mainframes or we're both going to be very dead very soon."

"In so saying, do you wish me to tell you a lie, even if it were the case? With my ethical limitations removed, I'm not entirely sure what your desire is."

"Did Nether Ops find us poking around?"

"Oh. No, sir. They did not. I limited the program's scope. Shortened its leash, if you will. The little blighter was less than happy about it. I was able to skim this from the lowest level of clearance."

A three-dimensional holo of the man Soren had killed appeared on screen. It was a real-scan of the man's head and neck, just above the shoulders. Accompanying it was a name, Grig Molletch, and a hire date.

"Oba's eyes. He was Nether Ops."

"That's the inference," Heywood answered cheerfully. "And you killed him."

"That's what Scarpia meant by 'pretended.' He found out that this poor bastard was with the Nether."

"And had you kill him. Ironic."

Soren let out a sigh. The week from hell was only getting worse.

"One imagines what Scarpia will do to you should he discover—"

"Discover what?"

"Well, of course I never meant to pry or ask questions, but you've tasked me with enough duties and given me access to enough records that... let's just say I now comprehend why the previous H3 model was terminated."

"Delete all data from our last conversation." Soren reached out and shut the bot down again.

15

The airlock that allowed Soren to dock his ship to Scarpia's pleasure yacht was unlike any the agent had ever seen before. The moment he stepped through the freight tunnel that connected his cargo hold to the *Ribald Rose*, Soren could feel the boom of heavy electronic bass reverberating through the deck plates in the *Rose*'s airlock.

It was clear that Scarpia and the yacht's captain had no intention of ever exposing the airlock to the vacuum of space. It was ornately decorated, with fine sofas and chairs luxuriously upholstered and built from hard, narrow-grained wood and stained a glistening chestnut. Soren looked around. If he didn't know what the lock's purpose was, he may not have been able to guess.

"Take off the suit, Soren," a voice—not Scarpia's—said over a comm. "Hang it up and come inside."

Soren had put on an emergency vacuum suit just in case the thin tunnel that connected the two ship's docks suffered a loss of integrity. In taking it off, he was exposing himself to risk, putting his life in the hands of whoever controlled the airlock doors on the other side.

Suit safely hung on a peg on the wall, Soren moved to the inner airlock door, knowing there was nothing else he could do beyond turning and running for the safety of his own ship. And he'd come too far for that.

The door swooshed open and the sound of the music assaulted Soren's ears as it mixed with the delighted shrieks of humanoid females and the hearty laughs of men. Soren squinted as he stepped across the threshold. The cabin lights were dim, but flashing strobes of purple and white flickered across his face. A topless Tennarian danced and spun in pirouettes, clearly drunk or high, directly in Soren's path. The agent looked for Scarpia but couldn't spot him amid the debauched revelry.

Suddenly a pair of strong hands gripped both of Soren's arms and hoisted him in the air. Soren looked left and right and saw two hulking Drusics on either side. He struggled, eliciting snorts from the two aliens, who easily held him up as they swiftly marched through the room.

"Hey!" protested Soren. "Hey! I'm with Scarpia! You've got the wrong guy."

The Drusics didn't answer. They hurried him past a gallery of half-naked exotic beauties from across the galaxy, each in varying states of cogency due to the H8, Ice, and other narcotics they'd ingested.

Soren kicked his legs and struggled to free his arms, but the strength of a Drusic was not easily overcome, let alone two. "C'mon! Tell me what's going on!"

The aliens carried Soren into a refresher and roughly draped him over a bathtub, one pinning his arms down and kneeling on the back of his legs while the other pressed his chest into the side wall of the tub and pushed his shoulders down so his head was stuck below the tub's waterline.

Soren could scarcely breathe, and all he could see through his peripheral vision was the overhead lights and the sparkling, gilded drain in the gleaming white tub itself. His eyes began to bulge from the pressure the two Drusics put on his body. His face reddened. The veins in his neck swelled.

Another figure came into the room, one Soren could sense and hear but could not see. Then he felt something cold and metal press into the back of his head, followed by the familiar sound of a shotgun charging.

"No," croaked Soren, struggling to shake his head in case his words were two weak to be heard above the booming din of the house music. "Don't."

The shotgun stayed firm.

"You know, Soren, I used to be a very trusting person."

It was Scarpia.

Soren opened his mouth to speak only to have it clamped shut by one of the Drusic's massive paws.

"The galaxy, with all its flaws, made sense to me," Scarpia continued. "People pursued what they wanted, and usually credits were a suitable substitute. Don't be fooled, Soren. Love, loyalty, belonging... not to mention a three-million-credit luxury yacht... all can be bought—and maintained—for credits."

The shotgun pressed into Soren's head didn't waver. If anything, it seemed to press down harder. As if Scarpia—if he were the one wielding it—was attempting to push it inside his skull.

"But there are men in this galaxy too principled—or too stupid, it's one in the same—to properly use credits for what they want. Zealots. Uncompromising crusaders for piety, justice, vengeance... take your pick.

"These people are dangerous, my boy. Like a rabid canix. And the only way to deal with that type is to put them down."

The shotgun was pushed even harder into Soren's scalp. He was sure the end was right now. That he was going go to die with his brains splattered all over the inside of a bathtub that probably cost more than what he earned in a month working for Nether Ops.

And he had no advocate. No backup. No way to make a case for himself or protest. And what would he be protesting? The truth? Scarpia had him—somehow—and Soren had already seen what fate was in store for 'pretenders.'

Soren squeezed his eyes shut, if only in the hopes of not having his final vision be that of his own gore splattering viciously before him.

And then the shotgun was pulled back ever-so-slightly, though the Drusics did not lessen their grip.

"You killed a man in the deserts of Ackabar, Soren. And I don't want you to feel bad about it. He was with Nether Ops. Have you ever heard of Nether Ops, Soren?"

The Drusic released its grip on Soren's jaw to let him speak.

"No," Soren gasped. Because most people had no idea Nether Ops existed. And if the galaxy knew what Nether Ops did—what it was—that wouldn't be good for Nether Ops. "I don't know... I don't know what that is, but I swear I'm not. I'm not here to do you wrong, Mister Scarpia."

"Shh, you're embarrassing yourself in front of my guards, Soren."

"Mister Scarpia, I swear it."

"Nether Ops are fanatics. Sometimes for credits— those are the easy type. Sometimes for power. Those too are easy enough because credits *are* power. Most of them are bureaucrats who fancy themselves visionary kings. But a few, Soren, a few believe that they're serving a Republic which has long abandoned its principles in pursuit of credits."

Scarpia leaned down and spoke softly in Soren's ear. "The dangerous ones. The rabid... canix. Now you come sniffing, asking if you can be one of my dogs. And all my dogs know how easily I can put them down. And now so do you.

"Let him up," Scarpia said to the Drusics.

The guards released Soren and pushed him down, causing more air to escape form his lungs and flinging his head farther into the basin of the bathtub. Slowly, Soren rose to his feet. He wrapped an arm around his ribs, which felt bruised to the point of cracking.

Scarpia smiled broadly. "We good, my boy?"

Soren looked down, his breathing ragged. "Yeah, Mister Scarpia. We're good, sir."

"Ha ha! That's more like it!" Scarpia pulled Soren in for a great bear hug, slapping his back and sending new waves of pain to Soren's ribs.

Soren wasn't sure whether to hug back or not, and the pain seemed to prevent him from doing anything beyond nursing his ribs. Neither did he speak. He felt as though he were undergoing test after test.

"You've done well, Soren," Scarpia said. "You knocked off that Nether Ops pretender on Ackabar. And you delivered Illuria *unspoiled*."

Soren looked at Scarpia, wondering how he would know that. He was sure there were no bugs installed on *Iago*. Probably something as simple as Illuria telling her matron, who told Scarpia.

The confusion on Soren's face must have been clear, for it caused another peal of laughter from Scarpia. "You're thinking right now, Soren, 'Didn't he say she was mine,' and yes I did. But if a man asks you to watch a cake for him, you sure as the nine hells down stick your finger in the frosting. And you didn't, my boy!"

Scarpia slapped Soren's arm. "You'd be dead if you had!"

The smuggler roared with a laughter that Soren imagined had to be fueled partly by the variety of drugs he'd seen circulating through the party. The laughing disappeared as abruptly as it arrived, and Scarpia was stone sober again.

"You're on the door, Soren. Your ship is being loaded with cargo for Utopion. Get that job done, and the sky is the limit."

"This is for the MCR? On Utopion?"

Scarpia rolled his eyes and the shooed away his guards. "The MCR blew its wad a few months ago with that little alliance it made with the zhee. They had the pieces set in place to make a difference—you know what happened on Kublar—and they swung for the fences and now Dark

Ops is on them so hard that there's no way they'll ever get back up. Mark my words. They're done beyond a few problem planets."

"Sir," Soren said before correcting himself, "Mister Scarpia, I told you I'm not in this for credits. I *want* the Republic reformed. I want to see it made what it once was. I thought the MCR was—"

Scarpia lowered his voice. His eyes seemed to dilate and then constrict, as if some bizarre combination of alcohol and narcotics had him constantly changing speeds. "The MCR is the smoke screen. The little red herring we use to keep the Republic busy. The man I'm working for now, *he's* the one who will remake the Republic."

There is no way Scarpia would be telling me this if he were in his right mind, Soren thought to himself. And there was no telling if he'd recall this conversation and have Soren killed as a result. Though the agent desperately wanted to know more, he had to be careful.

"I want to meet this man."

"Sky's the limit," Scarpia said with a wink. He turned and ushered Soren out of the refresher. "But for now... enjoy yourself! Find yourself a cute little Endurian who hasn't already been used and have some fun until your ship is loaded up. You'll have a hard time of finding anything like *this* on Utopion unless you're friends with a senator or delegate, ha-ha!"

Soren followed Scarpia out of the bathroom, stifling the urge to pull him inside and choke the life out of him. Men like Scarpia were monsters and the galaxy was full of them. But there would always be more monsters. The one who held Scarpia's leash... he was the one Soren needed to discover.

The dark man. It had to be him.

Soren found a lonely corner and nursed a scotch, thinking of the dark man and waiting for his cargo to load.

16

The Utopion system, home to the House of Reason, political heart of the Republic, was the model for all the star systems and countless trillions who lived within the body's borders. It was the standard by which every race and planet judged itself.

While this view was endorsed and spread by all sanctioned media outlets and popular culture influencers, anyone who had to actually experience Utopion came away with a different opinion. Especially when that opinion was informed by Out System Customs and Inspections station Zulu.

Zulu was an old star fort repurposed as a way station over a bland dwarf planet that used to be called Tombaugh but had been renamed every few years by the Senate to honor individuals, species, and even one professional sports team. As the balance of power in the House of Reason and Senate changed with each election, factions overruled the previous name in favor of their own designation. The Astronomics Committee in the House of Reason had not passed a bill in over two years due to filibusters over the last time not-Tombaugh had been renamed to, according to the tabloids, honor a senator's mistress.

The dwarf planet had come to be called Zulu across the galaxy, matching the customs station that formed a major loggerhead into the system, and no one breathed a word about changing the station's name lest a delegate or senator get a bright idea.

Soren looked out the *Iago*'s bridge to the tailpipes of a tramp freighter a hundred yards ahead of his ship. He'd been staring at the back end of that ship for hours as the inspection line moved forward ever so slowly.

"This is miserable," Heywood said.

Soren had turned him back on for company.

"It usually isn't this bad." Soren swiped through his holodisplay and dozens of lines of ships threading through linked sensor rings came up. The *Iago* was a half-dozen ships away from the front of the que.

"You should have demanded a higher rate from Scarpia," the bot said. "This is a holiday weekend and that there would be an increase in traffic into the system should have been anticipated."

"Wasn't really in a position to bargain." Soren glanced over his shoulder to the cargo bay. "Besides, all this may actually help us. Lots of ships to inspect. Lots of people wanting to attend the Unity Day Parade."

"And yet there are nine deactivated rings just sitting at the end of the chain," Heywood said. "Why doesn't Customs and Inspections have those up and operational? Did the holiday sneak up on them? It's on the calendar."

"Do you have plans?" Soren asked.

"We have a scheduled delivery time for six hours from now. I may be a lump of circuits in a chair that smells of flatulence, but I have my pride. And if we deliver on time, there should be a bonus. One large enough to buy me a new chassis. Right? Right?"

"This isn't about the money."

"You are a terrible smuggler."

The *Iago* lurched forward as the line advanced and it took another half hour before the ship finally entered the sensor rings.

Soren plugged Zelle's data core into the controls.

"Independent hauler... *Iago*? Is it?" a tired voice said through the comms. "This is C&I command. Heave to and prepare for inspection. A tax has been levied against your ship's tonnage. Pay that before the inspection begins. You have three minutes before you're denied entry and will be required to leave system or go to the back of the line."

"Affirmative, C&I," Soren said and the transmission ended.

"Pay up or sit through this all over again," Heywood said. "You are in the wrong business. The sure credits are in bureaucracy."

"All right, Heywood, time for you to earn your keep. Crack into their system when I wire over the... Oba, that is expensive. And... mark." Soren pressed his thumb against a sensor and transferred the tax along with a number of malicious lines of code.

"The firewalls have upgraded from the last time these viruses were written," Heywood observed. "It will take some time to gain access."

Soren looked up to the cockpit's ceiling. "Zelle, need you to come through for me..."

The rings around the ship spun to life and cast a pale light over the *Iago*. Heywood remained silent as he worked, only the subtle flashing of his optical sensor giving an indication that he was even still powered on. Soren drummed his fingers against his thighs as the sensors worked his ship over.

"Oh bother," Heywood said.

"What?"

"Seems one of the viruses has gone a little overboard and—"

A sensor ring stopped suddenly and the lights fluttered. Sparks shot out of a gear box and red warning lights snapped on.

"—and that. That's what's happening," Heywood concluded.

"Iago," the same tired voice returned with a sigh. *"There's been a malfunction. Obviously. Let's see... do you want to stay there until we fix it or d'you want a manual inspection?"*

Soren leaned forward and saw parts floating away from the sensor rings, then looked back at the long lines of ships waiting to go through the other painfully slow inspection.

"We are carrying—" Heywood stopped once Soren raised a finger.

"C&I, we'll go for a manual," he said. "You have an inspector on hand?"

"I'll get one assigned to you. Oba, this day will never end. Docking bay seventy-seven. Pay the additional fee before you leave the ring and slave your ship to central."

"Roger that, C&I." Soren cut the channel.

"*Another* tax?" Heywood asked. "I'm starting to see the appeal of the Mid-Core Rebellion."

Soren winced as he wired another payment over. The ship lurched out of the inspection station and made a slow turn toward the outer docking ring of Zulu station.

"Hopefully this is the last of the taxes."

"I will reiterate my earlier observation of you being a terrible smuggler," the bot said. "I assume you picked up illicit cargo from Scarpia on Asher's Star and now you're inviting C&I on board to find it. Panic would be appropriate."

"You don't know C&I like I do. What systems have the viruses managed to get into?"

"Plumbing, internal communications, duty rosters, maintenance bots—"

"Give me the active inspector duty roster," Soren said and five rows with pictures and data fields came up on his screen. "Day like this and they only have a handful on the job..." Soren touched a picture. "Him. Cut off comms from central to the other four. Do it now."

"As you like," Heywood said. "Want me to reverse the flow of every toilet and urinal on the station? That might be fun."

Soren sighed. "I have got to find a better setting for your ethics programming."

A message appeared over the profile of the inspector Soren had chosen. He touched the red box and the tasking order to inspect his ship appeared in the preview window. The agent waited as text messages snapped between the inspector and the control tower.

"He's pissed," Soren said. "Good."

"You *want* an angry inspector?" Heywood asked. "Wouldn't he take his frustrations out on poor old me? I mean the ship."

"He's about to end his shift." Soren stood up, drew his pistol and put it inside a lock box under the pilot's seat. "This is his last duty before a long holiday weekend."

"If he comes aboard with an exam glove, you'll have earned whatever happens to you next."

Soren gave a rueful smile. "Execute command code mushroom." The order shut down the bot's higher functions, leaving him able to regulate the ship's systems and unable to speak. "I honestly like you better this way."

The *Iago* rumbled as it docked with the station, guided to land by the C&I slave controls. Soren went to the bulkhead and opened the panel holding the flesh mask. He breathed deeply and pulled the polymer hood over his head and tucked it against his jaw, the bridge of his nose, and around the orbit of his eyes. The hood pinched his flesh as it tightened.

Facial recognition software was prominent throughout the galaxy, and changing just a few biometrics points on a face was enough to foil most detection systems. Naturally, Nether Ops had made a few modifications to the code to suit their needs.

Soren activated a screen inside the locker and swiped through several faces, all with percentage points in the profile. He chose one above ninety and squeezed his left earlobe. The wires in the mask pulled taunt, then closed like a vice against his skull.

Soren fell to one knee and stifled a scream as the mask reworked his features, puffing around the jowls, narrowing his nose and offsetting his left eye by the barest fraction of an inch. He huffed and pulled the gloves on, and a similar pain squeezed his fingers. He picked up a small vial from inside the locker and pressed the needle tip into the synthskin over his hands, injecting DNA markers. A quick look in the mirror and Soren saw a face many years older and very unlike his own.

"Oh, how I hate this." He looked at the voice modulator in the locker and decided against using it. He removed a hairpiece and closed the locker. The bulkhead panel it was mounted on flipped around, hidden until needed again. An identical locker filled with small bottles of alcohol and prescription drugs took its place.

Soren tightened the hairpiece against his scalp and the infiltration hood hummed against his skin. The agent ruffled his new hair and took a flask out of the cabinet. He swished alcohol around his mouth and spat onto the floor then rushed off the bridge and to a door on the side of the cargo bay. He made it to the dog, the round handle on the middle of the door, just as someone on the other side began banging against the hull.

Soren unlocked the door with a twist and pulled it open. Stale air wafted into the *Iago.*

The inspector was a rotund man with droopy jowls and a defeated look in his eyes. He patted a datapad against his thigh and frowned at Soren. A pair of C&I arms men carrying shotguns stood behind him, neither in much better shape and neither seeming any more excited than the inspector.

"By order of Republic Customs and Inspection decree number two thousand seventy-five..." the inspector began by rote.

"Yes, I consent," Soren said, cutting to the chase and sparing both a lengthy recitation of Republic law.

"Your ship will be manually searched for all contraband and duty-imposed items as outlined by Republic common law and code described in the House of Reason proclamation." The inspector took a deep breath, unwilling or unaware that he could just get on with it.

"I consent," Soren said again.

"Eighty-five of the four hundredth and... wait, did it change?" The inspector glanced at his datapad. "Ninth congress. Copies of which will be available to you before you consent to lawful search. Failure to consent will be considered reasonable grounds to obtain a warrant and then search your conveyance."

Soren nodded quickly. "I consent."

The inspector pressed his thumb on the datapad and held it up to shoulder level. "Captain gives consent as recorded by Inspector Iger, JD. Witnesses?"

"Witnessed," the first arms man said.

"Seconded," said the other.

"Where's the rest of your crew?" Iger asked.

"Just me and a mushroom bot." Soren stepped out of the way. "Lean crew means lean expenses."

Iger stepped into the ship and proffered the datapad to Soren. He put his hand on the screen until it dinged.

Soren hoped the faux bio skin he had over his hand was still valid. His Nether Ops identity should have been proof against any C&I scan, but if the traitorous elements worried he was still alive after Qadib...

"I see you're up-to-date on all your mandated union memberships and fees, Mr. Bismulla," Iger said. "Bob and Tom will check for contraband while I go through your cargo. Gentlemen?"

The inspector tucked his datapad under his arm and walked into the cargo bay.

Scarpia had indeed loaded some of the crates Soren had been tracking, along with several others that Soren neither had the time nor the inclination to work. Mainly because he felt that, at this juncture, Scarpia was capable of anything. Soren was apparently in Scarpia's good graces. He didn't want to risk leaving them. Not yet.

The inspector took a straight line for the crates of legionnaire armor, strapped down near the fore end of the bay, a refrigerated box the size of a small closet lying on its side was bolted to the aft end. The arms men took sensor wands off their belts and walked the perimeter of the cargo bay.

Soren handed a sheet of paper toward Iger.

"My manifest. Delivery for—"

"Doesn't matter." Iger brushed the paper away and went to the refrigerated box. "I need eyes on."

"Before you open it, may I suggest—"

"You open this in the next thirty seconds or I'll have your ship dismantled and handed back over to you as puzzle pieces. Not in the mood, buddy."

The inspector was proving to be a bit more thorough than Soren had anticipated, but there was still a chance he'd make it out of this.

"No problem." Soren hit three buttons on the refrigerated box and the top hatch sprang open. Fog billowed out from the seam.

Iger lifted the hatch and immediately dry heaved. A pungent odor stung Soren's nose and he didn't try to keep his composure. Inside the case were rows and rows of glistening pink fish the length of a man's forearm buried in ice.

The inspector slammed the case shut and turned away, gagging.

"Son of a bitch," Iger said. "Why didn't... oh by Oba, that cheesesteak for lunch was a mistake."

"Vikram smelt," Soren said. "A dwahser delicacy. The smelt don't have an anus so they secrete waste through their pores. The stronger the smell, the better the taste, I've heard. And a sushi restaurant in the capital is paying a premium to have these delivered at max... potency."

Iger pressed his arm to his stomach and groaned. His cheeks bulged and he vomited what Soren assumed was once a large cheesesteak. The inspector held up a middle finger.

"I was about to give you a nasal filter, but..."

"I'm not cleaning that up." Iger spat on the deck and righted himself with as much dignity as he could muster. "Give me your manifest."

He snatched the paper away from Soren and went over to the cases with the legionnaire armor.

"Costumes?" Iger asked.

Soren shrugged. "Some collector wants something for the Unity Day parade. Guy that makes these doesn't want to leave his studio on Asher's World and set up shop here. Artists."

Iger unlatched the top case then gave Soren a dirty look.

"No problem, boss," Soren said. "All the stink fish are in the reefer box."

Iger opened the case tentatively and sniffed the air. He lifted the top up and cocked his head to one side as he looked at the dark Legion armor inside.

"Looks rather functional for a costume," the inspector said. He lifted a helmet out with a grunt and tilted the face-plate toward him. Two credit chips fell out and bounced against the chest piece.

Soren looked back toward the bridge, watching the two armed men as they went inside. He kept his gaze off the inspector, but he heard a rustle as the chips went into a pocket.

"Big plans this weekend?" Soren asked Iger.

"The capital is an Oba-damned mad house." The inspector removed a stylus from the side of his datapad and began filling out a form. "House of Reason wants a parade and that's clogging up the entire capital. Tourists from all over the galaxy. Cost for everything skyrockets and customs hasn't upped my cost of living allowance in years."

"Hey, Iggy." One of the arms men stepped off the bridge. "You should see this guy's setup. Who needs one of those holo ship assists when you can just hack a bot head? And... by Oba, what the hell is that smell?"

"You done with your sweep or not?" Iger asked.

The arms man gave him a thumbs-up.

"Then I've got a shuttle to catch." Iger transmitted a form from his datapad and beamed it to Soren's. "Thank you for your voluntary cooperation as mandated by Utopion Customs and Immigration, which works to keep the system safe and crime-free."

The other arms man came out of the bridge and wafted his hand in front of his nose.

Iger smacked his lips and went to the side cargo door and hurried the two arms men out. He gave Soren a wink. "Enjoy your holiday weekend."

Soren bolted the door shut and hurried back to the bridge. He tapped in a code and brought up the station's internal comms again. Iger forwarded a complete inspection report and nothing else.

Soren sighed with relief. Lessons learned from his days as a navy logistician had paid off. C&I agents were a tight-knit group. It was a common understanding that they could have their skids greased every now and then. But if word got out that one took a little extra on the side and still caused trouble for the payee... that honest-not-so-honest inspector would have trouble from his peers.

"Heywood: Sunshine."

The agent's code word reactivated the bot.

"Oh, my olfactory sensors seem to indicate that I haven't been melted to scrap but am now back in a sushi kitchen," the bot said. "Yipee."

"We're cleared to leave." Soren acknowledged a message from the star fort and the *Iago* pulled away. "Set course for our spaceport in the capital and act like nothing's wrong."

"Is something wrong?" the bot asked.

"Plenty. If that inspector tells his buddy at Inclusive that I'm an easy mark, we're in trouble. Almost out of cash. You said your olfactory sensors were online?"

"Most unfortunately, sir. What is that? If I had tear ducts, they'd be in a crisis right now."

"Run the air scrubbers on max, I have to go clean up a mess."

"If I had arms and legs, I'd do that for you." Heywood wobbled from side to side. "Just a suggestion."

It was the first time that Soren thought getting the bot put back together might not be such a bad idea after all.

17

It seemed that the deeper Soren went into the Utopion system, the easier it became to move past Customs and Inspection. As though each succeeding ring of security was relying on the ring before it to catch any problems. By the time *Iago* was given a berth in a docking tower, security had gotten so lax that the bay inspector failed to even show up.

"We are three hundred stories up," Heywood observed. "One wonders how you are to deliver your cargo without a crew or a ship small enough to navigate Utopion's air lanes."

"All that's covered by Scarpia," Soren replied.

"That is most fortunate. I do not believe you would make your necessary delivery windows if left to your own devices."

"He's thorough. Frighteningly so."

The comm beeped and a text message notified them of the arrival of an outfit designated Morwen & Sons Freight Haulers.

"That's part one," Soren said, acknowledging the message and giving access to the sealed docking bay doors.

Soon a mixed crew of alien laborers and bots were off-loading pallets and crates, removing shipping labels and applying new ones. Updating manifests and cross-loading into a steady stream of repulsor trucks floating outside the exterior docking doors, waiting to take the contraband and all else to its final destination.

Soren watched intently. So far, the only crate he had a tracker on that was taken was the black armor. He made a mental note to follow its location once he finished his own tasks.

When the cross-docking had finished, Soren went to the cockpit to cycle the ship down.

"I take it you are now going to deliver the final shipment? Nothing like cutting it close."

"Yeah," Soren mumbled. He punched in the delivery address. "Find me a truck or van that can get me here."

"How much capacity is required?"

"Supposed to deliver by hand whatever the haulers left behind. Which amounts to one crate."

It was the weapons crate he and Zelle had been tracking since their time on Strach IV.

"I see several available repulsor vehicles that are authorized for air lane travel—"

"Great. Pick one."

"You interrupted me. Authorized for air lane travel that you can no longer afford due to your very un-smuggler-like propensity to willingly pay taxes. You will have to take street-level transport. Which is notoriously slow on Utopion according to my research."

Soren pinched the bridge of his nose. "Fine."

"You also cannot afford an inside pickup. You will have to use the repulsor jack to take the freight down the cargo speedlift to street level and onload yourself."

"Okay," Soren said. "Any other bad news you want to give me?"

"The fish smell has not left, though you likely have grown accustomed to it. It will require a full detailing. Which you likewise cannot afford."

"See you around, Heywood."

"Enjoy your delivery, sir!"

The alien quarter of the capital was a mishmash of architecture and species from across the galaxy. Simple and modern human buildings clashed with the twisting tiers of alien high-rises and the nest-like structures favored by species such as the Kaline. The streets were no different, with a dozen different species mingling together, colorful signs of Kimbrin dry goods stands at odds with the subdued tones of a dwahser fortune-teller next door.

The truck Soren rode in braked hard as a pair of zhee stopped in the middle of a narrow street and decided to have a conversation right in front of his bumper.

Soren looked at the woman driving.

"We have to wait?" he asked.

"You honk at zhee and they'll break your headlights. You payin' for that?"

Soren sunk deeper into his seat while the driver gripped her steering wheel tighter.

"These guys," she said, gesturing where she couldn't be seen through the windshield. "Can't sue them since the House of Reason ruled that them acting like damn savages is a-okay if it's in keeping with their culture. It's not just them, though. You have to honk at Hool to get them to move."

It was a mistake to take a street-level repulsor. Soren should have found a way to pay for something capable of traveling the air lanes. Maybe see if Zelle still had that bank-hacking program…

"Alien quarter's a pain in the ass," she said. "Always has been, always will be. I drive this because the insurance premiums are too high for the big companies to send robot drivers. Bot screws up and it's on the company. Anything goes wrong with me and it's my fault."

"And I thought hauling sushi was rough." Soren looked at a street sign and balked at the eighteen different languages bolted to the pole.

"This is you." She turned down a narrow alley and stopped next to an unmarked door. "And you want some free advice, don't stop and talk to nobody 'til your freight is delivered."

The truck was parked so close to a wall that Soren could barely open the door enough to get out. The city air was musty, faintly smelling of a variety of waste generated by various humanoids. He walked sideways to the back of the truck. The back door rolled up; the refrigerated case containing the weapons was the only thing inside. He lowered the truck's liftgate and pulled the repulsor jack to the receiving door as the truck left him to find his own way back to the docking bay.

Soren pressed a call button outside the door. "Delivery."

The unmarked door slammed open and a tall human male wearing a stained, sleeveless shirt and dirty apron came out. He was well muscled and had a faded unit crest tattooed on one shoulder. Former military. Soren could tell just by looking, even without the tattoo.

"Fish doesn't get delivered until the morning," the man said. "You think it'll stay fresh overnight?"

"Special delivery." Soren jerked a thumb at the case. "Vikram smelt, not-so-fresh from Asher's Star."

Recognition passed over the big man's face.

"'Bout damn time." He looked over his shoulder. "Curly! Donovan! Get out here."

Soren stepped away from the truck as a pair of lean young men in cook's garb came out the door. They activated the repulsors built into the case and unloaded it quickly.

"Right, so I'll be on my—" Soren stopped as the big man put a hand on the back of his neck.

"Got to do an inventory count before you go," he said.

Soren swallowed hard, acting nervous more for the sake of the bruiser than out of any real sense of danger. Scarpia didn't seem like the type to have his errand boys killed, not when he had ample opportunity before the mission. But... one never knew.

"Interesting accent you have," Soren said to the bruiser. "You from Pardith? I once dated a girl from there."

"Big planet. You think I'd know her?"

The bruiser guided him into a restaurant kitchen. The cooks all stopped their work as the case was set down next to a walk-in refrigerator. Soren did a quick once-over of the staff; all were young, fit human men. They looked at the case with eager eyes. The agent was sure they weren't hungry for the fish he'd just delivered along with the rifles.

"This it?" asked a well-built man in a button shirt and pressed slacks as he came in from the front.

"He says so." The bruiser banged a fist against the case.

"Close out the tickets we've got open and kill the stoves," the leader said. "We're closing early."

Soren recognized another Pardith accent. This was consistent with the MCR. Pardith was one of the more vocal critics of the House of Reason, and many of their young men joined the Kimbrin and other mid-core species in starting the Mid-Core Rebellion.

The cooks mumbled and went back to work, glancing at the case whenever they got the chance. The leader walked up to Soren, his eyes focused on the goods. He sniffed twice.

Soren produced a small jar and wiped clear jelly around his nostrils. He passed it to the leader.

"You came prepared," the man said as he dabbed at his nose. "You got a name?"

"Soren. Guess you're Lausa?"

"You guess right." Lausa tossed the pot to the bruiser and opened the case. He wrinkled his nose. "Thought the smell would be worse, even with the salve."

"I overcharged the cooling coils. Smelt's probably got freezer burn now, but I didn't think you were going to put it on the menu."

"Another good guess." Lausa thrust his hands into the ice and dragged out a rifle case. He knocked ice away and opened it up. Someone in the back whistled as he lifted an N-4 assault rifle out, pulled the charge slide back, and inspected the inner workings with practiced ease.

Lausa stuck a pinky into the charge pack well and removed it with a smidge of grease on the tip of his finger.

Lausa handed the weapon to the bruiser. "Fresh off the factory floor. Never been fired."

"Yet," the bruiser said, his mouth a big grin as he sighted the weapon against an empty wall.

"Packs?" Lausa asked Soren.

"In there too." The agent motioned to the ice.

"Sergeant Etta, get these weapons accounted for, cleaned, and stored," Lausa said. "We're done being cooks."

"Yes, sir." The bruiser opened the walk-in refrigerator. Inside were plastic bins full of frozen poultry, noodles, and vegetables. Toward the back were more military crates ringed with ice.

The rest of the staff left their work stations and walked toward the fridge. They all carried themselves like fighters. Even one of the prep cooks held his knife like he was about to get into a life-or-death fight with a frenzied alien, not that he'd just finished chopping up peppers.

Soren had a small pistol strapped to his ankle. He was sure he might get off at least one shot before these men killed him with ease. They had to be from an elite Rep Army unit... or even legionnaires.

"So, that's it for me, right?" Soren asked.

"Get off-world," Lausa said. "Be out-system by noon tomorrow and forget you were ever here." He pressed a pair of credit chips into Soren's hand. One was for a few thousand, his expected fee. The other was cipher-locked.

"I sold the place this morning," Lausa said. "All we earned goes back to the MCR. Scarpia's got your drop point and he'll have a bounty hunter on your ass long before you could ever crack that cipher if you think the money's worth the risk."

"It's not about the money," Soren said. "Death to the Republic."

Lausa smiled and slapped the agent hard on the shoulder.

"Now you're talkin'."

18

"Heywood," Soren said into his comm as he traversed the streets of Utopion. "I need you to trace those shipping containers and tell me where they all are."

"Did someone steal your cargo? I doubt Mister Scarpia will appreciate that."

"I know where that one is. Check the others."

"Checking now, sir."

Soren halted at a light, surrounded by a bustling gaggle of humanoids from seemingly every planet in the galaxy. He watched as a repulsor bus zoomed past, barely making the light before it changed. Repulsor transportation would be a faster way to get around Utopion, but the agent needed time to think.

What was that group of men, clearly military and open about their involvement with the MCR, going to do with the stolen N-4 rifles? It had to be something on Utopion, but Soren couldn't imagine an MCR cell large enough to cause any real threat to the government. Terrorism was the likely answer, and the Unity Day Parade was as obvious a target as any.

But security should be airtight, even accounting for the otherwise lazy standards on-planet. The Parade galleries would be stocked with House of Reason delegates and planetary senators. Their protection wouldn't be presumed accomplished by local security, personal guards, and potentially even Nether Ops attachments if the politician in question had the right connections.

"The crate containing the weapons remains at the delivery address."

"I said I knew that, Heywood. What about the others?"

"The crate containing the armor is no longer on Utopion."

"What?" Soren shook his head and stepped out onto the street together with the surging crowd of pedestrians. "That doesn't make any sense."

"It appears to have been loaded onto a waiting hauler that was scheduled for takeoff almost the moment the goods arrived, by my calculations. It seems Mister Scarpia uses layer upon layer to keep his contraband undetected. With the exception of the cargo you delivered. That seemed straightforward enough."

"All right. Thanks for looking."

"Your tone seems to indicate that you believe me to have had some choice in the matter, sir."

"I'll check in if I need anything else." Soren killed the transmission.

To this point, Soren had assumed that the weapons and the armor were a package deal. That perhaps the non-standard black and red, together with the mysterious allusions to 'Goth Sullus', were part of an MCR splinter cell. With Sullus being the code name of a commander or other high-ranking leader on the inside. Only a cursory search through a database of all military branches hadn't revealed anything relating to the name.

And now that armor was going elsewhere while the rifles seemed ready for immediate use from the way those make-believe cooks were acting. Scarpia had said that the MCR was a diversion. A nonfactor. Could it be that the rifles were a throwaway? Just some dead end on Utopion while everything else went off-world to parts unknown?

But then... those men in the restaurant. They didn't look like patsies. They looked like they had the knowledge and intent to use the weapons.

Soren stopped in front of a row of taxis waiting for passengers outside of a mega hotel. He was at the end of himself and at the end of what he could do on his own. He pulled out the credit chit he'd been paid for his delivery and transferred its balance into his datapad, then waved down a cab fitted for air lane travel.

"Where to?" the driver asked as Soren slid into the back seat.

"University of Utopion. Capital Campus."

The auditorium let out, and a thin man, dark-skinned and wearing tweed, nodded as he exited alongside an obese woman with thick black glasses and a stripe shaved down the middle of her hair to show herself as a non-human ally.

"Of course a five percent reparation fee against humans is justified," the woman said to her companion. "The damage alien worlds suffered put them far behind on their economic development."

"As a student and professor of history," the man said, "human worlds suffered the brunt of the Savage marines' attack and it was human legionnaires who finally won the war."

"Your facts aren't important." The woman—clearly another faculty member—nearly quivered with rage. "You've failed to internalize your inherent responsibility due to being human. Did we *not* just finish two hours of training on this subject?"

"I recorded eighty-five factual inaccuracies during the presentation," the professor said, a look of weariness on his face.

A man wearing a tweed jacket worked his way against the flood of faculty and brushed his hand past the professors, passing a small piece of plastic into his palm as he walked by.

"That half of the non-human Republic worlds live in poverty is well known," the fat woman said. "And it's humanity's fault they live like that."

"Perhaps. But the poverty rate was closer to eighty percent before the Savage Wars." The professor seemed almost reluctant to have spoken the words.

"I can't believe you're spouting this nonsense!" the woman squeaked. She fumbled with a jar of pills and popped two into her mouth, chewing loudly. "I need a personal day on top of this extended weekend, and it's due to your aggressions! I'll see that it comes out of your pay— humans are responsible for non-human suffering. It's immoral to do anything *but* pay the reparations."

"Doctor," the professor said, his voice remarkably even, "we already pay a mandatory five percent in galactic reparations before accounts are even credited. I wonder if you intend to pay the optional ten percent, or make do with just the mandated tax?"

"Triggered!" she pushed her way through the crowd, face red and breathing heavily.

The professor ran the tip of his thumb over the bit of plastic and read the message left for him in small dots. He tossed the note into a nearby garbage can and went into a stairwell. Three flights above him, he saw a shadow pull back and out of sight.

"Hello?" the professor asked as he made his way up the stairs, unbuttoning his jacket as he went. The stranger began to climb down, meeting him on a landing between floors.

The professor paused and squinted, looking the stranger in his eyes. "Soren?"

Soren nodded. "Nix."

He removed the infiltration hood with a slurp of synthskin as it let go of his face. The release seemed to give way to a massive migraine that beat through his head as Soren massaged his temples before rolling up the hood up and stuffing it into his jacket.

"Soren, that's..." Nix folded his hands over his waist, holding his briefcase in front of his thighs. "This is... this is not how you're supposed to reestablish contact after you've gone Onyx condition. My cover in the university is a bit of a pain but Nether Ops went to great lengths to set it up."

"There's more at stake here than your alias and back-stop," Soren said. He took out a datapad and pointed to a beacon on a map screen. "There is an armed team of insurgents on Utopion. They're loyal to the MCR. Senator Dryden from Pardith is involved somehow. I'm certain he's connected to a cell of traitors in the Legion and the military that tried to kill me on Rintaka."

"Son," Nix shook his head. "Son, you've gone too far. There isn't some grand conspiracy at work here. The MCR is on the run."

"I delivered N-4 assault rifles to men of military age—possibly former legionnaires—in a restaurant in the alien quarter. I'm positive they're planning an attack tomorrow."

"How's that?" Nix asked. "They're just going to walk up to the parade carrying N-4 rifles? Won't get very far."

Soren paused to consider how much more sense this all would have made had he delivered the black armor as well. But he hadn't. "Sir. I can only assume they acquired assets such as armor or uniforms to allow them to blend in prior to my making the weapons delivery."

"You need to listen to yourself," Nix said, putting a gentle hand on Soren's shoulder. "I know something about what you're going through. The loss of a partner can have a certain psychological effect on anyone. You've come in from the cold. Now let's get you back into Nether Ops for a proper debriefing."

"No, sir, you're not listening to me." Soren shook his datapad slightly. "I had trackers on the arms shipments from Strach. I infiltrated the smuggling network and was instructed to deliver them here. Same weapons, sir."

He fished legionnaire ID chips from his pocket. "Look at this. These belong the men who ambushed me on Rintaka. They were working for the station chief and they were all appointed by Senator Dryden. And the men I delivered to all had Pardith accents as well. That planet has been friendly to the MCR—that's a fact. I think Senator Dryden is working with the MCR from inside Utopion and I think the culmination of that work is happening soon."

Nix hissed and slumped his shoulders, examining the floor for a moment before bringing his gaze back upon Soren. "How many rifles could you have transported in your ship, son? And they're on a planet with billions of citizens. This is not a crisis, Soren."

"The man I delivered them to told me to be off-world by noon tomorrow. He sold off everything he and his team had. They're not looking to make a life here. They either have an escape planned, or they're on a suicide mission."

"And you think they're Legion? The Legion isn't known for suicide missions on Utopion, the capital of the Republic." Nix's voice rose slightly as he pulled his emotions back. "Just because they have the weapons and a military bearing doesn't make them Legion."

"But they could pass for Legion," Soren said. "Or marines, or anyone else who looks like they should be carrying a blaster rifle. And tomorrow at noon is the Unity parade on Capital Boulevard. Big fish like Delegate Karr will be there. So will the Senate. The entire House of Reason."

Nix was silent for a moment. "The MCR just tried to obliterate the House by ramming it with a ship full of explosives. Something like this feels like a step down for them."

"Orbital security is as high as I've ever seen it," Soren said. "At least at the point of entry. All the focus is on the skies and not on what's under our noses. The MCR's trying to infiltrate their own kill team to the parade. We need to inform the appropriate security detail. A senator we can trust. Someone."

"Not Nether Ops?" Nix asked.

Soren shook his head. "Sir, the agency is compromised. They sent a kill team after me on Qadib. Why? Because I was getting too close to whatever they have planned for tomorrow."

"If it was a Dark Ops team, you wouldn't be talking to me," Nix said with a slight shake of his head. "You'd be dead."

"There were plenty of people killed. The team screwed up and kicked a hornet's nest full of zhee. I got away in the chaos." Soren put the identification tags back in his pocket. "But I think it was a ghost team based on information my H3 bot provided."

"That was you on Qadib?" Nix stroked his chin.

"You heard about that?"

"Every department in Nether Ops heard about that disaster. Word gets around and fingers start getting pointed." Nix shook his head at the thought. "Let's say you're right. Maybe there is a conspiracy deep within Nether Ops—"

"We can root it out later." Soren pointed down the stairs. "We have to stop whatever they're planning for tomorrow first. Who do you trust? Someone in Rep-Int?"

Nix shook his head. "I wouldn't trust anyone in the intelligence community. And certainly no one in the Carnivale."

"How about a senator? Maybe Verdier. He's the one that sent more agents to outlaw space. He represents my home world, Oliphant, in the Senate. Our world is loyal, no love for the MCR. We can trust Verdier."

"Verdier... yes, let's take it to him." Nix unclasped his hands and waved Soren ahead of him. "Who else have you told about this?"

"No one."

"Not even your bot?"

"I destroyed my assigned unit's core and replaced it with something off the shelf. It doesn't have enough of the details to know anything more than he works for a smuggler." Soren started down the stairs and Nix followed.

"Good."

Nix snapped an arm around Soren's neck and pulled the agent backward. There was a click of a blade popping out of the sheath hidden beneath Nix's forearm and the senior agent stabbed Soren in the back.

The blade ripped through Soren's jacket, but turned aside when it struck the armored weave hidden beneath his clothes. The blade and Nix's arm shot past Soren's body. Soren grunted in pain from the force of the blow and clutched Nix's arm, struggling to free his airway. He twisted his hips to pull Nix off-balance and slammed him into the stairwell wall, still holding tightly to the older man's arm.

Nix chopped Soren's neck with his free hand, causing the younger agent to release him. He followed with a violent shove that sent Soren forward, stumbling down the stairs until he halted his progress by crashing flat onto the stairwell floor.

Soren had only moments to roll to one side as Nix jumped down the remaining steps to pounce upon him. The senior agent missed a plunging stab, sending sparks flying against the floor where Soren had been a second before.

Back on his feet, Soren lurched forward as Nix swiped at him with the knife, deflecting the attack with his armored triceps. As Nix rebalanced for another lunge, Soren leapt and slid down the next flight of stairs, fumbling for the blaster strapped to his ankle. His slide turned into a roll just as he got the weapon free.

The stop on the next floor was ugly, leaving Soren dizzy and battered. Still, he brought his pistol up and fired. The small charge blaster bolt smacked into the briefcase Nix clutched against his body as a sort of shield to accompany his knife attack. The professor threw the briefcase at Soren, knocking the blaster off target as Soren fired a second time, sending the bolt up the stairwell wide of its target.

The older Nether Ops agent kept up his assault, showing a speed uncommon for a man of his age. He followed up his briefcase toss by closing the gap between the men and kicking Soren in the wrist. The blaster went flying away, clattering down more stairs.

Soren gripped his wrist as he involuntarily reeled up on his knees from the force of the blow. The young agent stood up and pressed his back to the wall as Nix slashed at his exposed neck. He'd evidently wised up to the under-armor's presence and was seeking to land a surer strike. The Carnivale agent had no malice in his eyes, no emotion to his face, as he tried to murder his protégé.

As the plunging attack came down, Soren got an arm up in defense. The blade cut across his forearm, slashing through the tweed jacket but still unable to pierce the body armor beneath. Though his flesh wasn't sliced, the blow still sent pain up Soren's arm. He snaked a quick punch against Nix's solar plexus and earned a grunt from the older man.

Both men were sweating and panting from the effort.

Nix brought the blade back around in a reverse swing only to have it countered as Soren jammed his elbow against Nix's upper arm, killing the blow's momentum. Soren brought his fist over Nix's shoulder and punched him just in front of his ear.

The ferocity of the blow caused Nix to falter and for a moment Soren thought he'd knocked the man out. But Nix turned the stumble into a twist and stabbed Soren in the gut.

Again the decision to purchase armor back on Qadib saved his life. The vicious attack felt like a blaster bolt hit him, but the knife tip didn't punch through. Nix put his strength into his knife arm and rammed it home even harder.

Now the tip pierced the armor's synthweave. Now there was blood.

Soren snapped his head back and smashed his forehead against Nix's nose.

Nix gagged from the rushing onset of blood—a broken nose—and pulled back.

Knowing that above all else he needed to remove Nix's weapon from the equation, Soren kicked the man's shoulder, causing it to buckle with a wet pop. The older man gasped and collapsed against the guardrail, the knife falling over the edge.

Soren grabbed him by the neck and rammed his head against the railing, splitting Nix open and sending more blood streaming down his face. The older agent went down in a heap.

Breathing heavily, Soren touched his shirt and looked at the bloody fingers that came away. "What is this? I'm... I'm doing this for the... Republic."

Nix looked up at him from beneath a crimson mask.

"So am I." Nix pulled another knife free from the housing beneath his forearm and lunged at Soren's exposed throat. But he was too weak. Too slow. Soren parried the strike to one side and delivered an elbow to Nix's jaw that sent him to one side.

Nix bent forward at the waist as he impacted the railing. His momentum carried him forward and over the top. Nix let out a pitiful cry as gravity took over and he fell.

Soren grasped at his mentor's ankle but found nothing but air, and was left to watch Nix careen off a lower handrail and bounce against the stairwell side until he crashed to the bottom with a sickening crunch.

Watching Nix's twisted body from above, Soren's face contorted with pain as the blows he took made themselves known. The blood on his shirt was spreading.

"Oba's tears!" He beat a fist against the railing. "Oba, why is this happening?"

He hurried down the stairs, recovering his pistol and then coming upon Nix's knife on another step. He picked it up, seeing his own blood still on the tip.

Shrugging off his slashed tweed jacket, he tossed it onto the landing two floors down below the auditorium. Campus security would work their way up from the bottom and check that floor first when they found the jacket.

Soren shouldered his way through a door and found himself in a cafeteria. Banners with slogans for Unity Day hung along the walls. Most of the students had their eyes glued to their datapads.

He pressed a thumb against the side of his ear to activate the comm receiver.

"Heywood. Sunshine."

"Oh, hello, sir. I seem to be trapped in the same recurring nightmare. How are you?"

"I need a fire alarm in tower four of Utopion University. Now."

"As you like."

Soren thought he heard the bot humming a few seconds before the klaxons went off and overhead sprinklers sprayed fire retardant foam across the mess hall.

Soren scooped up the foam and wiped it against the bloody spot on his shirt and over his face.

"Acceptable?" Heywood asked.

"Zelle would be proud." Soren joined a throng of panicky students as they made for the exits.

"Imagine how proud I would be if I had any notion of who that person was."

19

The skin knitter hurt like the proverbial son of a bitch as Soren mended the knife wound to his abdomen. Nix had gone for the artery, which would have led to unconsciousness and a quick death within minutes if severed.

Soren was lucky to be alive, though he didn't feel like it at the moment. Skinpacks would be much less painful, but not as quick. And time didn't seem a commodity Soren was stocked with.

He ran his bloody fingers under the tap of the fleabag hotel he'd rented in the capital's red-light district. The hotel didn't have a staff, just pay-as-you-go cash kiosks and a strict no video policy. A janitor bot locked in the corner would spruce up the room after every customer. By the smell of the place, the bots were in need of an overhaul, and Soren wondered if the machines did any good at all given the general uncleanliness of the room. Any investigator that came looking for a trace of him here would be utterly confounded. A DNA sweep would pick up an uncomfortable number of individuals.

"Not bad, Doctor Voss," Soren said to himself as he checked his handiwork in the mirror.

Nix left a good scar and several bruises across Soren's body. The surviving agent set the knitter on the sink and scrubbed his face with a towel. The hotel room was tiny, with a bed much too large for it, pamphlets for all manner of in-room services, and a holoscreen that was entirely pay-per-view. A single window looked out toward the building across the street. But behind that were the skyscrapers and green vibrancy of One Voice Park in the distance.

The place where, tomorrow, everything Soren feared would become a reality.

Early dawn worked over the horizon, the sunlight mingled with the nighttime lights of the city, that ambiguous stretch between night and day.

The Unity Day parade would begin in a few hours.

He activated his comm.

"Heywood. Sunshine."

"Another day. Another disappointment. What do *you have against me being online?"*

"You can be detected while you're online."

"I'm more likely to be detected when you have me hacking systems."

"That's different. I can make sure you don't get into trouble."

Soren sat on the foot of his bed and looked out the window. A bowl of cold shaved beef and rice sat on the nightstand, barely touched.

"And who, pray tell, is doing that for you?"

Soren ignored the comment. Still staring out the window. "My parents brought me here as a kid."

"This is why you contacted me, sir? I could download a full suite of human psychiatric programs if you'd let me go online."

"We went to the Museum of the Republic. Saw the Founding Documents behind all those stasis fields and thick glass. I remember being on my father's shoulders for hours as we watched the Unity Day parade. This was back when it was more about the military than celebrating... well, anything but the military. My father would've complained nonstop about what it's become now."

"The parade or the Republic?"

"Both. More about the Republic. Oliphant was a neutral world until the Savage Wars. Not part of any of the old confederacies or alliances. The planet saw the threat coming and pledged their forces for the fight, even if it meant joining the Republic in the process. Oliphant coming into the fold during that time was... something special. My family fought in the wars."

"Not uncommon."

"I know I lost two great-uncles and a distant cousin to the Battle of Sylvan Beach. I grew up in love with the Republic."

"Your current business model of smuggling and illicit arms deals seems at odds with that sentiment."

"I keep forgetting which Heywood I'm talking to."

"I'm the one that deserves a shiny new chassis. Just because I'm the same model doesn't mean his failings are mine. Do your human religious beliefs in original sin somehow apply to me?"

Soren picked up a datapad and began tapping.

"Our situation has more to do with faith than anything else. I... had faith in the Republic. I, mean, I still do." Soren toyed with his datapad and then let it hang beside his leg.

"You don't sound convinced."

"You grow up with an ideal," Soren said as he began tapping the datapad again. "You have this picture in the mind of what the Republic is. What your family fought and died for. Then you join the navy and see the fraud, waste, and abuse rampant through the fleet. So you volunteer for something exciting that exists to protect the Republic during a time of crisis and... you see things aren't that different. In fact, they're much worse."

"Do you believe things were markedly better during the Savage Wars?"

"Planets in flames. Billions dead. Whole thing was a nightmare until the Legion got everything under control. Seems as soon as the war was over, society and the Republic just dissolved into squabbling groups of special interests. No one cared about the whole anymore. But there are those who still believe. Heywood, I need to see Senator Verdier."

Soren tapped a photo of the senator from his home planet and sent it over the encrypted link he had with the *Iago*.

"The senator's office is closed for the holiday. There is a waiting list for office visits."

"This isn't a social call. I want you to access the Senate's personnel records and show me everyone that's on Verdier's payroll." Soren pulled up a map of the city near where the senator kept his office and began tabbing through restaurant listings.

"*So I am being allowed back online. Excellent.*"

"Only so far as accessing what I told you to."

"*As you like. Am I looking for anything in particular?*"

"Just send me what you find." Soren highlighted two locations and picked up his small pistol from the nightstand. He had enough in the charge pack for nine almost pitifully small blasts. Or maybe one surefire, armor-punching killer. If he could get close enough.

The rest of his armaments included Nix's knife and his armor weave drying on a hanger. He picked up the knife and studied it in the light. A biocomposite of layered bone cells. Strong as steel and sharp as a razor, but engineered to evade Republic scanners.

"*Sent,*" the bot said.

Soren set the knife down and picked up his datapad and scrolled through profiles, stopping to read closer on a few then nodded when he found an awkward photo of a young man. Barely out of college. Prominent family name from the senator's planet. Listed as 'Assistant Administrative Specialist to the Assistant Secretary of Office Affairs.'

"*Have you found something?*" Heywood asked.

"The kaff kid. Send me his entire file."

20

Brent McCarty checked his holowatch and glanced at the knot of baristas behind the counter. They knew who he was. They knew who the order was for. And yet they still took their sweet time preparing the three fat-free-deffe-vmint-sprinkled- kaff whippers.

Honestly.

Sure, there was a line of tourists almost out the door waiting to pay premium prices for scalded kaff, but the baristas *knew* who he was. Bad enough he had to even stand in line.

"Brenny!" a girl in an apron called out and pushed his order across the counter in a paper carrier. She'd forgotten the fourth cup of dye-free sweetener packets and napkins. Again.

But there was no longer any time to wait.

Brent took the drinks away and stuffed a handful of neutrino additives into his pocket as he squeezed past waiting patrons. "Excuse me."

He brushed through the door and looked at his watch. Senator Verdier expected his drink in precisely fourteen minutes and this holiday was throwing everyone's schedule out of whack.

Brent hurried down the sidewalk, maneuvering around tourists taking selfies of the House of Reason dome in the background. Why people insisted on the real thing was a mystery to him. There were more than enough apps out there to make it look like you'd gone most anywhere in the galaxy for a snap.

A dwahser ahead of him ambled to the right. Brent went left and was almost hit by a delivery drone. He ducked back to the right to get around the elephantine alien, who bumped him off-balance and into an open door. Some unseen bystander grabbed him by the back of the collar and steadied him.

The saving motion caused Brent to jostle his tray of drinks, spilling some through its lid. "Careful, I've got *beverages* here."

The open door Brent detoured into was to a beauty salon. One that was empty for the day's festivities.

"Thanks," Brent said, looking the man up and down. He was well dressed with bruises and marks on his face, like he'd been in a fight the night before. Brent ran his hand over his perfectly coifed hair. He was always looking for the next hot stylist on Utopion, but this one seemed dangerous. "So... you own this place?"

"Ben McCarty?" Soren asked.

"*Brent* McCarty." The aide hesitated. Had he been in this salon before? He looked at his watch then at the lanyard around Soren's neck—he worked in the Senate building. Brent reached for his own ID tags stuffed into a coat pocket. "Do I know you? Aren't you from Dryden's office?"

"Nothing personal." Soren shoved a bottle under Brent's nose and spritzed him.

Brent's eyes rolled into the back of his head and he collapsed. Soren deftly caught the drinks before they could spill, then dragged the unconscious man to one of salon seats and lifted him into it. He pulled off Brent's coat and enerchained the man's wrists to the seat.

Soren pressed a palm against Brent's. Pain radiated through Soren's fingers as the infiltration sleeves he wore re-formed his biometric markers to match the staffer's.

Soren took a couple deep breaths then ran a scanner over Brent's face. Soren's face pinched and stretched, feeling like thousands of needles were knitting his skin and muscles. He gasped as the procedure ended.

"Test, test," Soren said, his voice re-modulating to match the staffer's. "Brent McCarty. There we go."

Finally, he pulled a sensor wand from the side of a datapad and ran it over Brent's well-coiffed hair. Soren's hood changed to match. Thankfully the two men had the same hair color and so there wasn't need for a wig.

He looked in a salon mirror and worked his jaw from back and forth, feeling the painful pinch against his entire face. Glancing down at the unconscious aide, he said, "If it's any consolation, you look so good it hurts."

Soren grabbed the drinks and left the salon as Brent McCarty, Senator Verdier's aide.

Offices in the Senate Chamber made up the outer rings surrounding the great auditorium where business was conducted. The more prominent the senator, the closer their office was to the inner chamber. And with each member planet of the Republic sending two senators to Utopion, those finding themselves with offices at the edges of the massive building were literally miles away from the inner elites.

Soren hurried by a knot of well-dressed men and women along with a bevy of other humanoids wearing their customary finest clothing. He walked along a hall whose one wall was an uninterrupted window overlooking the Senate floor. The gallery pointed at seats and tried to remember which belonged to which planet and representative.

Political junkies, Soren thought. *Ought to find a better hobby.*

Most of the foot traffic in the hallways was already flowing toward the exits to view the parade. Those this deep in the capital likely had assigned seats to watch the festivities, meaning they didn't need to leave early to find a place. That they were already moving told Soren he didn't have much time left.

He lifted his tray of kaff up to eye level as he sidestepped around a woman digging through her purse at the security station leading to Senate offices. A tired-looking guard took Soren's handprint and waved him over a red glass line in the floor. Scanners swept over Soren as he crossed the line and the same guard kept waving.

Soren got a step past him when he heard it.

"Hey, Brent," the guard snapped.

Soren turned around and traced the guard's eyes to the kaff cups.

"Sorry. Been one of those days." Soren held the tray up to the guard and he took a drink out.

"Looks like you had one of those nights, too," the guard said, a wolfish grin on his face. "Your eyes are bloodshot as all hell."

Soren winked. "Unity Day mixer went late."

The guard took a sip of his kaff and Soren smiled at him. "Tell me her name later."

Soren turned left, saw the directory with Verdier's office number and turned around.

"Went *real* late," he said as he hurried off in the proper direction.

The path to the senator's office was less crowded, but hardly empty. Soren did his best to appear a man on a mission, intent on delivering his drinks on time at all costs. He nodded at the smiling faces that all knew "Brent" by name until finally he reached Verdier's office and stepped inside.

Verdier's office had extravagant oil paintings depicting Oliphant from orbit, moving holo-images of the Finch Waterfall on the planet's main continent, and bowls full of little red candy balls that Soren knew tasted of cherries, strawberries, and rambutan. The candy was a local delicacy so expensive that Soren's parents only ever bought it during the holidays.

Past the lavish reception area was a cubicle farm with a wide pathway leading to the senator's door, a grand affair made of rich mahogany. Soren moved to the immense door, approaching a frumpy woman with horn-rimmed glasses who glared at him.

"You are almost late," she hissed.

"Sorry." Soren pulled out a kaff. She snagged it from him as he walked past her.

Pushing the heavy door open, he found Senator Verdier at the back of the room, looking through a slightly tilted glass window wall at the Senate chamber below. Verdier looked older than he seemed in the information holos, campaign bursts, and other social media blips Soren was subjected to as a citizen of Oliphant. In those images, he seemed barely in his fifties. In reality he appeared an older man with white temples and dark hair streaked through with gray.

"Thank you, Brent." The senator motioned Soren toward his desk without removing his gaze from the chambers below. The agent put the last kaff down on the desk and saw that Verdier was watching his reflection in the glass wall.

The senator turned, his posture now tense. "Brent, how is it you're three inches taller?"

Soren gently slid the kaff tray to the center of the desk and showed the senator his palms.

"I'm not Brent, sir," he said, seeking to keep his voice as calm and soothing as possible. Offering no hint of malice.

"Then my eyes don't deceive me. Who are you?"

"My name is Soren Voss. I'm a Nether Ops field agent. Number 99-337." He switched off the voice modulator on his neck and deactivated in infiltration hood, causing a painful ripple to surge across his face. "You and the Republic are in great danger."

The senator frowned. "That seems to be Nether Ops tech on your face, all right. But where is Brent? What did you do to him?"

Soren followed the senator's eyes as they glanced from Soren to his desk. He likely had a weapon there.

"Your aide is fine," Soren said, again holding out his palms to show he meant no harm. "I needed a discrete way into your office, which I think you'll understand once I explain the situation to you."

The senator's hands balled into fists and he looked ready to make a run for the door.

There was a creak behind Soren.

"Brent," the secretary hissed. "Why are you still in there? The senator has a—you're not Brent..."

"It's all right, Bertha," Verdier said. "We're just having a chat."

"... of course, Senator." The door creaked again, then clicked shut.

"I'll need to hear the compelling and *short* version now." Verdier walked to his desk, moving closer to where he kept his weapon. He sat down in his chair. "Why would a Nether Ops agent need to sneak in here to see me?"

Soren began to peel up the infiltration hood, pausing to say, "Senator, if you don't mind?"

Verdier nodded.

Soren peeled the hood off the rest of the way and rubbed his bare scalp. He rolled up the thin synthskin and tucked it inside his jacket.

"Thank you, Senator. Damn thing hurts and it only has a few minutes of power left. To the point, the short version: I have uncovered evidence that the MCR is planning a terrorist attack of some sort at the Unity Day Parade. I have further evidence that they are being helped by members inside the government and Nether Ops itself. Hence the need for secrecy in coming to you."

Verdier arched and eyebrow. "Perhaps I'd better have the long version, Mister Voss."

Soren recounted his operation from his initial assignment on Strach and got to the legionnaire ambush on Rintaka when the senator held up a hand.

"Stop, Mr. Voss." He shook his head. "Let me stop you right there. You expect me to believe that legionnaires—the Republic's elite defenders—are somehow involved in this?"

"Sir, not legionnaires per se. These were all appointed officers working as a collective cell. I can provide proof." Soren reached into a pocket and placed his hand on the desk, leaving four ID chits on the carved mahogany. "These weren't just four random rogues, sir. They—"

"Senator?" Bertha said from the door. "He's here."

"Show him in." Verdier swept his hand across the desk.

Soren quickly pocketed the ID chits.

A man with an unbuttoned jacket entered the room. His gait and the way he scanned the room, focusing on

Soren first, screamed 'bodyguard.' A thick vine of scar tissue crept out of his hairline and touched his right eye: a prosthetic that glinted in the light. Soren saw the handle of a pistol inside his coat. His trim physique was padded with flex-armor.

"That's enough, Pattar," called a voice from outside.

A man gave the bodyguard a pat on the shoulder and walked past him inside. He was elderly, only a few wisps of hair white left, liver spots prominent on his hands and temples, but he walked like a younger man. He bore a senator's pin on his lapel, but even without that, Soren recognized him instantly.

"Senator Dryden," Verdier said as he stood, arms wide and welcoming. "You know your man Pattar frightens my office ladies."

"Let them cluck." Dryden smiled and gave Soren a quick glance before sitting across from Verdier. "Besides, Pattar's a gentle soul. Isn't that right?"

"*He's* new." Pattar clasped his hands over his waist and stared at Soren. He inhaled slowly into a snort, like a dog taking in the scent of a stranger.

"Yes, a new hire from Oliphant." Verdier passed Soren a datapad and waved a hand toward a couch against a wall. "Looks to be very promising. He was just finishing up a report for me and I'd like for him to stay a bit if that's agreeable?"

Dryden shrugged. "It's your office."

Soren ducked his head slightly as any office drone might have and hurried over to the couch. He began tapping out further details of his journey to Verdier's office while he eavesdropped on the two senators' conversation.

"Is Delegate Karr going to do it today?" Verdier asked Dryden.

"During the parade," the older man said with a sniff. "His office lined up the usual media talking heads to broadcast the message just as some Army unit marches past. One thing I've always admired about Orrin is that he's always had a good sense of timing: announcing an entirely new corps of legionnaires and two new fleets fresh from Tarrago to deal with the MCR menace."

"Legion Commander Keller has been asking for a new corps for some time," Verdier observed.

Dryden rolled his eyes. "Well, the new corps is required to have an officer corps consisting of sixty percent appointees. Minimum. So Keller's joy at getting this new toy has been somewhat tempered."

Verdier nodded. "I am still uncertain as to the extent of this MCR 'menace' as you say, Senator Dryden. Outside of a handful of concentrated operations, they seem more focused on picking at isolated systems and performing terrorist operations on worlds already sympathetic to them."

"The loss of a destroyer is not something to simply shrug off."

"I know," Verdier said. "It's only that the MCR is a symptom of a larger problem. And it's my belief that spending Oba knows how much on new ships and legionnaires to fight the MCR will only make the problem worse. If the House of Reason tells the Republic we're arming for war, the MCR will get even more desperate."

"Let them," Dryden said. "The more terrorist acts they commit, the easier it will be to justify our response. Downplaying the exact nature and how close their attack was against the House of Reason was a mistake."

Verdier looked down. "We both know that had more to do with who they'd partnered with than anything else."

"The zhee could have been left out of it and the point would still stand." Dryden clapped his hands together. "It's not like the Legion needs convincing to kill someone first. But we need the taxpayers to take on a bit more of the burden that comes with sending those boys to do the job. And patriotism will always help sugarcoat that bitter pill."

"Karr can announce what he likes," Verdier said. "Taxes are already at an all-time high and it's not like he can snap his finger and create legionnaires or ships."

Dryden smiled. "Orrin wouldn't make an announcement if he didn't already have the necessary support in the House of Reason or Senate."

Verdier smiled. "True enough. Which leads me to wonder why you are even telling me this?"

"Because you're on record as something of a pacifist." Dryden gave a wry smile. "And... something of a tightwad when it comes to spending. No offense."

"I take that as a compliment."

"The media will go straight to you after the announcement and Karr wants you on his side for this."

"Karr *doesn't* have the votes to get the funding through the Senate," Verdier said. "That's why you stopped by my office."

"What would it take to get you on board to safeguard the Republic?"

"Save your spin for the networks," Verdier said, his face flushing with checked anger. "A spending bill like that won't solve anything. It will only serve to make matters much, much worse. If we simply put time and effort into fixing the rot in our institutions, the MCR won't have any reason to fight."

"They're mid-core barbarians." Dryden waved a hand in the air. "Barely better than the monsters we fought in the Savage Wars."

"The MCR are Republic citizens who are engaged in open rebellion. That is not the same as the Savage Wars. At all."

Dryden smiled slowly. "Well. I'm disappointed, naturally. But at least we have Unity Day to show our support for the Republic. Differences withstanding."

Verdier glanced at Soren and rapped his fingertips on his desktop.

"I'll do this much, Dryden," he said to the old senator. "Karr can count on me to only speak about this problem in his office. I'll keep my disagreement out of the headlines... for now."

"That can and will be arranged." Dryden got up slowly. "A media cycle of rah-rah-Legion, a little boost to defense sector stocks on speculation. Can't ask for more from a Unity Day, can we?"

Verdier glanced at the chrono on his wall. "See you in the box?"

Dryden shuffled toward the door. "Yes, yes. Delegate Karr's office will be in touch. Come, Pattar."

Dryden's bodyguard gave Soren a sidelong glance as he followed the senator out of the office.

Soren stood up. "The legionnaires I mentioned—they were all appointed by Senator Dryden."

Verdier stayed quiet for a moment, then said, "I have a hard time believing *he's* involved in this plot you've uncovered. He wants a *stronger* military. Wants the MCR crushed. Why work both sides of the conflict?"

"The evidence may be circumstantial," Soren patted the pocket with the legionnaires' identity chips, "but it is there."

Soren paused. Remembering the black and red armor that left the planet. "Senator, does the name or phrase 'Goth Sullus' mean anything to you?"

Verdier shook his head slowly. "Nothing."

Soren bit his lip and then handed Verdier the datapad where he'd brought up weapons schematics for the cargo he'd delivered. "Whatever connection Dryden had to those legionnaires on Rintaka, the reasoning can wait. What I know for sure, beyond any shadow of a doubt, is that there is a threat right now. Military grade N-4 rifles the conspirators wanted were delivered to this city."

"Weapons you delivered," Verdier mumbled, taking up the datapad. "Which is typical Nether Ops, in my experience. Make a larger mess and then cry for action and more funding. Mister Voss, the capital city has a billion people in it when the House and Senate *aren't* in session. Many more beyond that on a day like today. But you maintain that a case of blaster rifles comprises an existential threat?"

Soren frowned. This was essentially the argument Nix had made. Before he'd made the attempt to kill Soren.

"Senator, these weapons went to men with training. I'd bet my salary they were once Legion and are seeking to do as much damage as possible with them. I'm Nether Ops, sir. We believe a dagger in the dark is worth more than a thousand swords at dawn."

Verdier dropped the slate on his desk and rested his forearms on either side.

"It is hard to believe any of this," the senator said, "but I pushed the Security Council to seek appropriation for additional agents to investigate the MCR. My understanding was that while Dark Ops was on top of it, Nether Ops pushed back. Hard. Now you show up with evidence that there are corrupt elements in that institution…" Verdier shook his head. "It's good you brought this to me. No one else would have believed you."

"Then you need to—"

"This is where the weapons are right now?" He tapped the datapad.

"That's where the cases with the trackers are. If the rifles are still in there is speculation. I would suspect not."

"I have a contact in the Capital District PD. I'll send these coordinates as an anonymous source. If it's as you say, they'll at least find some evidence of what you're talking about. This planet is a gun-free zone. Even weapons cases are enough to arrest anyone on hand."

The senator stood up and put on his coat.

"If this contact of yours is reliable and to be trusted," Soren said, standing by Verdier's side, "then I agree. But I admit I've had some... trust issues lately."

"He's Oliphant born and bred, same as us. A family friend." Verdier made for the door and motioned for Soren to follow. "You're coming to the parade with me. I'll take you to Karr's office myself once this is all over with."

Soren followed, acutely aware of how unarmed he was.

"Senator, if anyone in Nether Ops sees me..."

"Aren't you dead?" the senator asked as they passed a very confused looking Bertha on their way out the door.

"Far as they know."

"Then appreciate that they aren't looking for you. If anyone pushes the panic button around you, it proves they're in on the conspiracy. Isn't that how this spy thing works?"

Soren smiled and shook his head. "Senator, I believe you may have missed your true calling."

"Sometimes I wonder. Now let me send a message to Brent so he doesn't panic when he recovers from... whatever you did."

21

Soren kept a step behind Verdier as they made their way through a narrow tunnel lit by glow pods in wrought iron frames.

"They don't mention this part of the capital in school, do they?" the senator asked.

"I took a tour once when I was a kid," Soren said, trying to make sense of the labyrinth all around him. "This wasn't a part of it."

Verdier smiled. "These tunnels run under the entirety of the capital compound and then some. Sometimes we want to be seen mingling with constituents. Sometimes we're late to a committee hearing and don't want attention along the way."

"And maybe sometime you'll have to escape..."

"Yes, that too."

Soren stepped over a puddle and hurried through an intersection. "Why is it that Senator Dryden has a security escort and you don't?"

"Fear is a state of mind," Senator Verdier said. "The more security you have, the less you're open to what's around you. If I have a former legionnaire glaring at everyone that comes near me, what good am I? I'm a representative of the people. The people need to be able to speak to me."

"If I could get through the House's security, so could someone else."

"Perhaps, but you had to disarm yourself to make it this far, remember?"

The senator turned down a hallway. Overhead, the pounding of feet echoed through the walls.

"But suppose you entered my office impersonating Brent and I had a bruiser like Pattar by my side? You'd be in a holding cell right now. Consider what refraining from a personal guard brought me."

The senator turned and gave Soren a warm smile. Something more than a politician's practiced face. Something genuine.

"Proof of rot at the very heart of Nether Ops. Perhaps the Senate itself."

"I'm grateful to have you as a senator rather than Dryden," Soren said, checking behind to be sure they weren't being followed.

Verdier laughed. "Pattar would've crushed your skull for laughs. Assuming Dryden's other guards didn't nab you first."

The senator stopped at an armored door and held a wrist up to a sensor. A light traveled around a bracelet and the door slid open with a pop. They stepped into a small alcove behind a semi-transparent holo-wall, fronds of a small tree on the other side. The sounds of cheers and beating drums were much louder now, echoing down the hallway beyond the faux wall.

"Everyone loves a parade." Verdier smoothed out his suit and adjusted his hair before stepping through the holo-wall.

Sunlight shone through domed archways at the top of a flight of stairs running along a hallway that curved in the distance. House of Reason and Senate staffers stood in little knots, vaping and checking their datapads, oblivious to the celebration happening just beyond the archways.

Security guards waved the senator up the stairs and didn't give Soren a second look.

The stairs let out to a raised platform wreathed with flowers. Senators and House delegates stood against the railing, waving at the parade marching past just a few yards below. A cheering throng could be felt as much as heard, as aliens and humans from throughout the galaxy mixed and added their diverse voices to the celebration. Music and a scripted account of the parade blared from floating bots mounted with amplifiers. A wide boulevard ringed the entire capital. The inner lanes were fenced off and manned by capital police, forming a thin line between the crowds watching the parade and those marching.

Soren's instincts went into overdrive as he searched for any threats. Following Verdier to the railing with his true face exposed made him feel as though he had a giant target on his back. He looked down just as a mob of college students carrying poorly written signs littered with spelling and grammatical errors walked past the review stand. Soren wasn't sure what they wanted, but they made up for the ambiguity with volume and vulgar slogans.

Small media drones crisscrossed back and forth along the stand, stopping to zoom in on the Republic's senior politicians as they waved and clapped.

The undisciplined mass of students paused to orchestrate an underwhelming shout of grief, where they stood in front of a gallery of House of Reason delegates, threw back their heads, and screamed in mourning for whatever was troubling them this semester. After a respectful period of observance, capital police wielding unpowered shock batons prodded them until they moved on.

Next came several ranks of horses ridden by men and women wrapped in bright-colored sashes and carrying flags with embroidered sigils.

"Should have put the cavalry in front of the protesters," Verdier said, leaning over so Soren could hear him. "Let them deal with some actual horseshit."

"They'd have thrown it at you, Senator."

Soren looked up and down the review stand, still scanning for anyone with a weapon. An N-4 wasn't easy to conceal, but neither was it impossible. But he saw nothing. And the skies were clear but for hovering capital police air sleds. Just how many snipers had a bead on his position was anyone's guess.

Verdier reached into the flower box stocked with fragrant, yellow-petaled annuals and flicked a pebble out. The pebble's progress halted with the hiss and snap of a force field.

"We're fine here," the senator said. "The appropriations committee lets a lot of pork slip through, but none of my fellows complain about spending taxpayer dollars on our protection. Isn't this grand, Soren? Relax your vigil and enjoy yourself. This is a once-in-a-lifetime view for you, I'd imagine."

Verdier waved to a lovely young woman on a horse as she ambled passed. She tossed a flower with brilliant silver petals at him that fell short of the force field.

"My father brought me to a Unity Day parade when I was a child," Soren said. "And we certainly didn't have seats this good."

"*This* is the Republic." Verdier said with a swelling of pride. He set his hands on the railing as a formation of dwahser followed the horses. The elephantine aliens had drums slung in front of them and beat out a marching pace with a stick grasped in their trunks.

"There's ugliness in it," the senator continued, "but if you look hard at anything, you'll find something not to like. The Republic can be glorious, just as unified as it was in the final decades of the Savage Wars, but it takes those of us that believe in what we *could* be to have that vision, that drive to lead people to a better future that remembers what made us so great in the past."

"I believe you, Senator." Soren glanced around to be sure Verdier wasn't just opining for a camera drone, but the drones were focused on a tight group of dignitaries a dozen yards away.

Boos went up from the crowd as the dwahsers went by.

Elderly men and women in old Republic Army uniforms came next. The front rank carried a sign proclaiming them as the Savage Wars Veterans Association. These were the last of a generation, many relying on cybernetics to even be present.

The boos intensified as the veterans continued passed the review stand. Somewhere from the crowd, a unit of water was hurled at the old soldiers, nearly missing a spry little man wearing sergeant stripes.

"There's always a couple bad apples." Verdier tried to signal to a capital police officer on the street below to point out the individual who threw the objects, but the officer either couldn't see the senator or was ignoring him completely.

Soren looked down the gallery at the politicians, sick of the scene unfolding below him and wondering how they might respond to it. The knot of representatives broke up and Soren saw Delegate Karr and Senator Dryden standing together, smiling for a camera bot. Soren kept up on galactic politics as part of his Nether Ops duties—spies had to understand who they gathered information and acted for—and knew that the two men were long-standing icons in the House of Reason and Senate respectively. Each was quite capable of bending the body's will to their own.

A bot zipping from spot to spot around them had no media markings. Soren suspected it belonged to one of the senators and they'd cherry-pick the best photos for release later.

"Senator Verdier!" someone called from behind them.

Soren braced himself as Brent McCarty, Verdier's aide, made his way through the crowd. He wore a coat two sizes too big and his face was flush from running.

"Senator!"

Verdier spun around and grabbed Brent by the arms and spoke to the staffer in hushed tones.

Brent looked over at Soren, his eyes widening in recognition. He continued listening, his eyes growing wider still and giving way to a sneer before the aide nodded quickly.

The senator gave the young man a pat on the arm and went back to watching the parade.

Brent, the top of his lip quivering, stood beside Soren. "I want my coat back, dick."

Soren shrugged. "Sorry not sorry."

"You know you could have—"

"No."

"Seriously, you had my attention and—"

"Don't make me regret letting you live."

Brent's mouth opened and closed a few times, then he opted for silence.

The boos from the crowd grew louder and lustier. Verdier clapped harder as if seeking to counter them. The sound of marching feet, hundreds strong and in perfect time with each other, carried over the jeers. Soren stepped closer to the senator and looked over his shoulder.

A Republic army company made their way down the boulevard. The men in the ranks looked tired and some were pushing the upper limits of the army's weight standards. The first ranks went past the reviewing stand and Soren looked hard at the rifles they carried. Mock-ups and not a single N-4. Solid hunks of plastic meant to look like the real thing. The uniform patches on their shoulders were for the logistics command, not a line combat unit.

"Couldn't they have found some poor bloody infantry for this?" Verdier shook his head. "Unity Day parade and the joint chiefs send... what would you call them, Soren?"

"Rep Army would call them REMFs," the agent said. "Read Echelon Mother..."

A glint of silver through the back ranks caught his eye. He leaned forward slightly to get a better look.

The boos died away to near silence as the next element of the parade passed by.

Two rows of a dozen total legionnaires in gleaming silver armor followed the Rep Army soldiers. The legionnaires stomped the heels of their sabbatons against the road, each footfall promising violence and fury.

Soren didn't doubt that the crowd hated what the Legion represented as much as the army. But the Legion commanded a certain respect. Perhaps even a certain fear. As though, in response to the boos, they just may decide to take target practice on those delivering them.

They all carried N-4s. Real N-4s with charge packs loaded. Fraggers hung from their belts and a legionnaire on either end of the front row had an aero-precision missile launcher strapped to his back.

"Oh no." Soren looked back to the exits and saw Senator Dryden leaving Delegate Karr. A few others went with the senator.

Verdier clapped, his face beaming with pride as the legionnaires marched closer. The bot floated slowly from Karr toward the Oliphant senator.

Soren grabbed Verdier by the elbow. "You need to leave. Now."

Verdier pulled away and shook his head. "Don't be ridiculous."

"Senator, they're carrying the rifles I delivered," Soren said, pointing at the men in the new gleaming "shinies" now standard in the Legion. "Those aren't legionnaires. *This* is how they managed to bring them in. I'm telling you, we need to leave right—"

A legionnaire called out, "Detachment... halt!"

The crowd mumbled with confusion.

Another group of student activists behind the legionnaires slowed, causing an accordion affect that made its way down the rest of the parade.

The legionnaires with the rocket launchers slipped them off their backs. A capital police officer timidly approached the legionnaire leading the element. He opened his mouth to speak and promptly received a backhand that knocked him to the ground.

The crowd gasped at once.

Verdier took a step forward at the surprising spectacle.

"Senator!" Soren grabbed Verdier's shoulder to pull him back, but McCarty wrapped his arms around the agent's waist, wrenching him away.

"Leave... him... alone!" the aide managed to huff out as he dragged Soren a few steps away from the railing.

"The Mid-Core Rebellion will not be extinguished!" shouted the legionnaires, the amplifiers in their helmets turned to maximum output.

Soren sent an elbow in Brent's temple and shoved the stunned man away. He leaped toward the senator as a legionnaire fired a rocket at the review stand.

Soren tackled the senator and covered him with his body as an explosion burst against the force field. The blast immediately caused the shields to fail and collapsed part of the review stand, spraying members of the House of Reason with shrapnel and hunks of concrete.

It felt as if knives raked across Soren's back as pulverized permacrete dust washed over him and the senator in a cloud of a gray dust. He coughed and pulled Verdier to his feet. The older man's face was covered in gray soot and his eyes were wide with shock, but he appeared otherwise unharmed.

Screams from the wounded and panic from the crowd washed through the haze.

"No," the senator managed, "not the Legion too."

"That's not the Legion." Soren grabbed Verdier by the wrist as a second rocket screamed through the air over their heads and smashed into the outer wall of the House of Reason itself. The marble façade cracked and crumbled, burying a senator and her aides before they could escape back into the building.

The hum of powered batons from capital police sounded from the street as they swarmed to face the false legionnaires. They were answered by quick bursts from N-4 assault rifles.

22

"Still want to stay?" Soren pointed to a partially blocked opening back into the House.

Verdier broke into a run. "Where's Brent?"

"Doesn't matter!"

Soren looked up as the unmarked bot from earlier trailed Verdier. He picked up a hunk of masonry and hurled it at the drone. The throw clipped the machine and sent it spinning away.

Verdier struggled over the broken marble as more shots from the legionnaires' rifles broke through the din of terrified people. Utopion police were woefully unprepared for something like this, never imagining that they would need blasters in a blaster-free zone. It would be precious minutes until the tactical unit—or better still, the Legion garrison—could respond to the threat.

Soren grabbed the senator by the belt and manhandled him through the gap. They had nearly outrun the firing angles afforded to the attackers down on the street when a legionnaire opened fire.

Pain blossomed in Soren's left calf and he rolled down the other side of the rubble, hitting every sharp angle on the way.

There was a smoking blaster hole in his pants and his lower leg throbbed with agony, but the armor weave had stopped the round from tearing through his flesh.

Senator Verdier sat in the middle of the hallway, bewildered. Staffers ran around in a panic. Capital security ran around seemingly at random.

Soren got up and limped to the senator and hauled him up. "Passageway."

He prodded Verdier toward the holographic wall. The senator vanished on the other side of it and Soren heard a sudden girlish shriek. He rushed inside and found McCarty cowering against the armored door leading to the underground passageways.

"Senator?" the aide asked. "I-I came here to get the door for you." He gave the control panel a quick pat.

A rifle fired from somewhere in the hallway and Soren put himself between the senator and the holo-wall. Armed personal security arrived with blaster pistols and joined the firefight as red-hot blaster bolts sizzled by the opening. A round bounced into the polished floor and then whacked into the alcove.

Brent yelped and shrank into a ball.

"Door!" Soren twisted the senator to unlock their escape route.

Verdier held up his bracelet and the mote of light ran around it, but the door didn't open. "What?"

He tapped it against the sensor again. "They... they've got the capital on lockdown. Wait, there's an override code..."

Verdier slid a panel aside and stared at a keypad.

More gunfire streaked through the holo-wall. Soren saw a legionnaire move through the holographic opening, firing all the way. He twisted to one side, arm hanging loose, then jerked as more bolts from the private security hit home.

"I don't," Verdier put his hands on his hips, "I don't remember my damn code."

An N-4 opened up just feet from the doorway, close to the wall that ran flush with the recessed security panel. Soren slid Nix's knife out from his belt and raised his arms to his head. A legionnaire backpedaled right in front of him, engaged in a firefight with more security.

Soren slammed his arms onto the legionnaire's shoulders and stabbed the knife into the synthprene around the man's throat. The blade slipped into the seam, but stopped when it bit into the chest armor with just barely the point through.

Soren used the shock of his sudden attack to wrench the legionnaire off-balance and into the alcove wall. The legionnaire's gleaming helmet took the brunt of the blow and cracked from the force. Still, the man was able to jab an elbow into Soren's chest that knocked the breath out of him.

The agent slapped his palm against the butt of the knife and rammed it up into the legionnaire's throat. There was a wet gargle and the legionnaire shoved Soren into the other side of the alcove, pawing at the knife in his throat as blood poured from the wound in gouts. He tried to lift his rifle but instead dropped it to the ground. He sank against the wall, chest heaving, then went still as his head lolled to one side.

Soren snatched up the N-4 and checked the charge counter on the buttstock. Mostly full. He pulled charge packs off the dead man's webbing and looked at the senator and the aide. Both stared at him slack-jawed.

"The door!" Soren shouted as he removed three fraggers from the legionnaire. He pulled the knife free with a wet slurp.

"Your wife's birthday backwards!" Brent said and Verdier snapped his fingers.

"Watch out! Watch out!" came from the hallway.

Soren turned to look only to have a blast wave smack him off his feet. More rifles opened fire, all directed at the private security and bodyguards that the MCR must have hit with a fragmentation grenade.

Verdier leaned against the armored door, his eyes unfocused. The control box had six of eight numbers in it.

"Thirty-seven!" Brent squeaked.

Soren finished the code and Brent pushed his way through the door as it opened before the agent could get the senator through. Soren hit a button to shut the door and looked for anything in the dark and damp tunnel to bar it.

"This can't be," Verdier said. He was bleeding from his arm now and seemed disoriented. "Why? Why are they doing this?"

"Worry about how we get you out of here." Soren flipped the grip on Nix's knife and stabbed it into the seam of the door's frame. He beat the pommel with the rifle's buttstock.

"There's a series of panic rooms nearby." Brent pointed a shaky finger down the tunnel.

"No." Soren whacked the knife again and wedged its blade deeper into the door. "That's the first place they'll go. And if they could get in this deep, they'll have a plan to get inside even those rooms. We need to get into the city, disappear into the crowd while Cap cops or the Legion get this under control."

"There's a shuttle pad on the roof," Verdier said, breathing hard. "The local police should be on their way here in force."

"Want to trust just anyone we see?" Soren grimaced and touched his back, feeling where shrapnel had torn through the jacket. He brushed past a rip in the flex weave and his hand came away with blood on it.

"Clearly the Caps are on our side," Brent said. "They're sworn to protect the senator and—"

The armored door groaned against its gears. Soren grabbed the senator by the back of his neck and pushed him down the tunnel.

Brent paused. "Wait, that could be the police and—"

A sudden explosion from the other side of the door sent showers of dusty debris and fragmentation as the MCR on the other side blew off a corner, exposing a shaft of light from the other side. It was followed by a volley of blaster bolts that burned into the tunnel walls.

Soren heard the aide scream and scurry after Soren and Verdier.

The sound of blows pounding against the door dogged them as they ran down the tunnel. Prepared as they were, it didn't seem the MCR were carrying cutting torches.

Soren felt the slow build of pain from his injuries as adrenaline wore off. They came to a narrow staircase. Soren pushed the Verdier up a few steps and then took cover against the wall, rifle up and covering the way they came. The stairs ended at another armored door.

"Where's this one go?" the agent asked.

"The west atrium, I think," the senator said, shaking his head. He looked pale.

"There's a speedlift to the roof close by," Brent added.

Soren glanced at him and gave him a dirty look.

The aide gave an apologetic smile and ducked his head. "Yeah, those are probably disabled because of the shooting."

"This atrium leads outside?" Soren asked.

Down the tunnel, the doorway they'd fled from exploded and Soren could hear shrapnel blasting the surrounding passageway. The MCR had been able to rig enough of a charge to get through all the way. He leaned out and saw a billowing cloud of smoke.

Soren leveled his N-4 and fired blindly into the smoke, only to be rewarded by a voice-modulated yelp of pain. That was good, it meant the Legion had cut off the MCR's stolen comm system and the men were relying on external speakers. Hopefully a Legion quick reaction force would be on hand soon to put this insurgency down for good.

A burst of blaster fire answered Soren and tore away at the brick edge of his cover.

"Get out!" Soren called as he pulled a fragger from his pocket. He quickly inspected it: a thermobaric. A grenade like that in this enclosed space would fry the flesh and crush the organs of anyone not in decent legionnaire armor—which meant everyone in this tunnel would die from its use.

Soren cursed and pulled out another one, a normal fragmentation grenade. He pulled the pin and looked back at the stairwell to check on the senator and his aide. The door was open and they were gone. Soren reached around to toss the grenade but a blaster bolt clipped his hand just as the explosive went flying.

Soren stifled a scream and practically flew up the staircase, seeking to gain distance on the grenade. He leaped out the doorway just as the fragger's dual blasts went off. The narrow confines funneled the blast back up the stairs causing a loose brick to hit Soren in the ear where he lay.

"Ah," Soren moaned through gritted teeth. He hurt all over, but the primary pain receptors were ringing from his head and hand. He looked down at his left hand where he'd taken the blaster bolt. The meat below his pinky was a ragged mess and bleeding with the skin above it blistering. Still, he was thankful it hadn't hit the rifle; he held the weapon as he got up to his knees.

"Soren!" Senator Verdier called to him from behind a large, blown glass vase.

The atrium had spindly trees with gentle branches arching down throughout the room. Sunlight beamed in through wide windows that ended at waist-height on the far wall. Soren made out a wide parking lot full of sleds jammed together as too many tried to flee for the exits at the same time. The sound of muffled blaster fire beat through the air, albeit much less frequently than it had before. Attrition had taken a toll on the MCR terrorists.

"The speedlift." Brent hustled over and tapped the call button repeatedly.

Soren got to his feet and shook his bleeding hand out. Blood speckled his pants and the floor. He looked back. The atrium ended in a double staircase leading down from either side of the landing.

The sound of shuffling feet and sobs came from below the stairs.

"The roof," Soren said as he tried to close his bleeding hand.

"But that's twelve floors up," whined Brent.

"Lifts won't work," Soren said as he leaned against a pot almost as tall as he was and pressed his body weight against his forearm, trying to stem the bleeding while he fumbled with his belt buckle to make a tourniquet.

A ding sounded from speedlift's control panel.

"Don't worry about it." Brent pointed to the counter over the lift's door, a smile on his face.

There was another ding and the lift opened.

Brent's smile vanished as he came face-to-face with three of the marauding MCR legionnaires.

They shot him in the chest before he could say a word in protest. The aide fell back on his hands, blood and smoke pouring from his mouth. A legionnaire stepped out and kicked him in the face, sending the aide flat.

Soren ducked low against the vase and tried to get his left hand to grip the front of his rifle. Three fingers moved, but they were weak.

"There you are," announced a legionnaire through his helmet as he looked at Verdier.

Soren recognized the voice as Lausa's from the restaurant.

Lausa pointed at the senator and another MCR insurgent stepped out and grabbed him by the coat.

"Do him here?" the man asked Lausa.

"Tunnels," the cell leader replied. "Need to make it look like he was running. A coward."

"I—" The senator squirmed like a child being dragged away by an angry parent. "I will not stand for this," he said loudly while roughly carried along.

Soren set his rifle to full auto.

Lausa's head snapped toward the noise.

Verdier's voice was defiant. "Not standing for this in three, two… one!"

The senator kicked his legs out and fell, pulling the legionnaire off-balance.

Soren came around the vase and opened fire. The rifle bucked wildly as he charged, spraying the legionnaires and sending rounds sizzling over the senator. The man holding the senator took two rounds to the chest and crumpled.

A bolt caught Lausa in the helmet and he spun around and pitched forward.

The N-4 went quiet, its charge pack empty as the third legionnaire ducked back into the elevator. Soren gripped the rifle by the barrel and swung it like a club as he rounded the elevator doors. The legionnaire inside blocked the strike and with his own weapon, but the blow caught him off-balance and knocked his N-4 out of his hands.

The agent rammed his shoulder into the legionnaire's chest and pinned him against the elevator wall. Soren got a good look at the man's armored fist just before it hooked into his mouth and sent him backpedaling. A copper tang flooded Soren's mouth as he bounced off the wall and fell just as the legionnaire followed up with a thrust of his combat knife.

The attack was high—aimed for the space Soren's head and neck had just occupied—and the blade buried itself up to the hilt in the metal wall as Soren reached for the still loaded weapon the legionnaire had dropped. He grabbed the rifle and swung it up just as the imposter legionnaire pulled his blade free and plunged down onto Soren before the agent could get the weapon on target.

The legionnaire's forearm hit the rifle, stopping the blade tip inches from Soren's face.

Soren could see himself in the reflection of the legionnaire's shiny helmet as he tried to push the rifle up like a barbell and put space between the knife and himself, but the legionnaire was far too strong.

"Going to kill you fast," the traitor said. "Kill the old man slow!"

There was a crack and the back of the legionnaire's helmet exploded, spraying the elevator with hunks of cheap armor and bloody matter. The legionnaire collapsed onto Soren and the knife fell out of nerveless fingers.

In the atrium, Senator Verdier held an N-4 and stared down at the smoking barrel. He tossed the weapon aside as though he'd just realized he was holding a snake. Soren pushed the legionnaire off of him and the body flopped in the doorway, blocking the door from closing.

Soren spat out a wad of blood and grabbed his foe's rifle, thinking it held a full charge.

"Behind you!" he shouted at the senator.

Verdier spun around and fixed his eyes on Brent lying in a puddle of blood. "He's still breathing!"

The senator went to his aide.

But Soren was speaking of Lausa, who had made it to his hands and knees, blood dripping from a crack in the front of his helmet. Soren aimed and shot the man in the chest, finding the weapon to be set on full auto. The weak, reflective armor buckled and the legionnaire collapsed. The N-4 dry fired and Soren's vision swam as he fumbled with a fresh charge pack from his pocket. He used one hand to push the button to eject the spent pack, and struggled to pull it free when it got stuck.

Verdier grabbed Brent by the shoulders and tried to drag him back to the open elevator. The aide sighed a meager moan and one hand rose and fell against the ground. Verdier waddled back, pulling Brent into the speedlift.

Soren leaned over the aide and heard irregular wheezing coming from burnt and blistered holes in the man's chest. He was deathly pale and his eyes were lost, staring into infinity. The young man had minutes to live if even that.

Soren put one hand on a blaster wound and did what little he could to stem the bleeding. He squinted, in a daze as his raw and pulpy finger blended in with the gore in Brent's chest cavity. The agent looked back for the senator and saw him hurrying across the atrium for the rifle he'd tossed away earlier.

Soren opened his mouth to protest. A sharp pain from a broken jaw stopped him from vocalizing anything more than a groan.

Verdier picked up the rifle then froze. He let go with one hand, surreptitiously holding back the other palm for Soren to see, as if to keep him away. The senator gently set the rifle back on the ground and raised his hands.

"Senator Dryden," Verdier said, a lump catching in his throat. "Why does Mr. Pattar have a gun pointed at me?"

Soren got the cue instantly. Two men. Only Pattar was armed. He hastily activated his datapad's recording suite, smearing the screen with blood.

"All this confusion," Dryden called out.

Soren realized Pattar and Dryden had to be at least a dozen yards away. Not an easy shot in his current condition. He fumbled with the magazine but it slipped out of his bloodstained hands and bounced off the dead legionnaire.

"My aide has been shot and needs help." Verdier pointed back to the speedlift.

"We'll get to him in a minute," Dryden said. "Can't have any witnesses that might complicate the narrative."

Verdier dropped his hands to his sides.

"Dryden... we've been in the Senate together for years. Why are you doing this? Do you know how many innocent people have—"

"This Republic is not what you want it to be," Dryden said flatly. "Never was and never will be. Men like you need to be out of the way so it can be rebuilt as strong as it once was during the Savage Wars."

Verdier looked around at the destruction. "Does all of this give an impression of strength? Dryden, you've always been a hawk. And now what are you telling me? That you helped orchestrate this attack with the MCR?"

"The MCR desired an opportunity to save face. I desired an opportunity to wake this sleeping galaxy from its malaise and finally put forward a military capable of countering all threats. Tell me, Senator Verdier, do you know how many *actual* full combat fleets are at our disposal?"

Verdier tilted his head. "I don't... you did all this— you committed treason—just to ramp up the war with the rebels?"

"They must be crushed! Every enemy of the Republic should be trod under foot. Only when the galaxy sees how close we stand to the brink, how weak we've let ourselves become, can we remake the Republic how it ought to be. This isn't personal."

Soren slid the charge pack into his rifle and got to his feet as fast as his could. He slipped in Brent's blood and almost dropped the rifle.

"Don't do this." Verdier sounded on the edge of panic. "Who else is behind all this?"

A blaster shot echoed through the atrium and the bolt burned a hole out of Verdier's back. He rocked on his feet and twisted toward the elevator. Soren could only watch as another shot rang out and tore through the senator. Verdier fell to both knees, looked Soren in the eyes, and tried to speak. He pitched forward, dead.

Stunned, Soren felt the rifle slip through his bloody fingers to the ground with a clatter.

"Finish off the aide and make sure the remaining assassins are dead," Dryden's voice carried through the atrium. "No witnesses."

Soren reached into his jacket and pulled out the thermobaric grenade with the thought of pulling the pin and rushing Dryden and his bodyguard. Even if Pattar cut him down, he'd take them both with him.

He looked at Verdier, a man who truly believed in the Republic and was cut down for it.

Die here... or fight on and make a difference.

Soren pulled the infiltration hood out of his jacket and stuck it over Brent's head. He squeezed the loose earlobe and it tightened against the dead man's skin.

"I'll make it worth it." Soren stuck the barrel of his rifle around the door and emptied the charge pack with wild shots toward Pattar and a single aimed shot at a nearby window, partly shattering it. He tossed the empty rifle next to the dying aide and pulled the pin on the thermobaric grenade.

Soren ran from the speedlift and toward the windows. He flung the grenade behind him, hearing the metallic click as the spoon released. He ran, forcing his body to compensate for the blaster bolt he'd taken to the leg, feeling the pain of every injury with each jarring stride as he closed on the windows.

He heard the grenade bounce off the ground and panicked shouts.

Soren dove into the remaining glass and broke through, cutting his hands and head in the process. He fell just beneath the windowsill when the grenade went off and blew out the rest of the windows in a gout of flame.

Soren didn't notice that his legs were on fire as he fell.

His body seemed to shut off all sensation of pain.

His ears rang.

His vision blurred and threatened to go dark. He had his eyes fix on the top of an ambulance ten feet below and sent a quick prayer to Oba that he'd land on top of it.

He missed the ambulance's raised back but the windshield broke his fall, cracking into a thousand spider webs with the impact, safely cradling him with a molecular safety webbing designed to save lives in a collision. Still, Soren heard and felt bones break.

He rolled off the ambulance and onto glass shards blown out of the House of Reason.

Soren lay on the ground, head spinning as fuzzy shapes moved around him. He felt something slapping the fire on his legs, a hand against a deep gash on along his scalp. Blood ran into his eyes and he tried to speak. He felt his body bump around and then a face he knew looked down at him.

"You're going to be okay, you hear me?"

Zelle? He could only think the words.

She looked away, and when she looked back, she was no longer Zelle. She was a different person. Or perhaps the person she always was. Soren closed his eyes and slipped out of consciousness.

23

Pattar picked his way through the scorched atrium. The trees were little more than blackened husks, their burnt branches lay across the floor, still smoldering. The bodies of Verdier and three legionnaires were burnt beyond recognition, and the smell was enough to cause even a hardened operator like him some pause.

He'd survived some tight scrapes in his time, but this took the prize.

A badly burnt body lay inside the speedlift. The corpse's clothing had ignited in the heat wave, leaving what remained almost unrecognizable. Pattar leaned over and poked at the body's face, which looked like a half melted candle.

"Small favors," Dryden said from behind Pattar.

The senator had a breathing mask over his mouth and nose. The edge of his suit was slightly burnt and one half of his face was lightly tanner than the other. "Fire makes falsifying coroner reports that much easier. Not that we'd have to do anything for the kaff boy."

"This wasn't the kaff boy," Pattar said. "He was wearing an infiltration hood when he died. This is the one who was with Verdier in his office."

"Indeed?" Dryden asked peering over his bodyguard's shoulder as if to verify the claim. "He certainly seemed to be a credible fighter, given the reports of how well he protected our late friend Senator Verdier. Hardly a new intern, eh?"

"My guess is that he's the Nether agent who caused us so much trouble back on Rinkata." Pattar worked the toe of his boot against the burnt pool of blood around the body. "He was hurt. Must've decided to go out with a bang in hopes of taking us with him."

"Another small favor," the senator replied. "Keep search and rescue away from here for a time. The longer Verdier is missing, the more his death will feel like a tragedy. And martyrs are always useful."

Heywood sat in the co-pilot's chair, power lines humming as his subroutines managed the *Iago*'s systems.

"Sunshine," came a voice over the speakers. It sounded strained and raspy, as though the speaker was communicating through clenched teeth.

The bot's optics lit up. "Yes, hello, sir?"

A light flashed on the *Iago*'s dash, indicating the ship's cargo ramp lowering.

"Heywood, I need you to—" Soren's raspy voice cut off with a hacking cough.

The bot heard uneven footsteps approaching and followed the sight of his master moving through the ship via internal holocams.

Soren stopped in the bridge entrance. Skinpacks covered his face and scalp, one hand was splinted and wrapped up. His clothes were torn up and marred by tiny little burn marks.

"Sir, you look worse than I do. How's it feel?"

Soren practically fell into the captain's seat and groaned from the landing.

"Prep for takeoff," he said. "Then I want you to access the Republic's medical records and swap my DNA and dental profile with a Senate aide named McCarty."

"Sir, that act carries several mandatory prison sentences," Heywood said.

Control panels came to life and a rumble carried through the ship as the engines cycled power.

"I don't really care." Soren looked at his mangled hand and then at the flight controls.

"You look as though you still require medical attention, sir."

"I do. But I needed to get here more."

"And how did you manage that?"

"The hospital I went to was overwhelmed with casualties. They did a quick and dirty job on me and the meds I got are wearing off. So just get what I asked done."

"I don't care, either. I'm just pointing that out in the hopes you might feel some measure of gratitude once the act is complete and buy me a proper chassis," the bot said. "According to the Republic personnel database, Brent

McCarty is listed as missing as part of a terrorist attack on the House of Reason... My word, were you involved?"

Soren looked at the bot and let the bandages do the talking.

"You were!" The bot's head twisted to Soren, then back at the controls. "You're not a smuggler, at all. Then what is it you do? DNA profile forgery complete."

"Set course for... for I don't know where." Soren opened the comms station with his good hand and read a message from Scarpia. "Asher's Star. Get us back to Asher's Star."

"The port authority says all airspace has been shut down," the bot said.

Soren looked out the window and saw dozens of ships lifting off.

"Guess all those didn't get that message," Soren said.

"And neither did we," Heywood said and the *Iago* lifted off.

Soren sat on his bunk, staring at the datapad in his hands.

He saw a portrait of himself in his navy uniform, the corners draped with blue-black Wellis flowers from his home world. Next to his portrait was Senator Dryden, reading from a podium covered in a black cloth.

"...and then naval officer Soren Voss died in a tragic explosion. His final act was to save my life, and for that I will be forever humbled, and forever grateful."

The screen cut from Dryden to bot footage of Soren leaping to save Senator Verdier on the review stand. Holorecordings of him leading Verdier into the House of Reason. A blurred security camera feed of him knifing a legionnaire, then an older holo of Soren on vacation with his then fiancée, looking happy and suitably heroic while on a lake cruise.

"The Order of the Centurion is the Legion's highest honor," Dryden continued. "I would that Lieutenant Soren Voss were here today so that I could express the depths of what I—and the Republic—owe him for his service."

An appointed Legion lieutenant colonel lifted up a gold and platinum medallion attached to a blue ribbon run through with gold thread. "The Order of the Centurion is the highest award that can be bestowed upon an individual serving in, or with, the Legion. When such an individual displays exceptional valor in action against an enemy force, and uncommon loyalty and devotion to the Legion and its legionnaires, refusing to abandon post, mission, or brothers, even unto death, the Legion dutifully recognizes such courage with this award. Today, on behalf of the Legion and a thankful Republic, I award this honor to Lieutenant JG Soren Voss."

He laid the award down solemnly in front of Soren's portrait and made a very poor salute.

Soren yelled and hurled the datapad into the bulkhead. He kicked a locker and beat a fist against the door so hard it popped open. The roll with Zelle's ashes fell out onto the deck.

"Ah, by Oba." Soren sat down and picked up Zelle's remains. "I'm starting... I'm starting to believe you, Zelle. The Republic is... is not what I believed. All that I fought for, what got you killed... it just feels like ashes."

On the cracked screen by the locker, a teary-eyed Dryden shook hands with Republic dignitaries beside Soren's portrait. There hadn't been a word about Senator Verdier in the news since the attack.

Soren set Zelle down next to him and buried his head in his hands for a time. The intercom clicked on.

"Sir, a Mr. Scarpia is on the holo for you," Heywood said. "And we've arrived at Asher's Star."

Soren lifted his head up, determination on his face.

"Be right there."

24

"Is that you, Soren?" The holo of Scarpia's head and shoulders leaned forward slightly. "You look terrible!"

"Had a rough time on Utopion," Soren said. The poorly healed cuts on his face and scalp had set into thick scars due to the rush job done by the hospital. Truth be told, he probably removed the skinpacks too soon, as well. At least the bruises around his eyes and jaw had a yellow halo now.

"You don't say," Scarpia shrugged. "Obviously you made your delivery. And you should have something for me."

Soren held up the encrypted credit chip. "Right here."

"Good." Scarpia smiled approvingly. "Bring it to my yacht and then we can talk about you taking on another run. Unless you'd prefer a little vacation?"

"No vacation. I want you to follow through and introduce me to that other shaker—the real deal you mentioned." Soren took a leap and spoke aloud where he felt the evidence brought him. "Goth Sullus."

Scarpia raised an eyebrow, intrigued. He wagged a finger at him. "Now now, my boy. Don't think that one good run for us means you're in the club, ready for the secret handshake and all that."

"I know what I've done for you," Soren said.

"Do you?" Scarpia sounded agitated. "Because all you did for me was make a delivery when I was short on bodies for the run. Don't make the mistake of thinking you're something special, boy."

"Utopion is a worm-infested dump right now. It's in chaos. I've proven myself. For him."

Scarpia sighed heavily. "All right. Come on board—with the chit—and I'll see about getting you connected."

Soren remembered his last encounter on Scarpia's pleasure yacht. "I'm thinking maybe it's your turn to come over for a visit."

Scarpia gave a half-smile. "If that's what you want, I'll be on board as soon as our ships are docked."

Soren nodded and ended the comm transition. "Heywood, prepare to dock with Scarpia's yacht."

"Yes, sir," the bot responded. "And while I understand that you are *not* a smuggler, I must say that you still remain a terrible example of the type. I can't imagine your employer being thrilled with your brusqueness. I suspect he will kill you."

Soren held up the chit he'd received from Lausa upon making delivery of the N-4s. "Not while I have this."

The bot attempted to shake its head. "I would not recommend you keep that on your personage."

Soren got up and moved to exit the bridge. "I don't disagree. Time to see how good of a smuggler I am. It's all hide-and-seek, right?"

Soren stood a distance from the *Iago*'s docking door and took a deep breath. He'd reached the end of himself, and he was either literally or metaphorically at the end of his life. He heard the pound of a rifle butt slam against the door.

"Open it, Heywood."

"They are armed Hools and they look more vicious than normal."

"Open it. Sometimes you have to take a beating for what you believe in."

"So long as it is only your funeral..."

The door swung open and four Hools armed with N-4 rifles stormed inside. Two of them peeled off to clear the ship, the same as the last time Scarpia had come aboard. But now two more were coming straight for Soren.

"Tell Mister Scarpia—"

The wind that carried Soren's words were violently forced from his lungs as the lead Hool slammed the stock of his rifle into the former agent's gut. Soren dropped to his knees, struggling to find a way to suck in air while evacuating bile from the force of the impact. The strain gave him an immediate headache.

A Hool roughly pulled him to his feet, his venomous quills bristling. He squeezed Soren's cheeks and hissed in jilted standard, "Where isss chit?"

"Hidden," Soren managed to rasp out. "Until I talk to Scarpia."

The Hool drove a knee into Soren's groin, then threw him down to the deck. The snarling bodyguard delivered a strong kick to the ribs while Soren was down.

Throughout the ship, Soren could hear a tremendous racket. The other Hools didn't seem to be clearing so much as tearing everything apart. Searching for the chit.

A comm sounded and the other Hool spoke to his partner in their native language. But Soren was able to decipher Scarpia's name.

A moment later, he heard the man's voice directly. "I'll need that chit, *Agent* Voss."

Soren struggled to his knees. "I have it. It's on the ship. But I needed to—"

Scarpia cut him off with a backhanded slap that rattled Soren's teeth and made his healing jaw feel as though it had been set aflame.

"Don't begin to think you can talk your way out of this, my boy!" Scarpia was incensed. "Your face is all over the news cycles right now. Lieutenant Voss of the Republic Navy. Only a lieutenant doesn't run rifles for the MCR, does he? So that makes you Nether Ops. And that makes you a dead man."

Scarpia held out a hand. A lit cutting torch was placed in his palm. Scarpia held the flame close to Soren. Close enough that the former agent could feel the heat drying his skin and singing his hair.

"The only question that remains is whether that death comes quick or takes a long, long time. So, give me the chit."

Soren gave a fractional nod, careful not to inadvertently burn himself. "I was never going to keep it from you, Mister Scarpia."

Scarpia smiled cruelly. "No shit."

"I only wanted to talk to you."

Scarpia nodded at his Hools, who lifted Soren back on his feet. "So you can talk while we go to wherever you're hiding the chit. Which way?"

"The bridge."

Scarpia motioned toward the front of the ship. "Let's go."

Soren looked around passively at the mess the Hools had made. It seemed everything was overturned and spilling out on the deck. They passed the mess to see foodstuffs spread across the floor, broken plates and scattered utensils.

"I could have taken the chit straight to Nether Ops," Soren said as he was pushed toward the bunk room. "But I didn't. I want you to think about all the things I could have done but *didn't* do. Because I'm done with the Republic."

"You'd be surprised how much Nether Ops is willing to do to keep up that little image," Scarpia said coldly. "What you did with the MCR on Utopion is nothing compared to what the last guy who tried this did. Believe me."

They passed the bunks and Soren stopped short. The Hools had spread Zelle's ashes everywhere in their search. A lump came into his throat. This… this also was nothing. It was the passing of an old life. That was all. And if not… maybe he'd see her again soon.

"I don't doubt that. But I'm finished with Nether Ops. And the Republic." Soren tried to keep his voice even, but the emotion over seeing Zelle's ashes pulled at his vocal chords. "My handler, a man named Nix, was part of the MCR conspiracy on Utopion. He tried to kill me."

Scarpia only grunted.

"Ask yourself why a kill team isn't storming this ship right now, Mister Scarpia."

"I don't worry about kill teams any longer, my boy. Friends in high places."

They reached the bridge, which was just as torn apart as the rest of the ship. The chairs were slashed and ripped, the dismantling of Heywood complete. The bot lay on the floor, its runtime completed and its head in pieces. There would be no repairing him this time.

"Here's the bridge," Scarpia said. "Now get me my chit."

Soren nodded and took a step toward the main console, gently releasing himself from the Hool's grip. Rifles went up in response, but a nod from Scarpia allowed Soren to keep going.

The former agent typed in a code onto an old alphanumerica keypad, causing a pneumatic box to hiss open. He reached inside and pulled out a small, velvet bag.

Scarpia leaned forward and caught the bag from mid-air as Soren tossed it to him. He scowled a moment and then handed it to one of his Hools. "Open this."

The Hool untied the string and dumped out six chits into his hand, offering them to Scarpia.

"What the hell is this?" Scarpia asked. "You forget which one they gave you on Utopion?"

Soren shook his head. "None of those are the chit."

Scarpia rolled his eyes. "I don't have time for this. We'll scrap the ship and find the damn thing on our own. Kill him."

"Bomb!" Soren shouted. The guns hesitated. "My lifes-cans are tied to the core of the *Iago*. I die and this whole ship goes up."

"Sounds like a bluff."

"An easy one to get around," Soren said. "You can kill me after you leave. I only want to make my case, Mister Scarpia. I don't want any of us to die today."

"So make it then," Scarpia spat.

"Those chits in your hand are legionnaire ID tags. They're from appointed officers who ambushed me and my partner—whose ashes you found in my bunk—on Rinkata. Every one of them was appointed by Senator Dryden. And Dryden was the man who arranged for the MCR to attack Utopion."

Scarpia raised an eyebrow. "And you can prove that? That Dryden was involved?"

"The evidence from Rinkata will lead to him. And I was there when Dryden killed Senator Verdier."

"So what? You want me to take you to the Utopion police?"

Soren shook his head. "I remember what you said, Mister Scarpia. That the MCR were dead without know-ing it. Just looking to make a name for themselves but on the other side of relevance. But Dryden was involved. He picked the wrong side. And I know that a man like you can use that information to your advantage."

For the first time, a hint of Scarpia's roguish smile came to his lips. "That may be of use. But it's nothing with-out that chit. Aside from the money for the delivery—and it's a lot of credits—it has information I procured about the nature of the MCR's current leadership. Information that I won't lose."

"But the MCR is a lost cause," Soren said.

"It is. But that doesn't mean it can't be of use to me. Or my employer."

"I want to meet him. I want to meet Goth Sullus."

"You said that. It isn't happening."

Soren shook his head. "Fighting against the rot in the Republic is the only thing I have to live for right now. And I'm fine dying if it's denied of me. Are you?"

Scarpia frowned. "Listen. Sullus isn't the type to be found unless he wants to be. I was hired—not by him—to supply him with whatever he needs to build an army."

"But you can trust that he'll at least review any messages you send?"

"Eventually, yes."

Soren took a deep breath. "When I took Illuria back to her homeworld, she talked about a dark man who could read her thoughts. I only recently figured that this man and Goth Sullus are one in the same. Was she telling the truth?"

A shiver seemed to run up Scarpia's spine. "She was."

"So let me speak to him. He'll know I'm telling the truth. That I'm done with the Republic. That I'm committed to him."

Soren reached into his mouth and dug open a laceration on his inner cheek, a sort of pocket of flesh. He pulled out the chit and held it out for Scarpia. "Here's what you wanted."

Scarpia walked to Soren and took the chit. "Thank you."

He turned and, when he was clear, said to his men, "Stun."

Soren was hit by no less than three stun bolts. He fell hard onto the *Iago*'s deck, wrapped in darkness.

25

Senator Dryden looked in a mirror and adjusted his mourning black jacket and straightened his matching tie. The multi-colored pin in his lapel showing solidarity with all the victims of the terrorist attack on the House of Reason stuck out as almost garish, but that was the point. It needed to be noticed.

"That was a fine speech today, Senator," Delegate Orin Karr, similarly dressed, said from his desk.

"'For such a life to be lost for the Republic is a victory.'" Dryden rolled one hand forward. "How did the *actual* Legion take the news that another Nether Ops agent will receive the Order of the Centurion?"

"Badly," Karr smirked. "With the last one, that Maydoon, there were legionnaires who provided witness statements. With Soren, his medal depends largely on your testimony and hours of observation bot holovids."

"Soren Voss saved my life," Dryden said. "He killed the Mid-Core Rebels posing as legionnaires that had just murdered Senator Verdier and were about to do the same to me when he wrestled that thermobaric grenade from a terrorist's hand. A pity to lose one such as him."

"Curious," Karr said, knitting his brows in suspicion.

"I beg your pardon," Senator Dryden said.

"There is something of a deeper mystery," Karr said, pressing his fingertips together in a steeple. "Voss's handler, a man named Nix, was found murdered."

Dryden shrugged his shoulders. "Perhaps he was targeted by the MCR?"

"Odd that the MCR would know of him. Nether Ops is rarely so sloppy in keeping its agents undercover."

Dryden cleared his throat and changed the subject. "Our media assets are doing a tremendous job. Such a shame that MCR terrorists managed to work their way into the parade."

"Yes, I'm afraid my measure to increase the Legion's funding won't pass," said Karr from behind a frown.

Dryden wore a shocked look on his face. "Even after all of that? I was sure it would all but guarantee it."

Karr shook his head. "Then you misread your peers and the state of galactic politics. While the MCR is the culprit, the image of the 'rogue legionnaires' opening fire on delegates and senators will be the lasting image in the Republic's mind."

"But—"

A comm chime sounded at Karr's desk and he held up a hand to silence the venerable senator. He spoke softly to whoever was on the other line. "Truly? Yes, if you're confident you can find the man. Yes." He looked up at Dryden, who fidgeted uncomfortably before him. "He's here with me now. Perhaps. If that is required, I'll be the one making that determination."

The comm discussion ended and Karr once again inclined his head to face Dryden, a smile on his face as they resumed their discussion. "Now, where were we?" Karr asked. "Ah. I fear that has damaged the Legion's reputation, though they do not deserve it. They will be stretched further than they already are and will have to do without more men and equipment. All the while the Republic will demand the MCR be punished. A shame."

Dryden's face was pale. "Surely, we can still assemble the votes?"

"This is not a hill worthy of dying on. Though I suspect a good number of deaths will come of this debacle with the MCR. But there may be a silvene lining: an associate of mine—you wouldn't know him; the man works on the fringes—seems to have come by a collection of legionnaire identity chits. They apparently lead to Rinkata. I have asked Commander Devers to oversee a naval raid to ensure all the traitorous elements working the MCR are discovered and eradicated. Legion Commander Keller informs me that Dark Ops is likewise standing by to assist."

Dryden swallowed hard. "I see."

"I'm quite sure you do... Senator." Karr leaned forward, a stern, commanding smile on his face. "Tell me, Senator Dryden, have you ever witnessed the ferocity of a Dark Ops kill team as they storm a building? Through sheer violence of force, they seem to bend the very air and make *your* home... theirs."

Dryden shook his head. "Orrin... I... surely some good to the Republic may yet come of all this?"

"It is my job to see that all things work together for the good of the Republic."

"Delegate Karr, I will do anything. I will resign from the Senate. Only... protect me if it is in your power. I made a mistake. I shouldn't have acted so boldly."

"I would not call the death of a longstanding senator and allying oneself with the MCR 'bold,' Senator Dryden. I would call it treason."

"Please!" Dryden wrung his hands together, pleading. "I am in your debt. At your mercy."

Karr nodded. "I will await Commander Devers's report. It is possible that those who infiltrated Utopion alone will be responsible for this terrorist attack."

"I... do hope the report shows what is best for the Republic."

"I'm sure it will," Karr said, attending to matters on his desk. He was finished talking with Dryden. The man was now permanently in his debt. His hold on the Senate and House of Reason that much stronger as a result. "There is an appropriations vote regarding the Legion's request for expanded security on the Tarrago moon."

"Yes, Delegate Karr. I know of it well. It all seems in order."

"Perhaps at first glance. You will receive a memo from my office detailing why, in my opinion, those resources are better spent elsewhere."

"Of course. And... thank you."

Soren found himself coming to in a pitch-black room. But he was alive. Alive and imprisoned, meaning his fate was still in the air. Still, he couldn't help but feel that he was in a much better situation now than he had been however long ago it was when he'd been put down with stun blasters.

There was a rattling from somewhere outside, and then the shape of a manual door appeared in the darkness as red light blazed around the portal's frame and the great door swung outward. Soren shielded his eyes from the sudden light. He squinted and blinked until he could make out the black silhouettes of three figures, a man and two Hools.

Behind them in the red-light glow were couplings and engine housings. He was being held in a makeshift prison somewhere aboard a ship's engine room. Probably Scarpia's yacht—this certainly wasn't the *Iago*.

"Good news, my boy." It was Scarpia. "My employer— the man above the man you wish to speak to—found your information *most* helpful. He's agreed to give you the opportunity you requested. You'll be granted an audience with Goth Sullus. Or one of his generals if Sullus so desires."

Soren pulled himself to his feet. His body still ached from the events on Utopion, a pain compounded by the beating he'd taken at the hands of the Hools. But this made it all seem worthwhile.

"Thank you," he said. "Death to the Republic."

"Save it for the true believers," Scarpia said. "A word of warning: if you go see Goth Sullus and you're... found wanting, you'll wish you were back among the Hools and cutting torches."

"I won't be." Soren took a step toward the open door. No one attempted to stop him. "I'm fueled up for as long a trip as it will take."

"Motivated. I'll give that to you," Scarpia said. "Since you lost your bot, you'll have to rely on your ship's nav computer. It has one set of coordinates. One. Now, maybe you've memorized coordinates for some other spots just out of repetition. But these coordinates come with a sizeable explosive device and a tracker. You jump out anywhere but to where I tell you and boom. You engage your comms systems and boom. Got it?"

"Boom."

"Sure hope Goth Sullus likes you. Your boom and the coordinates are waiting for you."

Soren passed through the yacht, taking servant's passages and crew corridors. Absent were the beautiful humanoids and stimulants, though it sounded as though a party was still going on. Soren wondered if it ever stopped. If a man like Scarpia could ever tolerate life were he to slow down and reflect.

Perhaps if Scarpia did, he would understand the privilege of what he was doing. Working for a man capable of remaking the Republic. Everyone Soren had encountered who knew Goth Sullus, from the sailors on Qadib to Illuria herself, spoke of the man with reverence and fear. And that was what this rotting galaxy needed. A man for the ages. One could face the monster of corruption and complacency and slay it without remorse.

Iago set down on a dry lakebed. Ochre dust billowed out and powder-coated a small ground sled with three armored men waiting outside of it.

Soren came down the ship's ramp, hands laced behind his head and his pistol holster empty. A man in black Legion armor with red trim—the very same Soren had once smuggled—aimed a blaster rifle at the agent and motioned to the ground. Soren went to his knees.

The dark legionnaire did a quick and rough search of Soren's person, then motioned into the ship with a nod of his head. One of the dark legionnaires rushed up the ramp.

Soren stared into the barrel of the dark legionnaire's gun and waited. The dark legionnaires were silent; whatever conversation they shared was from helmet to helmet.

A black isolation hood went over Soren's head and they cuffed his hands. Stripped away were all sensations of sight and sound as Soren traveled with the hood over his head. He knew that some found this maddening. He found it peaceful.

He knew not how long they traveled. They changed sleds at least once and marched him until his feet grew fatigued. And then they left him.

Outside.

Soren knew that much because of the wind whipping by him. It was an odd sensation, feeling the wind ruffle his clothing, feeling the sting of the sand it carried against his naked hands and wrists but not being able to hear its howl through the isolation hood.

I know you...

The words floated through Soren's mind like whispers from a dream. He struggled against the wind and turned slowly, as though in so doing, he'd somehow be able to see through the darkness of the hood which kept his breath hot and stuffy close to his face.

I know why you're here. Why you've come so far... but you don't know yet. Not fully.

"Who's there? What is this?" Soren shouted into the darkness. No one would hear him. And he should be able to hear no one. And yet the words were very real.

He tried to calm himself, ran through the mental exercises to brace against torture Nether Ops had taught him. Memories of Zelle came unbidden to his mind, then Illuria, then Verdier in his final moments of life.

Bend... don't break.

"What is this!" Soren screamed.

But he knew. Deep down. This was what Illuria spoke of. This was the dark man entering his thoughts, his mind. It was terrifying... and captivating. For there came with it a probing, a reveal like the peeling back of layers.

The raw fury of Senator Dryden awarding the Order of the Centurion came over him and he strained against his bounds, grunting unwords. He saw Nix's betrayal, saw him slam the blade into his armored back as though watching it unfold from above. Zelle's murder at the hands of the appointed legionnaires.

There it is. There is the truth.

The emotion vanished and Soren gasped. He sensed a someone approach and the hood was gently lifted off.

A man in a gray robe and tight belt looked down at him, his eyes dark, his presence overwhelming. Soren fell to his knees.

"Look what the Republic has done to its true son," Goth Sullus said at just above a whisper. "You were loyal. Brave. You used your gifts to fight for what you believed in, and how did the Republic answer?"

Sullus knelt and put his hands on either side of Soren's face. "You know the answer."

"They betrayed me," Soren said, his voice ragged. "Used me."

"They turned you into a paragon of their own sins." Sullus traced a finger down one of Soren's new scars, and the nagging pain faded away. "Will you save that Republic you believe in?"

Goth Sullus motioned to the restraints and they fell away.

"That Republic is gone." Soren lifted his hands and studied the ugly stitchwork on his skin. "It never was real."

"Then what will you do?"

Soren got to his feet. Goth Sullus rose with him. He squared off against the man in gray.

"You'll end it?" Soren asked. "Bring the end to the lies?"

I will. Not only end it, but I will save it from the threat which is to come.

"Then death to the Republic." Soren clenched his hands and felt the power of Goth Sullus, his new master.

JOIN THE LEGION

You can find art, t-shirts, signed books and other merchandise on our <u>website</u>.

We also have a fantastic Facebook group called the Galaxy's Edge Fan Club that was created for readers and listeners of *Galaxy's Edge* to get together and share their lives, discuss the series, and have an avenue to talk directly with Jason Anspach and Nick Cole. Please check it out and say hello once you get there!

For updates about new releases, exclusive promotions, and sales, visit inthelegion.com and sign up for our VIP mailing list. Grab a spot in the nearest combat sled and get over there to receive your free copy of "Tin Man," a Galaxy's Edge short story available only to mailing list subscribers.

INTHELEGION.COM

GET A FREE, EXCLUSIVE SHORT STORY

THE GALAXY
IS A DUMPSTER
FIRE...

Richard Fox is the winner of the 2017 Dragon Award for Best Military Science Fiction or Fantasy novel, author of The Ember War Saga, a military science fiction and space opera series, and other novels in the military history, thriller and space opera genres. He lives in fabulous Las Vegas with his incredible wife and three boys, amazing children bent on anarchy.

Jason Anspach is a best selling author living in Tacoma, Washington with his wife and their own legionnaire squad of seven (not a typo) children. In addition to science fiction, Jason is the author of the hit comedy-paranormal-historical-detective series, *'til Death*. Jason loves his family as well as hiking and camping throughout the beautiful Pacific Northwest. And Star Wars. He named as many of his kids after Obi Wan as possible, and knows that Han shot first.

Nick Cole is a dragon award winning author best known for *The Old Man and the Wasteland, CTRL ALT Revolt!*, and the Wyrd Saga. After serving in the United States Army, Nick moved to Hollywood to pursue a career in acting and writing. (Mostly) retired from the stage and screen, he resides with his wife, a professional opera singer, in Los Angeles, California.

FROM THE AUTHORS

Hello to you, dear and gentle reader. Thank you for reading *Through The Nether*. When Nick and Jason approached me to write in their Galaxy's Edge universe, I was a bit daunted as they had this grand space opera unfolding, and I didn't know where I could fit in a story.

But after a bit of thought, I wondered just why anyone would side with Goth Sullus in the grand conflict and how a character would react to the dumpster fire that is their galaxy. Then I got the idea for Soren and found a rabbit hole he could go down and transform from Nether Ops agent to one of Sullus' soldiers.

A bit different than most Order of the Centurion stories, for sure, but I found a corner of the sand box I wanted to play in and Nick and Jason let me have all the fun I wanted. I am grateful to them for the opportunity, and for letting me contribute to Galaxy's Edge.

Is this the last you'll here from Soren? I doubt that very much. Spies are a tricky lot.

I write my own space opera, and if you'd like to get a free book from my Ember War Saga, please click on the link below and sign up for my spam free newsletter.

I do enjoy hearing from readers, drop me a note at richard@richardfoxauthor.com.

-Richard

Follow Richard at:

Facebook: https://www.facebook.com/pages/Richard-Fox-Books/1377447982503883

Goodreads: https://www.goodreads.com/author/show/7771765.Richard_Fox

My Website: http://www.emberwar.com

Amazon: http://www.amazon.com/author/richardfox

Join my mailing list to stay up to date on new releases and receive a FREE book:
https://dl.bookfunnel.com/3qwdyf3qth

ALSO BY RICHARD FOX:

The Ember War Saga

The Ember War Saga Volume II: Terran Armor Corps

Terran Strike Marines

Terra Nova Chronicles
1. Terra Nova
2. Bloodlines
3. Wings of Redemption
4. Hale's War

The Exiled Fleet Series
1. Albion Lost
2. The Long March
3. Finest Hour
4. Point of Honor
5. The Last Ditch

Read The Ember War for FREE

The countdown to the invasion of Earth has begun.

A merciless alien race bent on human extermination has pointed its armada towards Earth. The countdown to their arrival begins.

A mysterious intelligence warns only a young scientist, Marc Ibarra, of our impending doom. Together, the two create a plan for humanity to survive the invasion. Even with the aid of advanced new technology, Marc is faced with a major problem. The plan—if it works—can only save a fraction of us.

Who survives? Who dies? How can humanity win the battle against almost certain annihilation?

With what will only be an ember of humanity left, will it be enough to rekindle our chance for survival and strike back at the Xaros?

The Ember War is the first novel in an epic military sci-fi series. If you like The Legacy Fleet by Nick Webb or Omega Force by Joshua Dalzelle, then you'll love this explosive adventure with nail biting sci fi battles across the stars. Read this now!

Sign up for my spam-free mailing list and read it for FREE
(BookHip.com/FLHWMX)

Here's a sample for you:

THE NEAR FUTURE

Humanity's only hope of survival entered the solar system at nearly the speed of light. The probe slowed as the sun's heliosphere disrupted the graviton wave it rode in on from the abyss of deep space. Awakened by the sudden deceleration, the probe absorbed the electromagnetic spectrum utilized by its target species and assessed the technological sophistication of the sole sentient species on Earth.

The probe adjusted its course to take it into the system's star. If the humans couldn't survive—with its help—what was to come, then the probe would annihilate itself. There would be no trace of it for the enemy, and no chance of humanity's existence beyond the time it had until the enemy arrived. The probe analyzed filed patents, military expenditures, birth rates, mathematical advancement and space exploration.

The first assessment fell within the margin of error of survival and extinction for humanity. The probe's programming allowed for limited autonomous decision making (choice being a rare luxury for the probe's class of artificial intelligence). The probe found itself in a position to choose between ending its mission in the sun's fire and a mathematically improbable defense of humanity—and the potential compromise of its much larger mission.

Given the rare opportunity to make its own decision, the probe opted to dither. In the week it took to pass into Jupiter's orbit, the probe took in more data. It scoured the Internet for factors to add to the assessment, but the assessment remained the same: unlikely, but possible. By the time it shot past Mars, the probe still hadn't made a decision.

As the time to adjust course for Earth or continue into the sun approached, the probe conducted a final scan of cloud storage servers for any new information...and found something interesting.

While the new information made only a negligible impact on the assessment, the probe adjusted course to Earth. It hadn't traveled all this way for nothing.

In the desert south of Phoenix, Arizona, it landed with no more fanfare than a slight thump and a few startled cows. Then it broke into the local cell network and made a call.

****

Marc Ibarra awoke to his phone ringing at max volume, playing a pop ditty that he hated with vehemence. He rolled off the mattress that lay on the floor and crawled on his hands and knees to where his cell was recharging. His roommate, who paid the majority of their rent and got to sleep on an actual bed, grumbled and let off a slew of slurred insults.

Marc reached his cell and slapped at it until the offending music ended. He blinked sleep from his eyes and tried to focus on the caller's name on the screen. The only people who'd call at this ungodly hour were his family in Basque country...or maybe Jessica in his applied robotics course wanted a late-night study break.

The name on the screen was "ANSWER ME".

He closed an eye and reread the name. It was way too early—or too late, depending on one's point of view—for this nonsense. He turned the ringer off and went back to bed. Sleep was about to claim him when the phone rang again, just as loudly as last time but now with a disco anthem.

"Seriously?" his roommate slurred.

Marc declined the call and powered the phone off. He flopped back on his bed and curled into his blanket. *To hell with my first class,* he thought. Arizona State University had a lax attendance policy, one which he'd abuse for nights like this.

The cell erupted with big-band music. Marc took his head out from beneath the covers and looked at his phone like it was a thing possessed. The phone vibrated so hard that it practically danced a jig on the floor and the screen flashed "ANSWER ME" over and over again as music blared.

"Dude?" said his roommate, now sitting up in his bed.

Marc swiped the phone off the charging cord and the music stopped. The caller's name undulated with a rainbow of colors and an arrow appeared on the screen pointing to the button he had to press to answer the call. *When did I get this app?* he thought.

Marc sighed and left the bedroom, meandering into the hallway bathroom with the grace of a zombie. The battered mattress he slept on played hell with his back and left him stiff every morning. Dropping his boxers, he took a seat on the toilet and answered the call, determined to return this caller's civility with some interesting background noise.

"What?" he murmured.

"Marc Ibarra. I need to see you." The voice was mechanical, asexual in its monotone.

"Do you have any frigging idea what time it is? Wait, who the hell is this?"

"You must come to me immediately. We must discuss the mathematical proof you have stored in document title 'thiscantberight.doc.'"

Marc shot to his feet. The boxers around his ankles tripped him up and he stumbled out of the bathroom and fell against the wall. His elbow punched a hole in the drywall and the cell clattered to the floor.

He scooped the phone back up and struggled to breathe as a sudden asthma attack came over him.

"How...how...?" He couldn't finish his question until he found his inhaler in the kitchen, mere steps away in the tiny apartment. He took a deep breath from the inhaler and felt the tightness leave his lungs.

That someone knew of his proof was impossible. He'd finished it earlier that night and had encrypted it several times before loading it into a cloud file that shouldn't have been linked to him in any way.

"How do you know about that?" he asked.

"You must come to me immediately. There is little time. Look at your screen," the robotic voice said. His screen changed to a map program, displaying a pin in an open field just off the highway connecting Phoenix to the suburb of Maricopa.

"Come. Now."

Marc grabbed his keys.

****

An hour later, his jeans ripped from scaling a barbed-wire fence, Marc was surrounded by desert scrub. The blue of the morning rose behind him, where his beat-up Honda waited on the side of the highway.

With his cell to his ear, Marc stopped and looked around before deciding how to continue. Spiked ocotillo plants looked a lot like benign mesquite trees in the darkness. A Native American casino in the distance served as his North Star, helping him keep his bearings.

"You're not out here, are you? I'm being punked, aren't I?" he asked the mysterious caller.

"You are nine point two six meters to my east south east. Punk: decayed wood, used as tinder. Are you on fire?" the caller said.

Marc rolled his eyes. This wasn't the first time the caller had used the nonstandard meanings of words during what passed as conversation between the two. Marc had tried to get the caller to explain how he knew about his theorem and why they had to meet in the middle of the desert. The caller had refused to say anything. He would only reiterate that Marc had to come quickly to see him, chiding him every time Marc deviated from the provided driving directions.

"If you're so close, why can't I see you?" he asked. He took a few steps in what he thought was a northwesterly direction and squished into a cow patty.

"Continue," the caller said.

Marc shook his foot loose and tried to kick the cow leavings from his sneakers.

"You know what this is? This is exactly what's all over my shoes, you monotone bastard. Forget it!" Marc shoved his phone into his back pocket and limped back toward his car, his right foot squishing with each step.

The route back to his car was comparatively easy; he just had to walk toward his headlights. That was the plan, anyway, until the lights on his car shut off.

"Marc, this is important." The muffled words came from his pocketed cell.

"How are you doing this?" Marc shouted into the night.

"Turn around, please."

Marc did as asked and a silver light like the snap of a reflection from a fish twisting just beneath the water flared on the ground ahead of him. No one was there a moment ago and Marc hadn't heard any movement.

"I swear if I get my kidneys cut out I will be so pissed about this," Marc said as he made his way to where he saw the light. He stood for a moment, then flopped his arms against his sides. "I'm here."

"You're standing on me." The voice came from beneath Marc's feet.

Marc skipped aside like he'd just heard a rattle-snake's warning.

"Holy—did someone bury you? Why didn't you tell me to bring a shovel?" Marc went to his knees and poked at the ground, which felt solid. "How deep are you? Do you have enough air?" Marc asked, using both hands to shove earth aside.

"Two inches ahead and three down."

Marc's face contorted in confusion as he kept digging. He moved a mound of gray dirt and pebbles aside and a silver light washed over his face.

A silver needle no more than three inches long rested in the dirt. Tiny filaments of lambent energy crept from the needle and undulated through the air like a snake in the ocean. Marc was frozen in place, his jaw slack as the filaments extended away from the needle, shades of white swimming in and around it.

"We don't have much time." The words came from the needle in the same mechanical voice as his mysterious caller. A point of light appeared in the air above the needle, sparked, and then lit into a flame no bigger than he'd seen on a match head. The white flame, which gave off no heat, rose and grew in size. A flame the size of Marc's head came to a stop a few feet in the air.

Marc, transfixed by the flame until now, got to his feet. The filaments from the needle had extended past him and formed a perimeter ten yards in diameter. Tendrils of energy writhed against each other and against an invisible boundary. His heart pounded in his ears and his innate fight-or-flight instinct made a decision.

"This is a different experience for you. Let me—"

Marc turned and ran away. He got to where the tendrils had stopped and ran into what felt like a wall of water. Air thickened around him as he tried to push through and find purchase on the ground ahead. It felt like he was moving through clay.

"Marc, you're being ridiculous." The air hardened and spat him back toward the flame. Marc tripped over his own feet and tumbled to the ground. He snapped back to his feet and looked for a way, anyway, to put some distance between him and the flame.

The flame, white on silver or silver on white—Marc couldn't tell as it morphed in the air—floated toward him slowly.

Marc made the sign of the cross with two fingers and looked away. He heard a sigh.

"Look at me." The flame, again.

Marc opened an eye. The flame was a few inches from his hands but he still felt no heat.

"I'm not here to hurt you. I'm here to help you. Understand?" The flame bobbed in the air gently until Marc nodded. "I am an emissary from an alien intelligence sent to save your species from extinction and I need your help to do it."

Marc pointed a finger at the flame and tried to touch it. His fingertip passed into the flame's surface without sensation.

"I thought unsolicited physical contact was against your species' norms," said the flame, the tendrils rustling with the words.

Marc snapped his hand back.

"Did you say something about...extinction?" The flame bobbed in the air. "How? Why?"

"An armada is coming." The flame morphed into an oblong shape with a half dozen tendrils sticking from it, like a misshapen spider. "They are the Xaros and they will annihilate your species with ease. Unless you and I work together, your extinction is assured," the flame said, floating closer to Marc, who stood dumbfounded. The flame came so close that he could see his reflection on it. Deep blue motes of light sprang from the flame and evaporated in the air.

"Why me? What am I supposed to do about an alien armada? I'm a B-minus grad student with a mountain of student loans, not some...some world leader!"

The probe returned to flames and a hologram of a white paper popped into the air next to it. Pages flipped open from the book, the mathematical proof he'd finished the night before.

"We expected that your species would have progressed to the edge of your solar system by now. To see such potential squandered on wars and Internet cat videos was disheartening, but this is well beyond what you should be capable of. The advancements you discovered in material science and energy storage are a springboard to technological advancement that will give you a 27 percent chance of survival, provided everything goes as planned. We can start here." The proof stopped with the picture of a lattice of carbon atoms. The last page had the words "No way!!!!" scrawled next to the diagram.

"I don't understand," Marc said.

"You will, but we need to get started right away."

"How much time do we have?"

"Sixty years."

Want to read the rest for FREE?

(https://bookhip.com/FLHWMX)

HONOR ROLL

We would like to give our most sincere thanks and recognition to those who supported the creation of *Through The Nether* by subscribing as a Galaxy's Edge Insider at GalacticOutlaws.com

Guido Abreu
Elias Aguilar
Bill Allen
Tony Alvarez
Galen Anderson
Robert Anspach
Jonathan Auerbach
Fritz Ausman
Sean Averill
Matthew Bagwell
Marvin Bailey
John Barber
Logan Barker
Russell Barker
Eric Batzdorfer
John Baudoin
Steven Beaulieu
Antonio Becerra
Mike Beeker
Randall Beem
Matt Beers
John Bell
Daniel Bendele
David Bernatski
Trevor Blasius
WJ Blood

Rodney Bonner
Thomas Seth Bouchard
Alex Bowling
Ernest Brant
Geoff Brisco
Aaron Brooks
Marion Buehring
Daniel Cadwell
Van Cammack
Zachary Cantwell
Steven Carrizales
Brian Cave
Shawn Cavitt
David Chor
Jonathan Clews
Beau Clifton
Alex Collins-Gauweiler
Garrett Comerford
James Connolly
James Conyers
Jonathan Copley
Robert Cosler
Andrew Craig
Adam Craig
Phil Culpepper
Ben Curcio

Thomas Cutler
Alister Davidson
Peter Davies
Ivy Davis
Nathan Davis
Ron Deage
Tod Delaricheliere
Ryan Denniston
Christopher DiNote
Matthew Dippel
Ellis Dobbins
Ray Duck
Cami Dutton
Virgil Dwyer
William Ely
Stephane Escrig
Hunter Ferguson
Ashley Finnigan
Steve Forrester
Skyla Forster
Timothy Foster
Bryant Fox
Mark Franceschini
David Gaither
Christopher Gallo
Richard Gallo
Kyle Gannon
Michael Gardner
Nick Gerlach
John Giorgis
Justin Godfrey
Luis Gomez
Gerald Granada
Gordon Green
Tim Green
Shawn Greene

Erik Hansen
Greg Hanson
Jason Harris
Jordan Harris
Matthew Hartmann
Adam Hartswick
Ronald Haulman
Joshua Hayes
Jason Henderson
Jason Henderson
Kyle Hetzer
Aaron Holden
Joshua Hopkins
Tyson Hopkins
Christopher Hopper
Ian House
Ken Houseal
Nathan Housley
Jeff Howard
Mike Hull
Bradley Huntoon
Carl Hutchens
Wendy Jacobson
Paul Jarman
James Jeffers
Tedman Jess
James Johnson
Randolph Johnson
Tyler Jones
John Josendale
Wyatt Justice
Ron Karroll
Cody Keaton
Noah Kelly
Caleb Kenner
Daniel Kimm

Zachary Kinsman
Rhet Klaahsen
Jesse Klein
Travis Knight
Ethan Koska
Evan Kowalski
Byl Kravetz
Brian Lambert
Clay Lambert
Grant Lambert
Jeremy Lambert
Dave Lawrence
Alexander Le
Paul Lizer
Richard Long
Oliver Longchamps
Brooke Lyons
John M
Patrick Maclary
Richard Maier
Brian Mansur
Robet Marchi
Deven Marincovich
Cory Marko
Lucas Martin
Pawel Martin
Trevor Martin
Tao Mason
Mark Maurice
Simon Mayeski
Kyle McCarley
Quinn McCusker
Alan McDonald
Caleb McDonald
Hans McIlveen
Rachel McIntosh

Joshua McMaster
Christopher Menkhaus
Jim Mern
Dylon Merrell
Robert Mertz
Pete Micale
Mike Mieszcak
Brandon Mikula
Ted Milker
Mitchell Moore
William Morris
Alex Morstadt
Nicholas Mukanos
Vinesh Narayan
Bennett Nickels
Andrew Niesent
Greg Nugent
Christina Nymeyer
Colin O'neill
Ryan O'neill
Tyler Ornelas
James Owens
David Parker
Eric Pastorek
Carl Patrick
Dupres Pina
Pete Plum
Paul Polanski
Matthew Pommerening
Jeremiah Popp
Chancey Porter
Brian Potts
Chris Pourteau
Chris Prats
Joshua Purvis
Nick Quinn

Eric Ritenour
Walt Robillard
Joshua Robinson
Daniel Robitaille
Thomas Roman
Joyce Roth
David Sanford
Jaysn Schaener
Landon Schaule
Shayne Schettler
Andrew Schmidt
Brian Schmidt
William Schweisthal
Aaron Seaman
Phillip Seek
Christopher Shaw
Charles Sheehan
Wendell Shelton
Brett Shilton
Vernetta Shipley
Glenn Shotton
Joshua Sipin
Scott Sloan
Daniel Smith
Michael Smith
Sharroll Smith
Tyler Smith
John Spears
Peter Spitzer
Dustin Sprick
Graham Stanton
Paul Starck
Maggie Stewart-Grant
John Stockley
Rob Strachan
William Strickler

Shayla Striffler
Kevin Summers
Ernest Sumner
Carol Szpara
Travis TadeWaldt
Daniel Tanner
Lawrence Tate
Tim Taylor
Mark Teets
Steven Thompson
William Joseph Thorpe
Beverly Tierney
Matthew Titus
Jameson Trauger
Scott Tucker
Eric Turnbull
Brandon Turton
Jalen Underwood
Paul Van Dop
Paden VanBuskirk
Jose Vazquez
Anthony Wagnon
Christopher Walker
David Wall
Andrew Ward
Scot Washam
John Watson
James Wells
Ben Wheeler
Scott Winters
Jason Wright
Brandt Zeeh
Nathan Zoss

Made in the USA
Coppell, TX
17 February 2021